★ "In this chilling tale, Marshall ties together regional folklore, urban legends, and ghost stories to craft an exquisitely unsettling dark fantasy." —*Publishers Weekly*, starred review

"Engrossing . . . [Readers] will enjoy this mashup of *The X-Files* and *The Blair Witch Project*." —*Kirkus Reviews*

"Marshall delivers a haunting tale about a childhood game that twists into a disturbing rescue mission." —*SLJ*

"Marshall keeps the twisty narrative intentionally murky, ensuring that readers, like Sara and her friends, may never find their way out." —*Booklist*

"A page-turner for anyone who loves a mystery tinged with the occult." —*VOYA*

OTHER BOOKS YOU MAY ENJOY

RULES FOR VANISHING

KATE ALICE MARSHALL

PENGUIN BOOKS

To the No Name Writing Group,
for walking the road with me.

PENGUIN BOOKS
An imprint of Penguin Random House LLC, New York

First published in the United States of America by Viking,
an imprint of Penguin Random House LLC, 2019
Published by Penguin Books, an imprint of Penguin Random House LLC, 2021

Visit us online at penguinrandomhouse.com

LIBRARY OF CONGRESS CATALOGING-IN-PUBLICATION DATA IS AVAILABLE

ISBN 9781984837035

Printed in the United States of America

10 9 8 7 6 5 4 3 2 1

Design by Jim Hoover
Text set in Apollo Mt Std and Courier

As requested, we have obtained access to the files of Dr. Andrew Ashford, specifically those concerning the incident in Briar Glen, Massachusetts.

We were unable to remove primary documents and materials from Dr. Ashford's possession without detection, but we have provided transcripts and descriptions of the file's contents, as well as a number of supplemental items not included in the file, which you may find helpful in providing context.

To our knowledge, Dr. Ashford remains unaware of your interest.

THE

ASHFORD

FILES

File #74

"THE MASSACHUSETTS GHOST ROAD"

Briar Glen, Massachusetts

April–May 2017

PART I

THE GAME

INTERVIEW

SARA DONOGHUE

May 9, 2017

ASHFORD: I'm starting the recording now. This is the first interview with Sara Donoghue concerning the disappearances in Briar Glen, Massachusetts. Today is May 9, 2017. Present are Sara Donoghue and myself, Dr. Andrew Ashford. Thank you for joining us today, Miss Donoghue.

SARA: You're welcome. I guess. I don't know what you expect me to tell you.

ASHFORD: The truth, Miss Donoghue. I think you'll find we are some of the few people who are willing to hear it.

SARA: So you believe me, then?

ASHFORD: Is there a reason I shouldn't?

Sara begins to laugh, a low sound that croaks in the back of her throat.

ASHFORD: Miss Donoghue—

Sara's laughter continues, her shoulders shaking. Her hands cover her face.

??: Pay attention.[1]

<Recording ends.>

....
1 Transcriptionist's note: Unable to identify the third voice. It is heavily distorted with static, and a droning sound appears on the recording simultaneously with the voice.

EXHIBIT A

Text message received by all Briar Glen High School students on Monday, April 17, 2017

DO YOU WANT TO KNOW WHERE LUCY WENT?

SHE WENT TO PLAY THE GAME.

YOU CAN PLAY, TOO.

FIND A PARTNER.

FIND A KEY.

FIND THE ROAD.

YOU HAVE TWO DAYS.

SARA DONOGHUE

WRITTEN TESTIMONY

1

THE MESSAGE ARRIVES overnight, and by Monday morning it's all anyone is talking about. People cluster around their phones, as if by reading the text again, comparing the identical messages, they might reveal some new clue about who sent them.

"Hey, Sara! Do you want to play the game?" Tyler Martinez asks, lunging toward me as I walk inside, the first bell ringing. He waggles his eyebrows at me and swings away, laughing at his own joke. I cross my arms over my ribs and lean forward, as if pushing against a current.

Whispers of *Lucy* are everywhere. And *the game*. People in clots, heads leaned together.

I've timed things so that I arrive just before the bell, and the hallway is emptying out as the threat of tardy slips overwhelms the urge to gossip. A few stragglers give me odd looks. Odder than usual. *I bet she sent it*, I imagine them whispering. *She's* obsessed.

The game. Lucy Gallows. And Wednesday is the anniversary. It doesn't take a genius. I'd probably blame me, too.

I slide into first period and take my seat, as close to the back corner as I can get.

"Hey. Sara." Trina sits at the group table in front of mine, and she has to twist around in her seat and lean to talk to me. Her blue eyes are piercing in their exquisite concern, her blonde hair swept up in a casual ponytail that looks more glamorous than anything I've managed since the days when she would sit behind me for hours, coercing my mousy hair into french braids and fishtails. "How are you doing?"

"Fine," I mutter. I can't look her in the eye. Her expression is too painfully sympathetic. It would be one thing if it was a performance, but it's genuine. And it's there every time she looks at me, like she's worried that I'm going to crumple under the strain of my personal tragedies at any moment.

"I don't think you did it," she says, leaning closer. Which means that people are already saying that I did.

"I didn't."

She nods slowly. "Don't let anyone give you crap for it," she says.

"How do you suggest I stop them?" I ask. She flinches back a little, but she's spared the need to answer by the second bell, marking the beginning of class. She straightens in her seat. I slouch down as Mr. Vincent launches into his daily preamble, complete with the terrible joke he inflicts on us every day.

"—and he says, 'Me? I'm a giant heavy metal fan.'" He wraps

up just as the door opens. Anthony Beck steps into the room to the sound of groans, and slaps a hand to his forehead.

"I missed the joke of the day?" he asks in exaggerated despair. He flashes a smile, his dimples deep, his brown eyes bright and half-hidden by his wavy black hair. Back when we were younger, when we were friends, he was skinny as a rail, all elbows and knees, his smile too big for his body. The last year or two he's started to add muscle, and the nerd who'd tripped over his own feet is co-captain of the lacrosse and soccer teams, an athletic scholarship waiting for him at Northeastern. He got his ear pierced over break, and the silver stud winks.

"I hope you have a good reason for missing out on my effervescent wit," Mr. Vincent says.

"It took me all morning to text the entire school. My thumbs are cramping like you wouldn't believe," Anthony says with a joker's grin. "Sorry, Mr. V. Won't happen again." His gaze roves around the room, and his grin wobbles a moment when he sees me. We're assigned to the same small group for our current project, which means we've been sitting together for the past couple of weeks, but we've managed not to exchange more than a dozen words. He's been responsible for eleven of them.

He slings himself into the chair beside me. It's much too cramped for his tall frame, and I shrink farther back into the corner, away from him. Mr. Vincent shakes his head.

Anthony sneaks a glance at me. I duck over my notebook, trying to ignore him. It isn't easy.

Anthony Beck and Trina Jeffries used to be two of my best friends. There were six of us—seven when we let Trina's little brother, Kyle, hang out—a roving gang of miscreants who stuck together from first grade until high school. We even had a stupid group name. The Wildcats. It was the Unicorn Wildcats until fifth grade, a compromise that Trina had worked out when the vote was split down the middle—my sister, Becca, and I on opposite sides of the debate, as usual. I was pulling for the Unicorns, of course. Back then my aesthetic was 70 percent glitter, before the severe color allergy I developed in middle school. Becca, though? She was fierce from the start.

We all linked hands, crossing our arms to grab the person on the opposite side, and shook on it. *We are the Unicorn Wildcats. Friends forever and ever. No matter what.*

To a bunch of first graders, it felt like an unbreakable bond. Forever felt possible. It felt inevitable. But now Becca is gone, and I haven't spoken to any of them about more than the Cold War or sine and cosine for almost a year.

Mr. Vincent is starting to outline the day's agenda when a hand shoots up in the second row. He pauses, rhythm disrupted. The corner of his mouth tightens, but that's the only sign of irritation. "Vanessa. If you need help with your current project, we can talk during check-in."

"It's not about my w-work," Vanessa says. "It's about the t-t-text message we all g-got."

"Yes. I saw that. And obviously, it's intriguing," Mr. Vincent says. He settles back against his desk. "But I'm not sure how it's relevant to the Industrial Revolution."

"But it's r-relevant to history. Local history," Vanessa says, pushing her round glasses up her nose.

From my angle I can only see the curve of her cheek and the back of her head, but like most of the people in the room, I've known Vanessa Han since kindergarten, and I can imagine the familiar expression of intense interest she must have fixed on Mr. Vincent. She wears thick-framed glasses and leggings with wild, colorful patterns, a look both bold and self-assuredly nerdy, much like Vanessa herself.

"Local history," Mr. Vincent echoes. "You mean the reference to Lucy? Meaning Lucy Gallows." He rubs his chin. "All right. It has nothing to do with nineteenth-century methods of production and their impact on the idea of the nuclear family, but what the hell. All right, who can tell me the story of Lucy Gallows?"

Half a dozen hands go up. He points. Jenny Stewart speaks up first. "Wasn't she, like, this girl from a hundred years ago? Her brother killed her and buried her body in the woods, and now the woods are haunted."

Vanessa gives her a withering look. "Th-that's not—" The next word tangles itself up in her mouth, and she falls silent for a beat before continuing in a firm, steady tone. "That's not true."

"Now, that's an interesting thought," Mr. Vincent says. "What's true, and what isn't? And how do we determine the difference? Let's set aside the supernatural for the moment. Whether or not there's a ghost in the woods of Briar Glen, it's part of local legend, and it must have come from somewhere. So was that somewhere a complete fiction, concocted by some creative soul and embellished over the years? Or does it have a seed of truth?"

I shut my eyes. No one knows what *really* happened to her.

Which is probably why she's stuck around in the town's memory for so long.

"Sara."

My eyes snap open. Mr. Vincent is looking at me.

"Last semester, when we were doing the project on assessing unusual historical sources, you used the legend of Lucy Gallows for your paper, didn't you?"

"I don't—" My mouth is dry. I lick my lips. I was hoping he wouldn't remember. Not that anyone is likely to have forgotten, when I spent months burying myself in stories of Lucy and making no attempt to hide it. "Yes," I say.

"And what did you find out?"

All eyes are on me, heads swiveling, bodies turning in their cramped seats. Except for Anthony, looking off into the distance conspicuously. Trina catches my eye and smiles a little, encouraging. I clear my throat. If there's anyone left who doesn't suspect me already, they will now. "There wasn't a girl named Lucy Gallows. But there was a girl named Lucy Callow, and she did go missing in the forest," I say haltingly.

"And her ghost kidnapped your sister, right?" Jeremy Polk says. Attention snaps to him. Anthony makes a sound in the back of his throat a little like a growl, glaring daggers at his best friend and co-captain. Jeremy's smile flicks off like a light. "Sorry," he mutters.

"What the fuck, Jeremy?" Anthony says.

Mr. Vincent pushes off from the desk, his voice pitched low and level. "Jeremy, I know that you're aware that's an inappropriate comment. We'll talk about it after class. And, Anthony? Let's all try to keep things civil."

Jeremy ducks his head, muttering another apology and rubbing his neck just under where one of his hearing aids sits, a habit he's had as long as I've known him. My heart pounds in my chest, my mouth dry as the surface of Mars. *Do you want to know where Lucy went?*

Yes.

Because Becca went there, too.

"Sara is right," Mr. Vincent says, redirecting with hardly a hitch. "Lucy Callow was fifteen in April of 1953, when she went missing. The name change came later, as the ghost story evolved. In cases like this, it's important to go back to official, contemporary records as much as possible. With Lucy Callow, there's still a great deal we don't know, but many of the popular stories are easily disproved. But even if those stories aren't factually true, they can help teach us about the people who told them. What was important to them, what scared them. Ghost stories are a vibrant, essential part of local culture."

He keeps going, prompting students to supply other ghost stories and urban legends, coming up with ideas for how to track down their origins.

I hardly hear it. All I hear are the last words my sister spoke, muttering into her phone. On April 18, one year ago.

We know where the road is. We've got the keys. That's all we need to find her. I'm not backing down now. Not after everything we've done to get this close.

And then she turned and saw me. Slammed her bedroom door closed.

The next morning she was gone, and she never came home.

EXHIBIT B

"The Legend of Lucy Gallows"

Excerpted from *Local Lore: Stories of Briar Glen* by Jason Sweet

It was a Sunday—April 19, 1953—and Lucy Gallows's sister was getting married on a sprawling property at the edge of the Briar Glen Woods. Little Lucy, age twelve, was the flower girl. But following an argument with her mother, she ran away into the woods in her crisp white dress with its blue ribbon around the waist. Everyone expected she'd be back in a minute or two, as soon as she calmed down, but ten minutes later she hadn't returned—and then twenty minutes, and then half an hour.

Lucy's brother, Billy, was sent to fetch his sister. He walked into the woods. The only way forward was a narrow track, a deer trail through the trees. He called her name—*Lucy! Lucy!*—but received no answer except the calling of crows.

And then he saw it: the road. There were roads here and there in the woods, the remnants of the original settlement of Briar Glen, which had burned down in 1863. These roads were now often nothing more than a stretch of trees planted in too straight a line to spring from nature, or one stone pressed up against another where all the rest had long since been knocked astray. At first this road was like that, a dimple in the underbrush and a few scattered stones marked with the tools of men. But as Billy chased it, the road widened, and the stones knocked up against each other, beginning to form a smooth path through the thick forest.

He was certain that Lucy had followed the road, though he couldn't explain the strength of the conviction to anyone who had asked afterward. And yet for all that conviction, every step he took seemed to be more difficult than the one before. As the road grew easier, his way grew harder, as if he was laboring against an invisible force.

His feet got heavier and heavier. The air seemed to push against him. It became almost unbearable, and then—there was Lucy. He could see her ahead of him, around a slight bend in the road. She was talking to someone—a man in a patchy brown suit and a wide-brimmed hat. Billy called her name. She didn't turn. The man bent slightly to talk to her, smiling. He put out his hand.

Billy screamed his sister's name and thrashed toward her. But Lucy didn't seem to hear him. She took the stranger's hand, and together they walked down the road. They moved swiftly, not burdened as Billy was, and the road seemed to follow, vanishing beneath Billy's feet. In moments the road and the man and little Lucy Gallows were gone.

Townspeople searched the woods for weeks, but no sign of Lucy was ever found. But every so often, someone stumbles across the road, winding through the woods, and sees a girl running down it, dressed in a white dress with a blue ribbon. You can never catch up with her, they say, and you will find yourself alone in the bewildering woods, with no sign of a road or a girl or a clear way home.

So be careful what roads you take, and be careful who you follow down them.

INTERVIEW

SARA DONOGHUE

May 9, 2017

Sara Donoghue sits in the interview room. It is hard to tell what sort of building it might belong to. The walls are cinder block, painted a dingy white. An empty metal bookshelf stands against one wall; the table in the center is a cheap folding picnic table.

Dr. Andrew Ashford enters the room and settles into the chair opposite Sara Donoghue once again. Ashford is black, dark skinned, hair silver. A dark web of scars puckers the skin on the back of one hand. He carries a briefcase, which he sets beside him on the floor. Sara Donoghue, in contrast, is a slight girl with medium-brown hair. She wears black jeans, a black tank top, and a black sweater that has slipped down one shoulder, baring a freckled shoulder. She seems tucked in on herself and tense with nervous energy.

ASHFORD: I'm sorry about that. Our equipment is usually reliable, but we occasionally encounter technical difficulties around these sorts of events.

Sara looks to the side, as if uninterested.

ASHFORD: Tell me about your sister.

SARA: Becca?

ASHFORD: Do you have another sister?

SARA: No, it's just—what do you want to know? There's a lot in the reports. Official records.

ASHFORD: I want to know about your sister from your perspective. Before her disappearance. What was she like? Did she have a lot of friends?

Sara hesitates. She speaks carefully, as if worried Ashford will get the wrong impression.

SARA: She had us. The five of us.

ASHFORD: The "Wildcats"?

SARA: Yeah. But by the time she disappeared, we weren't really hanging out together anymore. We hit high school, and Anthony and Trina got involved with sports. Mel started spending all her time with the theater kids, and Becca . . . I don't really know what happened with Becca.

ASHFORD: Did she have other friends?

SARA: She was friendly with almost everyone. But she didn't have close friends, other than us.

ASHFORD: She didn't meet anyone new she clicked with?

SARA: You mean her boyfriend? I guess. But she was never serious about him.

ASHFORD: What makes you say that?

SARA: She liked him because he listened to her. But they didn't belong together.

Sara chews on her thumbnail.

SARA: You always got the sense she didn't belong here at all.

ASHFORD: Did that have anything to do with the fact that she was adopted?

SARA: What? No. I mean, it wasn't always easy for her, I guess. Briar Glen's about as white as you can get, and people can be pretty racist even if they don't mean to be, but at least at home, that was never a problem. It wasn't about *not* belonging, I guess. More like she deserved to belong somewhere . . . bigger. Better.

ASHFORD: Like where?

SARA: New York. LA. Paris. Someplace where her art could really take off.

ASHFORD: I've seen some of her photographs.

Ashford opens a folder on the table and spreads out several glossy photos. The top photo shows six preteens. A printed label has been affixed to the front, identifying each of the children. Becca and Sara stand at the center, arms around each other, Becca's outline slightly blurred as if she's barely managed to dash back into the frame. Despite their different ethnicities—Sara white, Becca Asian—there is something about their stances that marks them as obviously related. Anthony Beck and Nick Dessen, both white, stand to the left of the sisters, Anthony with his chin tilted up in a too-cool pose he hasn't grown into and Nick, a skinny kid in an oversize windbreaker, mimicking him. On the right, Trina Jeffries breaks the mood with a smile, her hand lifted to tuck her hair behind her ear, and Melanie Whittaker, a black girl in a denim jacket covered in iron-on patches, curls the corner of her mouth like she can't quite take herself seriously.

Ashford slides this photograph to the side, baring another. Sara frowns, a faint line of confusion between her brows. He taps the new photo, an image of a young man with his face in blank shadow. The light is odd at his shoulders, as if his outline is fracturing.

ASHFORD: What do you know about this photograph?

SARA: I haven't seen that one before.

ASHFORD: What can you tell me about Nick Dessen?

SARA: Aren't you going to ask about the other photo?

ASHFORD: Which one? This one?

He moves aside the photo of Nick Dessen and places another on the center of the table. It shows Sara, her hair damp and hanging limply around her face, standing next to a young woman wearing a white dress with a slash of blue ribbon across her waist. The girl has extended her hand; Sara has begun to lift her own, as if to take it.

ASHFORD: You find this photo remarkable?

SARA: Don't you?

ASHFORD: Not particularly. Two girls. About to hold hands.

SARA: But she's . . .

ASHFORD: She's Lucy Callow? She does bear a resemblance to the photos we have, but existing photos of Lucy Callow aren't high quality. This could be anyone. [*Pause*] But it isn't, is it? It is Lucy. You found her.

Sara meets Ashford's eyes. She's silent for a moment. Then she lets out a quick, choked-off laugh.

SARA: No. We didn't find Lucy.

ASHFORD: Then—

SARA: She found us.

2

BECCA TOOK PHOTOS for the yearbook every year, and you could always tell which ones were hers. Most of the other photos were posed or awkward, the lighting flat, the students interchangeable. Becca's photos were different. She captured the longing of unrequited love in the way a girl stared across the classroom, her chin resting on her fist as she slumped over her desk. In the long, lean line of Anthony's body, stretched out along the ground, the arc of the soccer ball unmistakable even in the still frame as he dove to meet it, she captured exultation and concentration. Becca had a way of making everyone feel seen.

It was remarkable, then, how little time anyone spent looking for her.

The official story is that she ran off with a boy. Zachary Kent. Bad news, according to my parents. He was older than her. My parents tried to forbid her from dating him—hated his pierced lip and dyed hair, the music he played, the car he drove. I only met him once, when I nearly ran into him and Becca coming out of the Half Moon Diner, his arm slung over Becca's shoulders. Becca introduced him, but all he said to me was "Hey" before they got into his car and drove away. I saw the way she looked at him, and

I saw the photo she took of him. One ankle over his knee, a note-book propped on his leg, his eyes squinting off into the distance.

It was the kind of photograph Becca loved the most. Peeling back the layers of a person bit by bit. Making a study of them. There was curiosity in that photo, but not love. No wild abandon. She might have left home, but it wouldn't have been for him.

Yet they disappeared, and they disappeared together, and there had been all the fights with Mom and Dad—months of them, Becca alternating between giving them the silent treatment and screaming at them for being too controlling, while they managed to find fault in everything she did: hang out with Zachary, drop out of choir, steal away on her mysterious late-night trips she would never explain to any of us. So when she vanished, they looked for her, but not too hard; they didn't think she wanted to be found.

I tried to tell them about the conversation I'd heard, and what Becca had said about the road—Lucy Gallows road, I thought, though I couldn't be sure. And my mother told one of her friends, and her friend's daughter overheard, and suddenly the whole school seemed to know. That was how the rumor started—half rumor, half joke. The kind of nervous cruelty that kids spit out without thinking, to cover up their own uneasiness.

Lucy Gallows took Becca Donoghue into the woods, and never let her out again.

No one believed it, of course. It was all just a morbid joke. But Becca wasn't the sort for jokes or urban legends. She believed. And that meant that either my sister was losing it, or I had to believe, too.

And so I started searching. For the road. For Lucy. For my sister. It never got me anywhere.

Until now.

By lunchtime the novelty of the messages has started to fade, but the whispers still drive me out of the cafeteria to the back steps, where I sit with my packed lunch, staring out over the back lot at the looming trees. A single crow sits in the high branches, riding the swaying of the wind.

The door behind me opens. The bird takes off. I shift to the side so whoever it is can get past, but they stay at the top of the steps. I turn, squinting. Vanessa stands there, her phone gripped in her hand, her backpack dangling off one shoulder. "Th-there you are," she says.

"Um. Hi," I say. "Can I help you with something?"

"Maybe," she says. "Are you going to do it?"

"Do what?" I ask.

"P-play the game," she says. "The whole thing. The road, and the k-key, and finding a p-p-partner." Her stutter is pronounced, but she doesn't fight it like she used to when we were younger, and it has its own relaxed flow to it. She likes to tell people it's worth the wait to hear what she has to say.

"Why would I?"

"Because of Becca."

She says *Becca* and not just *your sister*, and I think that's the only reason I don't leave right away. So few people say her name anymore. Like it's bad luck. "You don't really believe that stupid joke, do you? That Lucy Gallows took my sister?" I'm not even sure if *I* believe it.

"No. But you must be wondering if the t-texts have anything to do with her. With Becca."

"Of course," I snap. Her cheeks go red and she pushes up her glasses, which has the effect of half hiding her face behind her sweater sleeve. "Why do you care, anyway?"

"I d-don't believe in ghosts," Vanessa says. "But I like history. And mysteries. I want to know who wrote these. And what it's supposed to mean. I thought, since you d-did all that research, you might know."

"Oh." There's something wrong with me, since Becca vanished. If anyone so much as hints at what happened, I react like they're attacking me. Even with my friends. Which is why I don't have any left. "Here, sit down," I say, gesturing for Vanessa to join me on the steps. She perches on the top step, a little above me.

"So, Lucy Gallows," I say. "Real name Lucy Callow. Disappeared on April 19, 1953. Wednesday's the anniversary. Her brother was arrested for her murder, but since they never found the body, they couldn't really make a case and he was released. She was fifteen, not twelve, and she was a bridesmaid, not a flower girl, but otherwise the story's pretty much what they say."

"And the game is that stupid thing everyone played when we were little kids," Vanessa says.

"Not exactly," I say. "You've played it?"

"Sure. When I was, l-like, eight," she says.

"Me too," I say. With Anthony. Standing at the end of the road into the woods, on either side of the median line. *Hold hands. Close your eyes. Take thirteen steps.* Supposedly, this summons the specter of Lucy Gallows to walk beside you.

"Did anything happen?" Vanessa asks, leaning forward.

"Of course not." There are two ways the game "works": either you're young and imaginative enough that you conjure the brush of a breeze into the brush of Lucy Gallows's hand, the skittering of leaves into her footsteps, the creak of trees into her spectral cries—or you have friends sneaking up behind you to mess with you. Similarly, there are two kinds of people who play the game: kids young enough to still believe in magic, and teenagers trying to impress crushes.

"But you said n-not exactly. So what's different?"

"There's an older version," I say. "Or a different one, at least. You're still supposed to have a partner and take thirteen steps, but it doesn't have anything to do with Lucy. It's supposed to summon the road—or it's how you get down the road, or something. The road has seven gates. If you get through them all, you get—something. Like a wish. That story is older than the Lucy Gallows story—older than Lucy Callow. Some people say she might have known the story, and that's why she got on the road when it appeared."

"Some people?" Vanessa asks, eyebrows raised.

"Ms. Evans," I clarify. The town librarian was the same age as Lucy when she went missing, and she was my best source for all game-related lore. For a while, a seventy-eight-year-old woman was the person I talked to the most.

"I've never heard of that part of the g-game," Vanessa says, pushing up her glasses with the side of her thumb.

"It got dropped at some point, I guess," I say. "Maybe in the eighties when those kids went missing?"

"I thought that was a rumor," Vanessa says. "Satanic p-p-panic and stuff. Those kids just ran away."

"That's what everyone decided," I reply, voice flat. Vanessa bites her lip, her eyes dancing away from mine. I guess I'm officially Trauma Girl, with the black clothes and the antisocial reputation to match. I've gotten used to that particular reaction, since I refuse to politely pretend Becca never existed.

Vanessa clears her throat. "So you need a partner," she says. "And a key?"

That's the part that made my stomach lurch, when I saw the message. Because I've never mentioned the keys. I've never heard anyone but Becca talk about them. The only place I've seen them mentioned, other than that overheard conversation, is her notebook, left behind when she vanished. "The keys open the gates. They have to be your keys. They connect you to the gates—to the road. I think." Becca's notes were vague on that front.

"So all that's l-left is finding the road," Vanessa says. "The one just off Cartwright?"

"That's where people play the game, but the spot where Lucy's brother claimed he saw her was actually, like, five miles west of there," I say.

"Is there a road there?"

"Well, no," I say, shrugging. "But there wouldn't be, if it was a ghostly apparition, would there? Except when Lucy's out haunting." I keep my voice casual, like there isn't a hand tightening around my throat with every word. Because if I was normal, if

I had *moved on* and *let go of this fanciful coping strategy*, as my mother once suggested, none of this would bother me.

"I don't believe in ghosts," Vanessa reminds me. "Do you?"

I pick at the crust of my sandwich. I want to say no, but it isn't exactly true anymore. I have reasons to believe. Because of Becca, and because—

It's just not a simple answer anymore.

She tucks her hands under her thighs on either side. "I want to t-try. The g-game and the road and everything."

"Why?" I ask. "If you don't believe in any of it?"

"I want to know for sure."

"Are you asking me if I'll be your partner?" I ask, half hoping she is.

"N-no. I already have one. Sorry," she says, cheeks beet red now. "Thanks for your help."

"Yeah," I say as she hurriedly stands up. "No problem."

She's already disappearing back inside.

I take my phone out of my backpack and unlock it. The text message is already on the screen, waiting for me. A road, a partner, a key. And two days to find them, if you want to play.

Do I?

I remember that door slamming shut, Becca's unreadable expression. I knew something was wrong, but I didn't say anything. Not for days. Not until it was obvious that she wasn't coming home.

The casual answer I gave Vanessa was true—there isn't a road at that spot in the forest. What I didn't say was that I went there a dozen times in the months after Becca disappeared. I've wandered through the woods and called her name. Lucy's, too. No one has ever answered.

But what if I just had the wrong day? Becca went missing in April. It's April again now.

I don't believe in ghosts, not exactly. But I don't believe Becca is dead, either. Which means she's out there, and no one is looking for her but me.

3

SOME PARENTS, WHEN their child is missing, keep their room as a shrine, exactly the same as when they left it. As if by some sympathetic magic it will summon them back from wherever they've wandered to.

My parents aren't like that. Three days after Becca went missing, my mother went into her room and tidied it up. She did all of Becca's laundry, wiped down her desk, changed the linens on her bed, decluttered everything. Closed the door. Didn't go back in for eight months.

When she did, it was to box everything up. Thirteen boxes. Ten went to thrift shops or the dump. Three went to the attic, tucked next to the boxes of elementary-school projects and macaroni art: artifacts of things long gone. The bed and the desk went out to the thrift shop, too. It would have somehow been less painful if she'd gotten rid of all the furniture, purged the house of Becca's presence, but she kept the bookshelf and the chair, moving them into the living room. It was as if Becca was so thoroughly forgotten they didn't even provoke painful memories.

I didn't argue. My parents didn't blame me for Becca's disappearance, but they resented me for my part in what followed. The strange rumors, the ridicule. My refusal to admit that my sister abandoned us for a boy she'd only known for three months.

I didn't argue, but I sneaked in while my mother was in the bathroom and took the box from under my sister's bed where she kept her most treasured possessions. A few early photos, too embarrassingly amateurish to show anyone else, but full of the promise of talent to come; her journal—not diary—in which she jotted scattered thoughts and philosophical musings; a handful of trinkets from our infrequent travels; and our grandmother's wedding ring, saved for when Becca got married.

It was inside the cover of the journal that I found the inscription.

FIND THE ROAD. FIND THE GATES. FIND THE GIRL.

I'm sitting on my bed now with the journal open in my lap, turning the pages. Most of it is notes on photos she's taken, critiquing her own work or recording ideas for shots. In between are scraps of poetry, meandering bits of song lyrics. She wrote a few songs with Zachary, and his handwriting is scrawled next to hers, crowding it in. I resent every letter, every word.

But the last bit of poetry, or song lyrics, or whatever—they stop me dead every time.

I saw it again | Out of the corner of my eye. | Doesn't matter where I am. | Doesn't matter how hard I try | To get away.

It's waiting | Waiting for me.

And so is she.

After that, the journal changes. In big, blocky letters, traced over and over again until they blurred and grayed, it says THE ROAD. And under that, Becca had written:

Don't leave the road.

When it's dark, don't let go.

There are other roads. Don't follow them.

The pages after are dense with notes about Lucy Gallows and the game—about the keys, the forest, and a city Becca never names. In between the pages, she's tucked photos of the forest. Zachary is in some of them. There's even a photo of Lucy's tombstone—not that there's a body in that grave.

Eventually the neat, bulleted notes devolve. They turn into odd nonsense. Scraps of phrases, unsettling drawings of eyes and hands and a figure that seems stretched, legs and arms too long—a man's body, but with the head of another beast, triangular, antlers branching out and out, sometimes filling the whole page. I've read every word.

the birds come after the dark

seven gates

follow the rules

keep moving

And on and on. Many of the phrases read like instructions, but there are others that don't have any clear imperative, like the one written in a spiral bursting across a page. *In the house in the town in the woods on the road are the halls that breathe. The singing will lure you the smoke will infest you the words will unmake you the woman will hate you.*

I've spent hours paging through that notebook again and again, but no secrets have unlocked themselves for me. I've gone to the place in the forest where Lucy Callow disappeared, in daylight and in the dark, on the full moon, in a white dress, whatever any legend says.

Because I don't believe in ghosts, but I want to. I know Becca didn't run away. That leaves one possibility and one impossibility, and I long for the impossible. Because if she isn't dead, if she's only been *taken*, she can be brought back.

The front door opens, and I hear the familiar sequence of sounds that mark my mother's arrival home: keys clattering in the dish inside the door, shoes thumping haphazardly into the corner, quick steps to the kitchen and the *poik* of a cork popped from a half-full bottle. She must know about the text by now. She must have heard. It's a small town.

I shut the journal back in the box and shove it under my bed. I pull my feet up and tuck them under me on the bed, a thousand versions of the coming conversation playing through my head, a thousand versions of how I'll convince my mother not to worry about anything.

My mother's footsteps come up the stairs, and she knocks lightly on my door before swinging it open. "How was school?" she asks.

So she wants to build up to it. "Fine," I say.

She pauses. She seems to search my face, as if looking for an answer—but to what question? Does she want to know if the text upset me? Does she want to know if I was the one that sent it out?

"Good," she says. I blink. "I'm thinking of ordering out for dinner. Pizza okay?" Apparently we aren't going to talk about it at all.

"Yeah," I say.

"Or Chinese."

"Uh-huh," I say. Briar Glen's only Chinese restaurant is owned by an Italian man named Aurelio, so it isn't exactly authentic cuisine, but it's tasty. Henry Lin's parents run the pizzeria in a bit of gastronomical symmetry, and we order from one or the other most nights—and most of the rest, we subsist on the leftovers.

My parents aren't divorced, officially. But even before Becca, things were strained between them. Dad stuck around for three months after. Took a job in New York, and while he says he isn't seeing anyone, one of his coworkers keeps tagging him in joint selfies at "work events" with a borderline psychotic number of emojis. He still pays a private detective to look for Becca, gets updates every couple weeks—always another promising lead, never anything solid. Even if he's given up, he isn't willing to stop looking. Not yet.

Unlike Mom. She isn't going to ask about the text, because it would mean, inevitably, talking about Becca. And that is one thing we can never do. Silence is the only way she knows how to deal with pain. As if by pretending she's moved on, she can stop hurting. All it really means is that we're forced to endure the pain alone, without each other to lean on.

When I lost my sister, I lost my whole family. I don't know if I can ever get them back. But I can find Becca.

Or at least I can try.

I thought I wouldn't be able to sleep, but it seems like the moment I shut my eyes, I'm dreaming. I stand on a road—a normal road, white line down the median, asphalt shimmering with heat. I'm walking down the median line, and another girl is walking with me. I've never seen her before. She's my age, with long, dark hair and a tattoo of a feather on the inside of her left wrist. Five crows wheel overhead, calling.

"Is this it?" I ask.

"The road?" she guesses, and smiles. She has a dimple in just one cheek. "No. Just *a* road. A safe one, for now."

"I need to find the other one," I say.

"Less safe," she observes. I nod, the whole situation perfectly normal in the way that dreams are. "It'll find you. As long as you're all together and you're looking for it, it'll be there."

"You're sure?" I ask.

"I try not to be sure of too much," she says. Then she nods ahead. The horizon is growing dark—no, a darkness is growing, swelling, surging over the distant hills, the trees, rushing toward us like a tsunami. She reaches out her hand and I start to reach back.

And then I wake. I stare at the ceiling for a few minutes, waiting for my frantic heartbeat to slow down, and then I sit up. I check the time. Barely past ten, but if that's what's waiting for me, I'm not going to try to get back to sleep.

I take Becca's notebook and her old camera and sneak out the back door. It doesn't take much sneaking—Mom takes sleeping pills most nights. Since Becca.

I'm not sure where I'm going until I'm already walking that direction. There's a park on Galveston and Grand. A creek runs through the center of it, trees growing along the banks. It's as far from the wilderness as you can get and keep the green, but to the Wildcats, it has been Narnia and Middle-earth and the Amazon jungle.

We would always meet at the bridge. It's five feet across, with dull wood planks and handrails that would drive splinters into your palms if you tried to run your hands down them. Becca and I were almost always the first ones to arrive, and we'd sit chucking sticks into the water and watching them rush away from us. I lean on the railing, trying to feel her presence next to me. The way she always stood, elbows on the rail, spinning the ring around her thumb.

I thought that when you lost someone, you lost the details first, but details are what I still have—the crinkle at the corners of her eyes when she made fun of me, the way she'd chew on her thumbnail when she was really focused. It's the big things that are slipping away. Her face. Her voice. The way it felt to be around her.

Becca was—is—six months older than me. Our parents tried to have a child for five years with no luck, so they went through the long, arduous process of adoption. They had one birth mother change her mind in the delivery room before they adopted Becca, tiny and perfect and theirs.

It was less than a month later that they found out about me. They'd always wanted two kids. They shrugged and laughed and told themselves they wouldn't treat us any differently. Mostly, they managed it—but you could always sense how hard they were working at it: second-guessing themselves, overcompensating for any hint that they might not be treating Becca the same as me by lavishing her with just a little too much attention and praise to be genuine. Maybe that's why her relationship with them fell apart so much when she hit high school. Or maybe something else was at the root of her silences, her strange moods, the way she avoided home whenever she could.

Long before high school, though, I was always chasing after Becca. The week she stood on her own, I started trying to pull myself upright. I walked within a month of her. Anything she touched, I had to have. My first word was my sister's name, and I'd shriek it at night until my parents put me in her crib to sleep.

I always thought the two of us were the center of gravity around which the rest of the group orbited, but I was wrong. Becca was. She kept us together. She was the one who pulled away from the group first. And after she vanished, we fractured for good.

I lift her camera and snap a photo. The flash goes off. I look at the screen. The water is a confusion of reflected light, the trees indistinct shadows. I'm not nearly the photographer my sister was. Is.

Was.

"Sara?" I'm not completely surprised to hear Anthony's voice, but I'm not sure I'm happy, either. His footsteps crunch closer, then turn hollow as he steps onto the bridge.

"Hey," he says. He leans against the guardrail next to me, looking down at the water. The park lights lend just enough illumination to glimmer on the water's surface, the delicate folds where it runs over the rocks. "I kind of thought you'd be here. Or in the woods."

"No point going out there yet," I say. "It won't be tonight."

"You're sure?"

"It's on the anniversary. Wednesday. Two days from the

time the messages were sent is just past midnight, Wednesday morning."

His hands tighten on the handrail, and the hinge of his jaw flares out as he clenches his teeth. "Yeah. I know." He glances at me quickly.

"You think I did it," I say. My voice is flat, but the betrayal slices through me. "You think I sent the message."

"I don't think that. Maybe I did for a moment. But only a moment," he says.

"Everyone else thinks it was me," I say. I scuff my foot against the bridge, knocking a pebble off into the water with a barely audible *plink*. Anthony nudges my shoulder with his, startling me with a moment of friendly intimacy I thought was long behind us.

"Only the idiots," he assures me.

"You said you thought I'd done it, for a moment."

"And I was momentarily an idiot," Anthony says, grinning that grin that is impossible not to echo, for a fleeting second. "Trina doesn't think so."

"You talked to her about it?"

He shrugs. "She's worried about you."

"So you mean you talked to each other about *me*," I say.

Anthony makes a frustrated sound. He turns to face me, but I stay stubbornly put, looking straight out at the water. "Come on, Sara. We'd have talked to you if you'd say more than three words to any of us."

"What, it's all my fault?" I ask, turning my head to glare at him.

"We all loved Becca," he says. *Some of us more than others*, I don't tell him, because I'm not supposed to know.

"It doesn't matter," I whisper. "It doesn't matter now."

"No. It doesn't," Anthony says. "Because whatever happened then, I'm here for you now. I don't know if this is a prank or a trap or if there's really something hiding out in the woods, but I'm not letting you go alone."

I stare at him. I feel off balance, like I've lurched forward and haven't gotten my feet under me. For a moment, my body pulses with gratitude and relief—he's doing this for me, he's still my friend, he still cares. And then I draw back, feral anger scrabbling up my spine.

"You're not *letting* me?" I repeat.

"I mean I'm going with you," he says. "I'll be your partner, like the thing said."

"I didn't ask you to go with me," I say.

"But you are going."

"Of course."

He nods, like this settles things. "Then I'm going with you."

"You're just assuming that I don't have anyone else? That I want you to come with me?"

"Why wouldn't you?"

"Really? Let's look." I pull my phone out of my pocket, open up the messages. Scroll back and back and back, until I find the thread with Anthony's name on it.

The most recent message is months old. It's a birthday cake emoji. The one before that is nearly a year old. *You ok?* it reads.

I hold it out to him. "Two messages in a year. My sister vanishes and you don't even bother to text."

He grabs my phone from my hand. I squawk, but he turns his

shoulder to keep me from grabbing it back and taps the screen a few times. Pulls up Trina's messages.

All of Trina's messages. Once a month or so now, links to interesting news stories, funny pictures. Before that, a sparse series of texts telling me that she was around, when I was ready. And around the time that Becca disappeared? Dozens of messages. Maybe hundreds. Telling me she was worried about me. Sending me stupid memes to distract me. Asking me to come hang out. Complaining about her jackass stepfather, our homework, the weather. I answered maybe a half dozen times. Never more than a few words.

He switches to Mel's messages. Mel didn't say as much. She gave up earlier. But they're there. I'd never answered Trina because her kindness hurt too much. I'd never answered Mel because she wanted to be there as my friend, and I'd stopped being able to pretend that was all I wanted, too. And so I'd let both of them—all of them—slip into absence and disconnection.

Anthony hands my phone back to me. I cradle it, thumbing the screen off, and look away from him. "You never answered their texts. So I figured there wasn't any point trying. Which is why I came over. Your mom always told me you were sick."

I was sick. Sick with dread and with sorrow, curled on my bed with a fist against my stomach and nausea making me shudder. I survived the next few weeks and months in a haze. If my mom hadn't been reminding me to eat and shower and go to school, I would have just stayed in bed. Waiting for Becca to come home.

"I didn't want to respond to 'you ok' when you hadn't even

bothered to sit by me at lunch for a year," I snap. "Look, I get it. We were friends when we were kids. High school's different. You've got new friends, and you don't need a weird loser hanging around."

"You're not weird."

"You're in the minority with that opinion."

"Oh, come on, Sara. You can't blame people for thinking it. You barely talk to anyone anymore. You don't wear anything but black. Everyone knows that you go out in the woods by yourself all the time, and you're obsessed with the whole Lucy Gallows thing."

"I don't care what anyone thinks about how I dress. And I only care about Lucy Gallows because Becca did. She was looking for her."

"I know," Anthony says. The bitterness in his voice surprises me. He looks away. "She wanted me to help. She said—she said she could hear her. Lucy. She said she was dreaming about her, but I didn't believe her. I told her they were just dreams."

"Zach believed her," I say, understanding something that's never clicked before. Like why Becca picked Zach, when it was obvious she belonged with Anthony. "That's why she didn't tell anyone else," I say. "That's why she didn't tell me. Because you didn't believe her, and—"

Anthony glares at me. "You know what, Sara? You think people avoid you because you're weird. Did you ever stop to think that maybe they avoid you because you're a jerk?"

The breath goes out of my words. "Not being warm and fuzzy isn't the same thing as being a jerk."

"When you won't even talk to your friends, it gets hard to tell the difference," he says. He shakes his head. "Fine. If you have another partner, you have another partner. I can't force you to go with me. But I'm going to be there. Because I still care about you, even if I've sucked at showing it lately."

"You don't even know where to go."

"I'm sure I can figure it out," he says, and shoves off from the railing. It's started to rain; it patters against my shoulders and sneaks down the nape of my neck. Still I stand for a long while, watching Anthony stride back toward the street, his hands jammed in his pockets. My hands are shaking. I curl my fingers into fists.

Anthony abandoned me, when I needed his friendship the most. Even if maybe I did abandon him first.

I can't pretend that the others didn't reach out. Trina is still doing her best, and it isn't like I've made that easy. Even Mel, not exactly Miss Sentimental, tried to help, and I turned my back on both of them. I kept my grief wrapped tight around me. I kept them at a distance.

And now I might have the chance to get Becca back, and Anthony is right. I need his help. Because I need a partner, and I don't have anyone else to ask.

EXHIBIT C

Group chat transcript

April 18, 2017

TRINA (4:07 pm): Hey guys

NICK (4:08 pm): Sup

MEL (4:08 pm): I didn't even know I still had this app installed

TRINA (4:10 pm): I thought we should talk

MEL (4:11 pm): Are you sure it's safe? It might ruin your reputation.

NICK (4:12 pm): You only wish you were that edgy, Mel.

MEL (4:14 pm): I meant if she gets caught talking to you, nerd squad.

NICK (4:14 pm): Can you have a nerd squad of one?

MEL (4:14 pm): You are nerdy enough to count as four point seven nerds for the purpose of squads. Basic science.

TRINA (4:15 pm): Guys.

NICK (4:15 pm): Um, Trina, "guys" is a sexist term created by the patriarchy to imply that maleness overrules femaleness in a group setting

MEL (4:15 pm): Shut up I don't sound like that

NICK (4:16 pm): a) yes you do and b) you know I dig it

MEL (4:17 pm): Were I but heterosexual my friend

NICK (4:17 pm): You know you'd be all over me

MEL (4:17 pm): Hell yeah. my pasty-white love stallion.

TRINA (4:17 pm): As glad as I am that you two are still friends . . .

TRINA (4:18 pm): WHAT GROSS MEL WHY

MEL (4:18 pm): Where's Anthony?

MEL (4:18 pm): And sorry, I regret everything

NICK (4:18 pm): I don't

ANTHONY (4:18 pm): I'm watching you two reverse-flirt or whatever it is you're doing. Can't talk much. Hiding my phone during "family time."

ANTHONY (4:19 pm): Sorry, answering your question, Mel.

MEL (4:19 pm): We know how chats work. How's the rev

ANTHONY (4:19 pm): She's fine thanks. Wants to see you in church more.

MEL (4:20 pm): That's just bc she loves me more than you

ANTHONY (4:20 pm): Why isn't Sara in the chat?

MEL (4:20 pm): Oh snap

NICK (4:20 pm): Wait, what?

MEL (4:20 pm): Like she'd answer anyway

ANTHONY (4:21 pm): She wasn't at school today, either.

TRINA (4:21 pm): I left Sara off because we need to talk about what to do and I don't want her shutting us down.

TRINA (4:24 pm): So . . . what are we going to do?

ANTHONY (4:25 pm): I'm going. Whatever anyone else decides.

TRINA (4:25 pm): Me too.

NICK (4:25 pm): I was already planning on it. Vanessa wants to go. Going out for dinner in a few minutes, then out ghost hunting.

MEL (4:26 pm): Sorry, have to—NICKY HAS A GIIIIRLFRIEEEEEND.

NICK (4:26 pm): Is there a middle finger emoji? Wait. Found it. [redacted]

MEL (4:27 pm): I don't see what the point is. It's not like anything is going to happen. And besides, I have a date.

NICK (4:28 pm): MELANIE HAS A GIIIIRLFRIEEEEEND.

MEL (4:28 pm): [redacted] [redacted] [redacted]

MEL (4:28 pm): [redacted]

TRINA (4:29 pm): Does anyone know if Sara's going?

MEL (4:29 pm): [redacted]

ANTHONY (4:30 pm): Yeah. She is. She told me.

TRINA (4:30 pm): You talked to her? Is she okay?

ANTHONY (4:31 pm): Yes. Last night. And no. I don't know.
She's the way she's been.

MEL (4:32 pm): Someone should be there if she's going but
we don't all have to be. This isn't an intervention. She just
needs someone so she doesn't slit her wrists in the woods
or something.

TRINA (4:33 pm): That's insensitive and crass.

MEL (4:33 pm): Insensitive and crass is basically my
brand so

PRIVATE MESSAGE: MEL/NICK

NICK (4:33 pm): This is perfect—you show up and save
Sara from herself and she's so grateful she swoons into
your firm yet supple embrace.

MEL (4:33 pm): You know I will cut you if you say the
word supple in any context ever again and also shut
up.

PRIVATE MESSAGE: ANTHONY/MEL

ANTHONY (4:34 pm): Mel. Cut it out.

MEL (4:34 pm): It was a joke.

ANTHONY (4:34 pm): Kyle tried to kill himself a couple months ago.

MEL (4:35 pm): Fuck

MEL (4:35 pm): Really?

MEL (4:35 pm): KYLE?? That's why he wasn't in school? I thought he had the flu.

ANTHONY (4:35 pm): He's okay-ish. I think. Just lay off the jokes.

MAIN CHANNEL

MEL (4:35 pm): Sorry

ANTHONY (4:36 pm) There's always a chance she doesn't show.

TRINA (4:36 pm): Then it's on us.

MEL (4:36 pm): Uh. What's on us.

TRINA (4:37 pm): The game.

MEL (4:38 pm): IT'S NOT REAL

ANTHONY (4:38 pm): I'm bringing someone in case Sara doesn't show. Unless you want to partner up, Trina.

TRINA (4:38 pm): I already agreed to go with someone.

PRIVATE MESSAGE: ANTHONY/TRINA

TRINA (4:39 pm): There's something else I need to talk to you about.

ANTHONY (4:39 pm): What's up?

MAIN CHANNEL

NICK (4:39 pm): Cool. That settles it, then. Midnight in the woods, yeah?

TRINA (4:40 pm): I don't actually know where to go.

NICK (4:40 pm): Vanessa got the GPS coordinates. I'll text you guys.

NICK (4:41 pm): I mean INDIVIDUALS OF VARIOUS GENDER IDENTITIES.

MEL (4:44 pm): Don't bother. I'm not going. BECAUSE
NONE OF IT IS REAL. Becca's gone. She's dead or she's
shooting up in a flophouse or whatever, but she's not in the
woods and she's not the prisoner of some stupid ghost from
an old urban legend. You're all delusional if you think she is
for even a moment. You should do yourselves a favor and
admit that so you can move on.

<MEL has left the chat>

TRINA (4:45 pm): See you guys tonight?

ANTHONY (4:46 pm): Yeah. See you.

NICK (4:46 pm): I'll be there. Ciao, bitches.

<NICK has left the chat>

PRIVATE MESSAGE: ANTHONY/TRINA

ANTHONY (4:47 pm): Trina, what did you need to talk
about?

TRINA (4:47 pm): I

TRINA (4:47 pm): Fuck I really don't know how to say this

ANTHONY (4:48 pm): Are you okay? What's going on?

TRINA (4:48 pm): I found out something and I don't really know what to do

ANTHONY (4:49 pm): Do you want to call? Or come over?

TRINA (4:49 pm): No. I don't know.

TRINA (4:50 pm): I have to go

ANTHONY (4:51 pm): Wait

TRINA (4:52 pm): I have to go. Chris[2] is home.

<TRINA has left the chat>

---

2 Refers to Christopher Mauldin, stepfather of Kyle and Trina Jeffries.

4

WHAT DO YOU wear when you go to meet a ghost? What do you bring?

Every time I went into the woods before, I didn't bring anything more than a flashlight or a granola bar. I never had any hope of finding a sign of Becca. It was more about getting away from home, from town, from every other living soul. I never thought about what would happen if it was all real. If there was a road to walk down. Rationally, I still don't believe in ghosts, in roads that vanish. But I've begun to operate as if it is true, and that is close enough to believing.

In the end I dress warmly, with layers, and pack a lunch box, some water bottles, and a bunch of protein bars. I bring along my heaviest flashlight and extra batteries, Becca's camera, a change of clothes, and the notebook. And, of course, a key. I wait until I'm sure my mom is asleep, leave the note I've written on the kitchen table, and walk out.

If I vanish, I want her to know exactly why. Not like with Becca. Maybe it'll help. Maybe it won't. But at least she'll know why I've gone.

The duffel bag digs into my shoulder as I beeline for the forest. It's a cold night, though at least it isn't raining anymore. The sidewalk gleams under the streetlamps, and I think of black ice, surfaces that look solid until they plunge you into the depths. You could fall forever through darkness like that.

My phone buzzes with a message notification. I hold it face-down for a moment, convinced it's Anthony telling me he's staying home, destroying my chance at this before I even get to the woods. I flip the phone over in my hand and thumb the button to bring the screen to life. And nearly drop it.

One message, it says. From Becca.

I unlock the phone with shaking hands. And stare. The message is from a year ago.

Hey. Going to be out late. Don't worry. See you soon.

She sent that a few days before she disappeared, some night she was out with Zach. Why am I getting a notification for it now?

The phone buzzes. And buzzes again. The same notification popping up over and over until I feel dizzy, like my feet don't quite connect with the ground. I jam my thumb over the power button. The phone keeps buzzing, quick staccato pulses that writhe into the bones of my hand until the power shuts off at last.

My heart beats quick as a hummingbird's. The skin on my arms prickles with goose bumps, and I shake myself a little, trying to pull free of my one, endlessly looped thought—*this is impossible, this is impossible.*

I take a deep breath. It was just some quirk of technology. A coincidence. A fluke.

I turn the phone back on. For a moment I brace myself, certain the buzzing is going to start up again. Nothing. And then—

I'm here.

Not from Becca. From Anthony. He's waiting.

I let out a sound more like a sob than I want to admit and stuff a hand against my mouth. He's waiting for me. It's time to go.

I bury my phone deep in the duffel, where I can't hear it if it buzzes again, and set off at a jog.

EXHIBIT D

Transcript of 911 call

Placed from unknown number, 10:23 p.m., April 18, 2017

Briar Glen, Massachusetts

OPERATOR: 911, what's the address of your emergency?

UNKNOWN CALLER: [*Indistinct*]

OPERATOR: Hello? What's your emergency?

UNKNOWN CALLER: [*Indistinct*] him [*indistinct*] not moving.[3]

OPERATOR: Hello, ma'am? Are you hurt?

UNKNOWN CALLER: No. Not me.

OPERATOR: Is someone hurt?

UNKNOWN CALLER: I think you need to send someone. I think he's dead. I think I . . .

OPERATOR: What is your address, ma'am? Where are you located?

UNKNOWN CALLER: I think . . .

<Call ends.>

....
3 Voice is female, young. Words are difficult to make out; the caller seems to be crying.

VIDEO EVIDENCE

Retrieved from the cell phone of Kyle Jeffries

Recorded April 18, 2017, 11:37 p.m.

For a few seconds, the scenery is shadowy and indistinct, only the sound of footsteps trampling through the brush audible. Then the phone's flashlight comes on, and the camera tilts up, steadying. Trina Jeffries walks ahead, bobbing in and out of the edge of the frame. She looks down at her phone as she walks. The light from the phone washes her out and gives her a pallid cast. She stops, staring at the map on her phone, and doesn't move for nearly ten seconds.

KYLE: Hey. Trina.

She doesn't respond at first.

KYLE: Trina, you okay?

She jerks, eyes focusing on him.

TRINA: What? Sorry. I'm, um—we're almost there.

She scrubs her palm against her jeans, an unconscious gesture.

KYLE: Are we the first ones?

NICK: Up here!

TRINA: I guess not.

She flashes a tight, nervous smile at Kyle.

TRINA: Let's go.

Her voice is too loud, too brightly cheerful, and her brother doesn't respond. He follows her as she marches toward Nick's voice. Soon the light from the phone dimly illuminates Nick Dessen and Vanessa Han. Nick is gawky and lean. His sneakers are duct-taped together at the soles, and his shirt is much too light for this weather, but he doesn't seem to mind. His shaggy brown hair hangs down past his jaw. On someone else it might look roguish; he just looks young. Vanessa has a knit cap jammed down so low it brushes the top of her round glasses.

NICK: Hey, Kyle.

He gives Trina a questioning look. She shrugs, a hiccup of movement.

KYLE: I liked Becca, too. Besides, anything's better than staying home.

NICK: Oh, it's cool you're here. I kind of thought Trina'd bring a boyfriend.

Trina doesn't respond; she seems distracted.

NICK: So . . . no boyfriend, then. Uh, Earth to Trina?

Trina blinks. Shakes her head.

TRINA: I, um. Paul and I broke up.

NICK: I heard. The whole school heard.

KYLE: His voice got *very* high.

They share a chuckle, then stand awkwardly as Trina doesn't react, the brief burst of renewed friendship withering, becoming distant again. Vanessa examines her hands. Kyle pans the phone around the clearing idly.

KYLE: So this is where it happened?

VANESSA: R-roughly. W-w-we don't know exactly wh-where.

Another beam of light pierces the trees, and Kyle keeps the camera trained in that direction as two figures approach. Anthony Beck and Jeremy Polk enter the dimly lit area.

TRINA: [*Muttering*] Great.

ANTHONY: We're the last ones here, then?

He tries to catch Trina's eye, but she crosses her arms and looks at the ground.

NICK: Other than Sara. You brought Jeremy.

His voice is too neutral to read as anything but unfriendly.

JEREMY: So what do you think this is? My money's on prank or some kind of ARG, geo-caching-type thing. Good, you're recording. We can be internet famous.

NICK: Why *are* you recording?

KYLE: If something happens out here, we're going to want proof.

JEREMY: You don't actually think it's going to be, like, a ghost? Do you?

TRINA: Why did you bring him?

ANTHONY: Because he's my friend, and he offered.

JEREMY: He's also standing right here.

He signs to Anthony, looking disgruntled.

JEREMY: *Why didn't you tell her?*

ANTHONY: *I don't know. I didn't think it would be a problem.*

TRINA: *I sign, too, remember?*

JEREMY: *We need to learn Spanish.*

TRINA: I speak Spanish. Try German.

JEREMY: Da.

TRINA: That's Russian.

ANTHONY: Are you two going to argue the entire time? Jeremy's here to help.

TRINA: He didn't even know Becca.

The others look a bit taken aback at the vicious edge to her voice.

VANESSA: N-neither did I.

Trina shakes her head. Jeremy shrugs, but he looks uncomfortable.

ANTHONY: Trina, do you—should we talk? For a minute?

TRINA: No.

ANTHONY: Are you—

TRINA: We don't need to talk. Where the hell is Mel? Is she really not coming?

Anthony gives Trina a concerned, speculative look, which she ignores.

NICK: I tried texting her, but she didn't answer.

TRINA: I really thought she'd change her mind. I mean, Jesus, I know she hates me right now for some reason, but—

NICK: It's not your fault. It's just that you embody everything her parents want from her and that she can't give them.

TRINA: What?

KYLE: Yeah, you're too perfect. It's irritating.

Trina visibly blanches, her hands curling into fists for a moment before relaxing one finger at a time, the effort palpable.

TRINA: I'm not perfect.

KYLE: Captain of the girls' softball team, shoo-in for vale-dictorian, perfect attendance, perfect *teeth*, perfect manners . . .

NICK: And you want to be a doctor, and Mel's parents want her to be a doctor, and . . .

Trina throws up a hand to stop him.

TRINA: Enough! Jesus. I get it. But even if she hates me, she should be here for Sara.

NICK: Not Becca?

TRINA: We all know this isn't for Becca. She's gone.

JEREMY: Damn, this is getting heavy. Should I go stand over there by the not-friends-with-Becca tree?

ANTHONY: Which one is that?

JEREMY: I'll pick the one that looks the most ashamed of itself. For Trina's sake.

VANESSA: D-did you guys hear something?

Everyone falls silent for a moment. And then laughter breaks through the silence, along with crashing footsteps. Trina flinches and whirls toward the sound, prompting a startled chuckle from Kyle.

ANTHONY: Well. I think Mel decided to come after all.

VIDEO EVIDENCE

Retrieved from the cell phone of Sophia Henry

Recorded April 18, 2017, 11:41 p.m.

The phone's camera focuses on the dimly lit face of Sophia Henry. The background is indistinct.

SOPHIA: Okay. We're here. In the middle of nowhere. In the dark.

A flashlight beam sweeps across Sophia's face, and she winces.

SOPHIA: Hey! Watch that thing.

MELANIE: [*Laughing*] Sorry! It wasn't on purpose. So is this it?

Sophia switches to the forward-facing camera and pans around a small clearing in a dark forest. Two young women stand nearby. Melanie "Mel" Whittaker is tall and thin, her dark curls under a purple knit cap, the only splash of color in an otherwise black ensemble. She has brown skin sprinkled with dark freckles, and her features have the kind of elegant severity prized in models. Miranda, a white girl with long hair dark enough to look black in the poor light, stands next to her in a blue windbreaker, looking off into the woods. Mel holds a large flashlight, sweeping it around the trees.

SOPHIA: Surprise, surprise. A whole bunch of trees. I'm shivering in fear. Terrified.

MEL: Oh, come on. You have to admit it's pretty spooky. The dark woods at midnight . . .

Mel's eyes are a bit too bright, her gait sloppy, and her voice overly loud in the quiet woods.

SOPHIA: You realize the message didn't say anything about midnight.

MEL: That's because it goes without saying. Come on, Sophia. Get into the spirit of Christmas.

SOPHIA: It's April, and this is a waste of time. There's nothing here.

MIRANDA: We're in the wrong spot.

Miranda moves off through the woods, not waiting for the other girls or the light. They scramble to follow, Sophia muttering indistinctly under her breath as the camera bobs and weaves, picking up their silhouettes sporadically.

MEL: Hey, who's that?

Another light bobs between the trees.

MEL: Hey! Who's up there?

NICK: It's just us.

The camera stabilizes as the two groups meet. Trina's mouth is a tight, straight line, her lips pressed together. Anthony shakes his head as Mel staggers slightly, entering the clearing.

MEL: Nicky! The gang's all here. Plus bonus crew. Sup, Jer?

JEREMY: Mel.

TRINA: Are you drunk?

MEL: Noooooooooo. Maybe.

SOPHIA: Yep.

TRINA: And you are?

Trina crosses her arms and fixes Sophia with a flat stare. Nearby, Kyle is still recording.

MEL: She's Sophia. She's with me.

TRINA: She's your date?

MEL: Yeah. She's my date. This is a date. Is that a problem?

Trina shakes her head, a look of disgust on her face. Her voice shakes as she speaks.

TRINA: Only you. Only you would show up drunk and bring a *date* to—

NICK: Can we not fight? Just for tonight? Let's just focus on figuring out what's going on.

SOPHIA: Somebody's messing with us, that's what's going on. Getting a bunch of idiots out into the woods at night for the lulz.

Mel rolls her eyes.

JEREMY: Dumb question, but—why are there three of you?

MEL: How is that your business?

JEREMY: Well, you did just say it was a date. Which is normally a two-person affair.

VANESSA: W-we're supposed to be in pairs. Partners. Remember?

MIRANDA: It won't be a problem.

VANESSA: Are you sure?

TRINA: Seriously, Mel. You brought a *date*.

MEL: So did Nick.

TRINA: Nick brought his girlfriend. That's different. You brought a *date* to look for Becca.

SOPHIA: Wait, Becca? That missing girl? You know her?

TRINA: Mel. Really?

SOPHIA: You didn't say you knew her. You said this was just for fun.

MEL: It is. Because it's just some dumb prank.

NICK: You didn't come because of Becca?

Mel doesn't answer. She pushes her hair back from her face and lets out a breath.

MEL: Look, I . . . I don't believe in ghosts or in Lucy Gallows. So that means that I don't believe there's any chance that Becca is somehow . . . out here. I wish she was. But she isn't.

NICK: Then why come?

MEL: Because.

She stretches a manic smile across her face, her eyes flashing with pent-up emotion.

MEL: It. Is. Fun!

She lets the smile drop and scratches the back of her neck, a quick, nervous gesture.

MEL: Where's Sara, anyway? I thought she'd be the first one here.

SOPHIA: Unless she's the one that sent the message in the first place.

ANTHONY: She wasn't.

SOPHIA: I dunno. She's pretty weird.

VANESSA: She's n-not weird, she's j-j-just—

SOPHIA: J-j-just freaking bizarre. D-d-duh-damaged, if you ask m-m-me.

Mel wheels, eyebrows raised incredulously.

MEL: Wow. Okay. Sophia, this isn't a date anymore.

SOPHIA: What?

MEL: I don't date assholes. Firm rule there.

SOPHIA: Lighten up. It was a joke.

MEL: And the punch line was that you're an asshole. Thanks for letting me know.

SOPHIA: Fuck you. And fuck all of this. I didn't want to come out here in the first place. Have fun with your stupid ghost hunt.

The phone drops, hanging beside Sophia's leg as she walks, but continues recording for several seconds as Sophia stomps away through the trees.

MIRANDA: I told you it wouldn't be a problem.

5

THE LIGHTS AND voices up ahead draw me forward through the dark woods. My mouth tastes strange, like I have a penny tucked under my tongue. That's Trina's voice. Mel's. Anthony's. They're here. They came.

All of them.

I enter the clearing where they've gathered, staying in the shadows for a moment. They didn't come together—not a single one of them. But they've come. It seems like proof of something. Like we've been broken, but we can still be mended. Like we can be whole again.

Anthony sees me first. That seems right. A look like relief breaks over his face. He gives me a nod, a bob of his head that pulls the others' attention around, too, and then they're all staring at me, all silent.

"You came," I say.

"Of course we came," Trina says. No one seems to know what expression they should be wearing—Trina's smile teeters, strangely fragile; Mel stares at the ground; and Anthony keeps nodding a little, as if he can't bring himself to stop. Mel's refusal to meet my eye hurts more than I want to admit. I force myself to look away from her, to pretend it doesn't sting. She's here. That means something, doesn't it?

Not what I wish it could. But something.

Kyle waves awkwardly. I haven't seen him much since Becca, since we aren't in the same year, and I'm surprised at how much older he looks—fifteen now, but I'll probably always think of him as younger. His features are still delicate, almost like a doll's, his near-white hair making him look otherworldly. But that delicacy has sharper edges now, the suggestion of the man he is growing into beginning to appear in the shadows of his eyes and the line of his jaw. I remember something about him getting suspended, being on the brink of flunking out, getting into fights, but I haven't updated my mental image of him since he was the awkward kid who worshipped his older sister and wanted nothing more than to be cool enough to hang out with her friends.

The only one who looks perfectly comfortable is a girl I've never seen before, standing next to Mel. Her complexion is stark, her skin fair, and her rich mahogany hair hangs loose and straight past her shoulders. A crow's feather is tattooed on the inside of her wrist. Recognition sparks. She's the girl I dreamed about.

"That's everyone, then?" Mel says. "Um, this is Miranda, by the way. She's a friend." The faintest hesitation before the last word. Girlfriend, then? I try to ignore the spark of jealousy that thought ignites. I thought I was over that. And it should be the last thing on my mind.

I must have seen Miranda around before. But why my mind picked her to dream about, I have no idea.

"We're odd again," Trina notes.

I do a head count and realize she's right. A jolt of panic goes up my spine. Things are going wrong already.

What did I think going *right* would look like?

"It'll be okay," Anthony says. "We'll figure it out."

"What exactly are we expecting to happen here, anyway?" Jeremy asks. Anthony wasn't sure I would show up, was he? So he brought his best friend. His *new* best friend, since I got fired from the position. Or quit, depending on your perspective.

Jeremy isn't a bad guy. Clueless sometimes. Too much of a jock for my tastes. Has a tendency to talk about three times faster than he thinks, but it's not like I've never put my foot in my mouth.

"The road shows up. We walk down it. That's the idea, anyway," I say. "Everyone brought a key?"

A chorus of affirmatives and nods go around the group.

"So we just walk thirteen steps, right?" Trina asks. Her voice speeds up when she's nervous, rising in pitch. She's nervous now, practically shaking. We all are, probably. Even Jeremy, who's flexing his fingers like he wishes he had a lacrosse stick to hold on to. Jock version of a security blanket, I guess.

Vanessa shakes her head. "I th-think it's more complicated," she says, looking at me. "Anyway, if this really happens at m-m-midnight, and th-there's no r-reason to think it *does*, w-we'll know soon e-e-e—"

"Enough," Jeremy finishes for her.

"Don't do that," Anthony reminds him.

"It's okay," Vanessa replies with a little shrug that suggests that it isn't okay so much as so common she doesn't see the point in calling it out every time. Judging by Jeremy's expression, he knows the feeling, and he turns a bit red. With his hearing aids, he can understand most conversation—though it's easier if he's looking at you, to supplement with expression and lip-reading— but that doesn't stop people from trying the whole loud-and-slow- like-you're-stupid approach. Which just makes things worse, since it distorts the sound and makes lip-reading difficult—on top of being condescending and assholish.

"Right. Sorry," Jeremy says. "My bad."

"Two minutes to go," Kyle says. "I guess this is everybody that's going to show."

"Two minutes until we all feel really stupid," Mel mutters. She's studiously not looking at me, and I notice the sway to her stance for the first time. Questions bubble up, but I don't voice them. What matters is that we're here. All of us. For Becca.

Whatever happens.

"Guys?" Kyle's voice wavers. "I think something's happening."

Together, we turn. And the road arrives.

VIDEO EVIDENCE

Retrieved from the cell phone of Kyle Jeffries

Recorded April 19, 2017, 12:01 a.m.

The phone swings around. The image is out of focus; the field is a dark blur, streaks of black and gray, grainy and disorienting, refusing to resolve into a clear picture. There is a sound like wind across the microphone, or maybe Kyle's finger scraping against the phone's case.

The camera focuses as voices rise in indistinct murmurs of surprise. Between the trees, a narrow track stretches out into the darkness. At the feet of the teenagers, it's no more than a few scattered stones, a little too large and square to be natural. But they quickly draw together, like a torn cloth being gathered and stitched up. Despite the darkness of the forest, the stones seem to collect moonlight to them.

NICK: Holy shit. It's real. It's actually real.

TRINA: Oh my God. What do we do?

The camera jostles. Sara has pushed past Kyle, and walks quickly toward the road, as if she is afraid it will slip away from them into the darkness again. When she reaches a point where she stands on solid stone, she looks back over her shoulder.

SARA: All right. Who's coming?

INTERVIEW

SARA DONOGHUE

May 9, 2017

Sara taps her middle finger on the table. At first it seems random, but careful examination reveals a pattern, quicker sequences interspersed with pauses. 1-5-1, 1-4-3, 2-5-2. And then again.

The light overhead flickers slightly. It's out of frame, but the dinginess of the room makes the presence of old wiring unsurprising. Sara glances up toward it, staring blankly.

ASHFORD: Miss Donoghue?

SARA: Who else are you talking to?

ASHFORD: A number of people. Though the Jeffries family has retained a lawyer. We haven't been able to get an interview. Have you spoken to any of the families of—

SARA: No. I haven't spoken to any of them.

ASHFORD: Why is that?

She chews on her lip. The tapping continues. 1-5-1, 1-4-3, 2-5-2. She seems to realize she's doing it and stops abruptly, clenching her hand into a fist on the tabletop.

SARA: It's my fault.

ASHFORD: What is?

SARA: All of it. They wouldn't have been there if it wasn't for me.

ASHFORD: And you wouldn't have been there if it wasn't for your sister. So couldn't you say it was Becca's fault, by that logic?

SARA: None of this is Becca's fault.

ASHFORD: I'm not saying it is. I'm saying that it isn't yours, either.

SARA: Have you ever played the game, Dr. Ashford?

ASHFORD: *The* game? No. I haven't.

SARA: But you've played games before. In general.

ASHFORD: Of course.

SARA: Do you know what all games have in common?

ASHFORD: All games have rules.

SARA: Exactly. And what happens when you break them?

ASHFORD: It depends on the game, I suppose. Did you break the rules?

Sara doesn't answer. Her hand splays out on the table. After a few seconds, her finger starts tapping again. 1-5-1, 1-4-3, 2-5-2.

ASHFORD: Miss Donoghue? Did you break the rules?

SARA: We all did.

PART II

THE ROAD

EXHIBIT E

Children's skipping rhyme,
local to Briar Glen, Massachusetts

Little Lucy, dressed in white

Gave her mother such a fright.

Walked into the woods one day.

Where she went no one can say.

Down a road that no one found.

Or are her bones sunk in the ground?

How many steps did Lucy take?

One, two, three, four . . .

6

"ALL RIGHT. WHO'S coming?" I ask. I sound calm, despite my heart pounding so hard I can hear it. No one else says anything. They all stare at the road—or at me. Like I have answers.

You expect in a moment like this to have trouble believing or a need to search for a rational explanation. Maybe it's like that for the others—denial, trying to find evidence that they're dreaming or hallucinating or that it's some kind of trick. But for me, at least, it's like a puzzle piece clicking into place. A feeling that everything has finally aligned the way it should be.

The road is here, and Becca is waiting.

"No way," Jeremy says, shifting his weight back from the road. "Have you guys ever watched, like, a single movie? We get on that road and about thirty seconds from now some hook-handed motherfucker is wearing our guts like a scarf."

Trina's eyes are fixed on the road, her lips moving—praying. Finally she nods. Smiles. It's an unsettling smile, off balance, and her eyes are bright and watery. "Okay," she says.

Mel makes a disbelieving sound, half laugh and half cough. "What about this is okay?" She sounds more offended than afraid, like she's pissed the world would dare throw something so bizarre at her. I know in that moment she's with me—she won't let the road *win* by scaring her off—and the first tremor of relief goes through me. If I have Mel, at least, I'll be okay.

"It's real," Trina says. "It's real, and that means that Becca—doesn't it?" She looks at me. She's crying now, her tear tracks silvery in the light. I step toward her, not quite off the road, not wanting to leave it in case I'm all that's anchoring it here. She scrubs her cheeks with the heels of her hands. "I'm fine," she says, in the same voice I've used a hundred times.

The five of us are standing together now, in a loose ring; Vanessa and Kyle and Jeremy and Miranda are farther back, and it's just us, just the Wildcats.

"This is real," Anthony says. "I'm just—we all agree, right? This is really happening?"

"It's happening," Mel says, rough-voiced. "Becca was right. The road is real."

I don't know who's the first to do it—to reach out. One hand to the next, stepping closer, drawing tighter, but then there we are, linked. On one side I hold Mel's hand, warm and dry, on the other side Anthony's, skin cool.

"No one has to come who doesn't want to," I say.

"I'm not going back," Trina says forcefully.

"We're coming," Anthony says. "All of us." His hand squeezes mine. And then drops. We all shift back, our attention drifting to the others, a question in the air.

"Anyone who doesn't want to come should head back," I say, realizing as I do that I'm somehow in charge and that no one is objecting to this.

"I'm in," Kyle says. "I'm already past my curfew. Which means Chris is already going to hit the upper limit of pissed off, so I might as well go for broke, right?" He gives Trina a lopsided grin. Her mouth opens, like she means to say something, but she only shakes her head and makes a sound like a swallowed laugh.

"I'm in, too," Vanessa agrees, nodding vigorously.

"This is nuts," Jeremy says. But he doesn't leave.

No one asks Miranda. This doesn't seem strange to me, not yet.

"I guess . . . I guess we go, then," I say, knowing that no one is going to move until I do. I turn. Grip the strap of my duffel hard. And take the first step.

If I expect anything mystical in that first step, it doesn't happen. I let out a held breath and take another step, and another. But now that the road has arrived, it seems content to exist in a state of absolute reality. The trees lining it stand upright, its stones meet neatly, its surface is firm. Silence lies steadily against the road, and I am glad I do not walk alone.

"'Even larks and katydids,'" Anthony mutters, a few steps behind me, and I glance back.

"What?"

"Nothing. Just something from a book," he says.

"You read a book?" I ask in mock surprise, nerves knocking me into our old, joking pattern. "Look at Anthony, shattering the jock stereotype."

"Hey, watch it, or I'm going to make you repay me for all those Goosebumps books you 'borrowed' and never returned."

"Your mom told me not to give them back because they gave you nightmares. She called you a *sensitive child*," I remind him, and he laughs, wincing at the memory. I guess all it takes is breaking the rules of reality to make things feel normal for a moment.

Behind him, the others trail in a ragged line. Jeremy is last, still on the dirt of the forest floor, not yet on the stone. He looks like he is ready to turn, to head back to the street and the cars they arrived in, to decide that this is a dream or a mistake and return to a life where things make sense and roads don't stitch themselves together out of moonlight.

I wish more than anything that he had.

But his eyes meet mine, and a look like shame flits across his features, stark and clear despite the shadows. And he steps forward. Onto the road. *No turning back*, I think, knowing instinctively that it's true. The only way now is forward.

I don't know how long we walk. A few minutes or an hour. None of us say a word, not until we reach the first gate. Anthony and I have dropped back a bit, Mel charging out ahead, flashlight swiping furiously back and forth ahead of her, legs pumping like she's trying to escape something. Or maybe she's just trying to sober up. She gets far enough ahead of us that she goes around a bend and out of sight, a screen of scraggly-limbed trees blocking her from view.

When we come around the curve, she's stopped dead. She holds the flashlight up like a pointer, aiming it straight ahead, toward a wrought-iron gate that blocks the way. It's eight feet tall, spanning the whole road, but there's nothing but a low, crumbled wall to either side. You could just step around it. None of us ever suggest it. Some rules you don't need to be told.

"What's up?" Anthony asks as we reach Mel. "Is it locked?"

"I don't know," she says. "But look."

"What am I looking for?"

"Just *look*," she says again, and hands him the flashlight. He lifts it, squinting. Swears. And then I see it too.

The light from the flashlight hits the iron bars and it should appear beyond them. Turn the night gray, illuminate some stray mote of dust. Instead, it stops, as if it has struck a black wall, but there's nothing there. Only darkness, the utter absence of light.

"What do we do?" Anthony asks.

When it's dark, don't let go, I remember. "I think—" I pause. Everyone has reached us now. I look back at them and find myself taking a head count even though I don't see how anyone could have gotten lost. "Becca left a notebook. It has—I think they're rules," I say.

"What rules?" Trina asks.

"Don't leave the road," I say. "When it's dark, don't let go. And there are other roads—don't follow them."

"Don't let go?" Trina asks. "Don't let go of what?"

"L-like the game," Vanessa says. "That's why you need a partner, right? H-hold on to each other's hands."

"That makes sense," I say, halfway between a statement and a question.

Kyle's up at the gate. He shakes it. "It is locked," he says. "Do you think we can force it open?"

"You brought a key, didn't you?" Miranda asks softly.

"Just my house key," he says.

"Use it," she insists.

He laughs a little. Like it's any crazier than what we've already seen. "Okay," he says. He digs in his pocket until he finds it, and we all stare at him. Watching. "You guys are giving me the creeps," he informs us, but he turns and slides the key into the lock on the gate. It shouldn't fit. It's an old-fashioned lock, the kind shaped like a cartoon keyhole, a circle overlapping the top of a narrow triangle. But it clicks in and turns, and Kyle pulls the gate open with a groan that sounds like something dying.

Someone hums the theme from *The Twilight Zone*.

"Shut up," Mel says, but without it the whole thing would have been too much. The black still looms, and nothing stands between it and us now. Empty air, and that's no protection. It has a kind of pull to it. Like we can't help but lean forward on the balls of our feet. Like one of us is going to plunge in soon, whether we mean to or not.

"We could still turn back," I say.

"Can we?" Anthony asks.

"I don't know," I admit. But no one's going to anyway. We've all made our decisions. Even Jeremy.

"So we pair up," Mel says.

"There's j-just one problem," Vanessa says. "There are nine of us. We've g-got too many."

"Or too few," Trina says.

Vanessa nods. "Either way, it's a problem."

VIDEO EVIDENCE

Retrieved from the cell phone of Kyle Jeffries

Recorded April 19, 2017, 12:46 a.m.

The teens stand in a loose clump. Occasionally one of them rubs their eyes, or glances back the way they came, as if waiting for sense to reassert itself. The road remains. They remain. The darkness stands, unyielding.

ANTHONY: Okay. Nine of us. Odd man out. What do we do?

TRINA: Someone will have to go alone. I can do it.

SARA: No. No way. No one goes alone.

TRINA: Then what?

NICK: A group of three. That's safer. There's nothing that actually says you can't have two partners.

MEL: Careful there, Nicky. Not sure Vanessa's down for the monogamish thing.

Nick gives her a flat look and deadpans.

NICK: Ha ha. Your attempts at humor have absolutely put me at ease. I'm no longer terrified. Well done.

MEL: I live to serve.

ANTHONY: So it's Vanessa and Nick, Miranda and Mel, Trina and Kyle, and then Sara can come with me and Jeremy.

Sara looks quickly at Mel, then away, a touch of pink creeping into her cheeks.

SARA: Yeah. That makes sense.

ANTHONY: So everyone . . . hold hands, I guess?

The group shuffles as people move to stand next to their partners. Vanessa and Nick clasp each other's hands readily. Trina sticks her hand out, palm up, and gives the camera, and her brother behind it, an encouraging grin. He grabs hold, palm slapping against hers, still holding the phone in his opposite hand. It swings away from the group for a moment, then back, as he shifts his grip. Sara and Anthony are together at the head of the group, but Jeremy stands with his hand in Mel's. Both of them look vaguely startled, like they can't figure out how they ended up that way. Mel glances at Miranda, who holds her other hand, as if checking to see if she objects.

MIRANDA: It's fine. Let's get moving.

Anthony shrugs. He and Sara turn. Their shoulders bump against each other, and then their hands stray together, seeming to link one finger at a time, like the teeth of a key fitting against the pins of a lock.

Together, they step forward. One step. Then two. Then they are at the darkness. They look at each other, and each instinctively draws a breath, as if they are about to plunge into water.

They step forward. And vanish.

7

I'M SURE YOU want to know what it feels like, stepping into pure darkness. Have you ever stepped off a dock or a pier—not jumped off—stepped, one foot out and then the rest belonging to gravity? Even that isn't right, because there's a border between the air and the water, a surface to sink through, and it isn't like that with the darkness. You are simply on one side of it, and then the other. And there is no sensation of cold and wet to warn you not to take a breath. Gasp. Drag it into your lungs. It fills you. You don't choke, and somehow that makes it worse. You can keep breathing, keep pulling more and more of it inside of you.

That's the first step. There are thirteen. Each one is harder than the last.

We stop after the first. Hands clasped, breath ragged, not yet realizing that with every breath we take, we're making it harder to map where we end and the dark begins.

I look back, but all I can see is black. "Can you hear us?" I call.

"Yeah," Mel says. "But you're all echoey. Like you're in a tunnel."

"Maybe we are," Anthony says. How could we tell? I spread my fingers out on the opposite side from him, and I can feel him doing the same, through the way his grip shifts. My hand touches only air.

"Thirteen steps," Vanessa reminds us. "That's the g-game. Thirteen steps."

"And don't leave the road," Trina adds.

"I can't see the road, how are we supposed to stay on it?" Anthony asks.

"The stones," I say. "It's a stone road. You can feel them when you step on them."

Silence. Then, "Yeah. Sorry, I just nodded, but obviously you can't see that."

"It's okay. Twelve steps to go, right? Or have we taken the first one yet?"

"I guess there's only one way to find out," he says. "Count them?"

"Sure. So this is two," I say, and we step together, lurching. He's taking big steps, like he's trying to cover as much ground as possible, and I'm inching along, feeling for the stones beneath us. Our hands jerk against each other, and my grip spasms around his, frantic.

"Sorry. Sorry," Anthony says. "Just walk normally?"

"Okay. Three," I say, and we take another step, this time more or less in sync. But still there's a tug, his hand against mine. Not because of the step, but because *we're* tugging at each other, pulling, twitching. Like we're trying to let go. "Hold on," I say.

"I know," he says. "It's just—"

It's just that I want to let go. The faint niggle of a desire, like a fingernail pressed against the nape of my neck, twisting back and forth.

"Four," I say. We take a step. My skin crawls. I don't want him touching me. Don't want anyone touching me. "Five," I say. Another step, and I want to fling his hand away. I swallow.

"Hold on. Hold on," he says.

"I'm trying," I say.

"The others—"

I nod, remember he can't see. "Hey!" I yell back. "It's hard to hold on. It makes you want to let go." My voice echoes back at me. There's no answer. Five steps, but I have the disorienting feeling we've gone farther. Much farther.

"Six?" Anthony asks.

"Six," I say. Then, whispering, clutching each other so tight our bones creak, "Seven."

I don't know who lets go. Maybe me. By then the urge to do it is so strong it's a physical ache, pain through my wrist and shooting up to my elbow. It makes my teeth hurt, and I clamp them hard over the urge, but it isn't enough. Or maybe it's Anthony whose fingers slip away from mine. Maybe it's both of us. It doesn't matter. We start to take the step and by the time my foot comes down, my hand grasps nothing but air.

It lasts a second. Half a second. An instant of sweet relief, overpowering, and then panic sweeps over me, and I flail for his hand again. He catches mine, a moment of awkward grappling for each other before our fingers fit together again, and I let out a shuddering breath. I grip his hand with both of mine, getting my bearings.

"Sorry," I whisper. "Okay. Seven—no, this is eight."

We step forward. Faint vertigo makes me unsteady; I stumble.

Anthony's grip keeps me on my feet. I never want to let go.

"Nine," I say. I take another step, Anthony slightly out ahead, guiding me. My foot lands strangely, on the edge of a stone, tilting toward bare dirt that compresses under the edge of my sneaker. "Hold on," I say. "I think we're—the road curves or something."

Anthony doesn't answer. And then I hear my name.

"Sara!"

Anthony's voice. Behind me. Far behind me.

"Sara, where are you? Where did you go?"

I can't breathe. There's something in my throat as solid as a stone.

Whose hand am I holding?

"Anthony?" I say. Barely a whisper. Louder, "Anthony?"

"Sara? I can hear you, barely. Where are you?"

I make a sound like a sob. The hand in mine doesn't let go. Doesn't tighten. Doesn't do anything. I tug. It holds fast. "Let me go," I whisper. "Let me go. Let me go. Let me go." I pull. I twist my hand.

It holds fast. And slowly, slowly, starts to pull toward the edge of the road.

"Let me go!" I yell and strike out at where Anthony should be. Where *it* should be. My hand hits something. It tears under my fingers, sinewy but thin, warm and wet and shredding, filling the gaps between my fingers, like putting your hand through rotten fruit.

I scream. I rake at the hand in mine, my fingernails scraping over my own skin, digging painful furrows across my wrist and palm. The hand shreds, pulps beneath mine, still tugging me toward the edge of the road—and then there's not enough of it left to hold me, and I fling myself away. Back toward Anthony's voice.

"Sara! I'm coming!"

"No! Stay there! Just—just keep calling," I say, struggling to form words around the sob still lodged in my throat.

"I'm here." Closer now. But still farther, so much farther, than two steps. He talks to me as I creep closer and closer, my breath coming back to some kind of regular order, my feet shuffling, feeling for the edge of the road that doesn't come, doesn't come, doesn't come—and then his voice is right in front of me, and my hands creep up, cautious, finding him. His arm. His chest. His face, my fingertips testing the shape of him. "Sara?" he says.

I find his hand.

"What happened?" he asks.

It tried to—I want to say, but I don't know how it ends. Trick me. Steal me. Kill me. It wanted me to leave the road, to break the rules, but I don't know what it was.

I don't know if it's enough, that I escaped. Or if letting go means I've already lost.

"I'll tell you when we're out of here," I say. "Nine?"

"Eight," he reminds me.

"Eight," I echo, and we take another step. I want to let go. I want to let go more than anything in the world and that is the most comforting thing I have ever felt, and the more I want to let go, the tighter I hold, through nine and ten and eleven and twelve, and then, our fingers digging into each other so hard I'm sure I'll feel the trickle of blood down my hand any second, thirteen.

And we're out of the dark. Out of *that* dark, at least, the impossible dark. Back in the night, moonlight gleaming over us. I stagger. Lose Anthony's hand, fall to one knee, retching. I hold my hands in front of me in the silvery light. Clean. They're clean, no sign of what I felt beneath them, giving way.

No sign of the thing that tried to take me.

"We made it," Anthony says. "It's okay. We made it out."

I nod. We're safe. We're on the other side. It's gone. We broke a rule, but we escaped the consequences. It's fine.

I almost believe it.

"Where's everyone else?" I ask.

"Right behind us," Anthony says. "Just give them a minute."

And so we wait.

VIDEO EVIDENCE

Retrieved from the cell phone of Kyle Jeffries

Recorded April 19, 2017, 12:51 a.m.

The phone records only flat black. The sound of footsteps and breathing can be heard.

KYLE: I can't see anything. I can't even see the screen.

TRINA: Just hold on. That's—that's—

KYLE: Twelve. One more. You can do it.

TRINA: I can do it? Isn't this hard for you?

KYLE: I've kind of got a lot of practice lately ignoring my brain's bad ideas.

Trina laughs, a strangled sound, and then light floods into the camera. Everything is a blur as it adjusts; the forest is dimly lit when it settles, Anthony and Sara barely shadows ahead.

ANTHONY: Are you guys okay? Did you let go?

KYLE: Trina kept trying. Nice to finally be better at something than my sister.

TRINA: Shut up. Crap. I feel like I'm going to puke.

SARA: Me too. The others—

As if on cue, Jeremy, Mel, and Miranda stumble out of the wall of darkness. Jeremy pulls free of Mel with a string of curses, and vomits, bending over the side of the stone road. Mel sinks into a crouch, hands over her eyes, and Miranda steps away, pulls into herself.

Silence falls. Waiting gains a sharp edge. Mel is breathing through her teeth, gaze tipped up toward the stars. Sara wraps her arms around her middle, her hair hanging in front of her face, staring at the wall of dark. Ten seconds pass. Twenty. Thirty.

ANTHONY: Maybe we should go back in. They might have—you almost got lost, Sara.

TRINA: What?

ANTHONY: She let go.

SARA: I didn't let go. I don't think I let go.

ANTHONY: One of us did. The point is you went out ahead without me.

Sara swallows, nervous. But Trina's expression betrays only concern.

TRINA: Are you okay? What happened?

SARA: There was something—there was a hand, and I thought it was Anthony's, but it wasn't. It tried to lead me off the road. But I got away. I got back to Anthony. We both made it through.

Nick and Vanessa step out of the darkness. Nick lets out a groan of relief.

SARA: There you are. Everyone made it, then. We're all fine.

JEREMY: Hold on. We need to talk about this. You two let go. The rules said not to do that.

SARA: Maybe—maybe something was going to happen, but it didn't because I got away.

JEREMY: Or we're all going to get hook-massacred because you couldn't follow a simple rule.

ANTHONY: Lay off. We're safe. That's what matters.

The camera has been focused tightly on the three of them. Now it swings around to capture the rest of the group. Mel has gotten to her feet, though she still looks queasy. Miranda has moved farther out ahead of the group, looking down the dark road ahead. Nick and Vanessa stand with their heads together, hands linked. Vanessa is whispering something, and Nick nods.

KYLE: You guys okay?

Nick takes a breath, looking indecisive.

VANESSA: Hm? Yeah. We're fine. That was terrifying, though. I tripped and almost let go. And I lost my stupid glasses.

She squeezes Nick's hand, smiles at him. He gives her a shallow nod.

TRINA: Are you going to be all right without them?

VANESSA: I'm not totally blind without them. I can tell where everything is, it's just super blurry. I mean, don't ask me to read anything, but I'm not going to walk into a tree.

KYLE: Oh, shit. Look.

The camera focuses on the landscape behind Nick and Vanessa. The phone's flashlight barely pierces the darkness, but beyond it they can see the formless black is gone, and the teens stand just on the other side of the iron gate, at a distance of perhaps a dozen steps. No more.

Trina laughs, a high, nervous sound.

TRINA: Are we sure it's too late to go back?

Behind them, farther down the road, someone screams.

8

THE SCREAM COMES again. We bunch up. I look for Mel first, instinctively checking that she's okay, and catch her eye for an instant before I notice the others' reactions—who stands in front of whom, who hangs back, who lurches forward to investigate or help or stand guard. Jeremy out front, stepping twice toward the sound before halting. Vanessa fading back. Anthony moving in front of the others like a shield. Trina putting herself in front of Kyle, Mel a few feet apart, the most alone of any of us except for Miranda—Miranda, who stands farther out than even Jeremy, but makes no move toward the sound or away from it, listening, her hands lax at her sides.

"What do we do?" Trina asks.

"It sounds like a girl," Anthony says.

"Is she saying something?" Jeremy asks. His hearing isn't good at a distance.

"I don't think so," Anthony says.

"We can't just stand here," I say. "If someone's in danger, we have to help."

"It isn't Becca," Anthony says.

"I know." I know her voice. It wasn't her. "We still have to help."

"I'll go," Jeremy says immediately.

"We all go," I say, firm. "We're not splitting up."

"Never split the party," Kyle says softly, like a half-quoted joke.

We move forward cautiously. It's silent now. The stone road continues out ahead, our flashlights fading long before it does in the distance. The trees stand thick around us; mostly evergreens now, the ground littered with dry needles, bleached of color. I've never been this deep in Briar Glen Woods. If we're even in Briar Glen anymore.

"Do you hear anything?" Jeremy asks. "Is she still there?"

"I can't tell," I say. I try to speak loudly enough for him to understand easily, but it's hard with the night pressing back, a threat that makes my voice thin as paper.

"I don't like this," Mel says.

"Shh," Miranda says, holding up a hand. "Listen."

The scream comes again. We all jump. Mel screams, too, cutting it off with a hand clamped over her mouth, and our flashlight beams leap toward the sound, scrambling over roots and branches, and then mine finds it, pinned by the light where it crouches, hunching its black wings up toward its blunt blade of a beak. A solitary crow.

"Is that . . . ?" Anthony says.

"It was just a bird?" Trina says.

The crow screams again. We cinch together. There's a moment—a stutter, like a skipped frame, my stomach suddenly tight and sour, a desperate sensation tilting through me like there's something I've forgotten.

"Oh God," comes the voice from the crow's beak, distorted, raspy. *"Oh God, what is that?"* And then the scream again, as the crow flaps its wings, and the scream shatters into a broken caw. It flings itself into the air, into the night, too fast for our lights to follow. For a moment the beams rake at the trees in scattered confusion before falling, one by one, to stillness at our feet again.

I'm not sure how long it is before one of us speaks again. "This is fucked up," Mel says. "Just so we're clear."

"It was just a bird," Vanessa says, pushing up her glasses.

"A *deeply fucked-up* bird," Mel emphasizes.

I look down. I'm not holding my flashlight anymore; it's tucked into my bag, which is unzipped. I have Becca's camera in my hand. It's on, the pinprick lights steady. I don't remember taking it out. I lift it, focusing on the dark outline of Miranda, up ahead. She half turns to look at me as I snap the picture, the flash strobing once. The camera shows the shot for a few seconds. The flash flattens her against the dark background. All around her the light distorts, as if splashed across mist, though the air is clear. There is something odd about the image, though on the tiny screen, it's hard to tell. A discoloration to her skin, strange shadows.

I thumb the power off and tuck the camera back in my bag.

"What now?" Anthony asks. They're looking at me again, like I have answers.

"We keep going," I say, shaking off the feeling that I've forgotten something.

"Going where, though?" Trina asks. "Where does this lead?"

"To Becca," I say, hoping it's true.

"Becca," Trina echoes with a nod. We don't know where she is—where *we* are—but her name is enough of a talisman and a goal. The road leads to her. We only need to follow it.

The eight of us set out, walking two by two as if on instinct, close enough to catch each other's hands if the darkness returns.

We don't look back.

INTERVIEW

SARA DONOGHUE

May 9, 2017

The door opens. Abigail "Abby" Ryder steps in. She is a young white woman, her dark hair cropped to chin length, her features sharp and uncomfortably severe. She walks with a slight limp, favoring her right leg, but otherwise appears recovered from the Oregon incident.[4]

ABBY: You asked for these.

She sets a stack of papers on the desk. Ashford flips through them momentarily, nods.

ASHFORD: Thank you, Abby. That will be all.

ABBY: Did you ask her about the photos?

ASHFORD: Thank you, Miss Ryder.

SARA: Ask me about which photos?

ASHFORD: We will get to that in due time. Miss Ryder, please see to our other guest.

Abby gives a curt nod and exits, pulling the door shut behind her with a bang.

ASHFORD: I'm sorry about that. Miss Ryder's training is . . . informal. We're still working on her people skills.

---

4 Described in File #71. We have been unable to retrieve File #71 thus far, but will continue our efforts.

SARA: What did she mean about the photos?

*Ashford hesitates, indecision in his expression. Then he reaches
for the folder containing the photos he showed her earlier.*

ASHFORD: We looked at some of these earlier, but we haven't
had the chance to discuss them in detail yet.

*He sets two on the table. The first is the photo of Nick Des-
sen. The other he removes from the folder is one he has not
shown her before, a photograph of Miranda taken with a
flash, mist hanging in the air around her. There is something odd about her skin, and the shadows that lie on it.
The viewer can almost imagine that they see the faint lines
of the bones beneath her skin. Sara reaches for the photo of
Miranda, pulling it toward her across the table.*

SARA: Miranda. I remember taking this.

ASHFORD: Then Miranda was with you.

SARA: Yeah. She came with Mel. But you knew that.

ASHFORD: I did, I only . . . We'll discuss that later. You
haven't said anything about the other photograph. Earlier, you hardly looked at it.

SARA: That's because I've never seen it before.

ASHFORD: You don't remember taking it?

SARA: I didn't.

ASHFORD: It came from your camera.

SARA: Becca's camera.

ASHFORD: Yes, but it was taken when you were in possession of the camera. And look at the background. The same
tree is in both of them. These photos were taken in the
same place.

SARA: That's not possible.

ASHFORD: Why not?

SARA: Because whoever this kid is, he wasn't with us. And we hadn't met anyone else on the road yet.

ASHFORD: Excuse me?

SARA: We hadn't met anyone else yet.

ASHFORD: Yes, but—you said "whoever this kid is." You don't recognize Nick Dessen?

SARA: Who?

Ashford stares at her for a moment in silence. Then he reaches for the papers that Abby brought in, flipping through once more.

ASHFORD: In your written statements, you don't mention that Nick Dessen was with you.

SARA: I told you, I don't know who that is.

ASHFORD: Miss Donoghue, how many people were there when you walked through the gate at the beginning of the road?

SARA: Me, Anthony, Mel, Miranda, Trina, Kyle, Jeremy, and Vanessa. So eight.

ASHFORD: But there was an odd number. In your testimony, you state more than once that there were nine of you. And three of you had to go through the darkness as a group as a result.

SARA: No—I mean, yes. That's right.

ASHFORD: But you only listed eight names.

SARA: There were nine of us, though. You're right.

ASHFORD: So who was the ninth?

SARA: I—No, I must be wrong. Me. Anthony and Jeremy. Mel and Miranda. Trina and Kyle. Vanessa. That's eight. So there were eight of us.

ASHFORD: Then why did you need a group of three?

SARA: I don't know!

She shoves herself up to her feet, stumbling back from the table. Her hands cover her face. Her left sleeve rides a little lower than the right; inked letters on her wrist appear to form the tail end of a word in spiky script, though not enough is visible to determine what it might say.

ASHFORD: It's all right, Miss Donoghue. We don't need to talk about this right now. We can return to the subject later.

He sweeps the photographs together and slides them back into the folder, resting his hand on it as if to reassure her that it won't spring open of its own accord.

ASHFORD: Miss Donoghue?

Her hands drop. Reluctantly, she creeps back to her seat, sinking into it. Her eyes fix on the folder, and she chews on one thumbnail.

ASHFORD: You were telling me about the crow. That was before you found Becca, correct?

SARA: Yeah. Yeah, it was still early.

ASHFORD: When you described the gate, you called it the *first* gate. Can you explain that?

SARA: Yeah. Um. There are supposed to be seven gates. That was the first.

ASHFORD: What was the second?

SARA: You said there was another guest. Someone else is here? Who is it?

ASHFORD: Melanie Whittaker.

Sara nods, as if she expected this answer.

SARA: What has she told you? About the second gate?

ASHFORD: I would rather hear it in your own words.

SARA: The second gate was where things went wrong. Or where we realized how wrong they already were. The second gate was where we realized we weren't the only ones on the road.

9

WE WALK MOSTLY in silence for the next stretch. I find myself walking next to Mel, toward the back of the group. She's sipping from Trina's water bottle, tiny sips that barely seem enough to wet her lips.

"I wasn't going to come," Mel says after a while. Her eyes lift to mine, then cut away.

"It's okay. It's not like any of us knew this was real." It isn't okay. I have held this bitter anger between my teeth so long the enamel has been eaten away, and no matter how undeserved it is, I've forgotten how to let it go.

"You knew. Anthony knew."

"It's not that I knew it was real," I say. "It's that it didn't matter if it was real. I had to be here either way."

She screws the cap back on the water bottle. Half of it still sloshes back and forth. I have extra bottles in my bag. I don't think anyone else brought anything to eat or drink, but I hope we won't be on the road long enough to need it.

"I'm glad Sophia didn't come," Mel says.

"Who?"

"Oh. Yeah, she left before you showed. She was my date," Mel says with an awkward sort-of laugh. "I told her we'd go make out in the woods."

"I didn't know you were seeing anyone." I try to sound like it's an intellectual point of curiosity—and I mostly succeed. I got a lot of practice at it, before we stopped talking.

"No reason you would."

I bite my lip. Once upon a time, I was the first person Mel came out to. We were sitting in my room drinking lemonade that had gone watery, playing a game she'd invented on the spot. Trading a secret for an M&M. Little things. Thirteen-year-old things. The lip gloss I stole from Becca. The time Mel snuck out and then couldn't think of anything to do and so just sat in front of her house until she got cold. When Becca and I stole Mom's gin and got silly drunk off a few sips and decided it was a good idea to go belt out Christmas carols in the park at midnight. But the point of all of it was the last secret.

Who do you have a crush on?

I'd shrugged. Couldn't say *Anthony*, because he was our friend and that was weird and embarrassing and I wasn't sure it was a crush anyway. Mel probably assumed Anthony anyway, the way I always hung around him. I'd picked a name almost at random. I can't even remember who it was, now. And then she said, *Now you ask me.*

So I asked, and she answered—Nicole from English class—and she waited, and it was awkward and stilted but I said the right things I guess and we went back to M&M's and lemonade, and six months later she was stapling a pride flag to the back of her sweatshirt until a horrified Trina confiscated it and stitched it on properly.

My coming out, if you could even call it that, was more incremental. I never kept it a secret, but I never particularly volunteered it. There was no moment when I declared, *Oh, by the way, I'm bisexual.* Maybe it would have been easier if I had, so there was one clear moment when Mel could make it obvious she wasn't interested, instead of the months of me vaguely hoping that now that I was a little more open with it, a little more certain of it, she'd finally notice me as more than a friend.

"So, wait. But you came with Miranda," I say, remembering.

She snorts. "None of tonight can be counted among my finest hours. Sophia and I have been dating, sort of, but I met Miranda a couple days ago and . . . I sort of asked both of them to come? And forgot about it? I was pretty drunk." She pauses. "I'm sorry."

"You don't need to be. You came." I bump my knuckles against hers, smile. If friendship is what we have, I'm still glad to feel it creeping back in. "I've missed you," I say. I'm surprised how much it's true.

"Hey," Kyle calls. He and Trina are in the lead now, but they've stopped. "Guys? There's another gate up ahead. And I think there's someone there."

We hurry to catch up with the two of them. The trees have thinned, letting more of the moonlight spill over us. Our flashlight beams probe forward, catching against the tines of the wrought-iron gate ahead like a plastic bag catching on barbed wire; they seem stuck, pierced through. The gate is almost identical to the one we already passed through, except that it's taller, wider. At the base of the gate, slumped against the bars, is a person.

He wears dark clothes. His head hangs forward. His hands lie limp in his lap. There is a stillness about him that is less an absence of movement and more a sense of having settled, like a stone sinking slowly into the muck of a river until it can press no deeper.

"Is he dead?" Trina asks.

"I can't tell," Anthony says.

"What should we—" she begins; I'm already stepping past her. Someone is here, other than us. There are people on this road. It's the first hint I've had that this might not be a wild-goose chase. That we might be able to find someone—find Becca. "Hello?" I call. "Hey. Are you okay?"

He doesn't move. I'm not even sure it's a man. The flashlights flatten his face into a pale oval, featureless, leaving no shadows to shape it.

We creep closer, moving as a single organism, amorphous. We find each other's hands; who links with whom doesn't seem to matter right now. I might be holding Mel's hand or Anthony's or Trina's; later I won't remember, and neither will anyone else.

Once we're within fifteen feet or so, it's obvious that he's a man—a boy, really, our age, with blond hair that flops across his forehead and a long face, a soft face of few angles that will probably look young in fifteen years. He stares straight ahead. He's breathing, short, sharp breaths like an animal in pain. He looks normal. Like us, not like this place.

"Hey," I say. I drop the hand I'm holding and I crouch. Still well away, but down on his level now, tipping my head to try to catch his eye. "Are you hurt?"

He doesn't answer. I try again. Anthony talks to him. Trina does. I stand. Look at the others, helpless. And then I swallow, and step closer. The group sorts itself swiftly, like we're being unzipped: those who come forward, and those who stay back. With me: Anthony, Trina, Jeremy. Standing back: Vanessa, Mel, Kyle, Miranda.

I approach until I'm standing right next to him. He keeps up that shallow breathing, that in-out, in-out. It's a wet sound; I can hear the spit in his mouth. "Hey," I say. I reach out. "Hey." My fingertips brush his shoulder, the cloth of his black sweatshirt.

He moves so quickly I can't track the movement, his hand seizing mine, tightening until my bones scrape together. I yelp and lunge back, but he holds me firm, stock-still again, staring, panting between his teeth. Anthony yells and grabs his wrist, trying to pry his hand off mine, but it's pointless. Jeremy's there, too, grabbing the boy by the collar, shaking him, fist raised—and then just as suddenly as he grabbed me, he's letting go.

I fall back against Anthony, who keeps me upright as I cradle my aching hand. Jeremy backs up fast, arms spread out slightly like he's making himself a wall between me and Anthony and the boy.

The boy blinks. Turns his head at last and seems to see us for the first time. His fingers flex where they still hover above his shoulder. It's like the beat of a moth's wings.

"Don't you dare—" Jeremy begins, balling up his hand in a warning fist. But there was never any fight in the boy, not really, and he only stares placidly at us.

"Who are you?" he asks.

We glance at each other, like we're deciding who should speak, but we know the answer before we ask the question. "My name is Sara," I say. "These are my friends."

"Sara," he says. "Becca's Sara?"

Behind me, someone hisses. I barely hear over the wind-rush sound in my ears. "Yes," I say. "Yes, I'm Becca's sister. I'm Sara. You know her? You've seen her?"

"Becca," he says, like he's trying to remember. His eyes close. "Yes. I met Becca. She came by here. Or someone met Becca, and I think I'm still someone. But am I the same someone? Or are they me? Or are we someone else?"

"What's your name?" I ask. I kneel. Out of arm's reach, again. I'm not making that mistake twice.

He sighs. "I think I was Bryan or Isaac. I wasn't Grace and I wasn't Zoe, so I was either Bryan or Isaac. Bryan met the bramble man, so I must be Isaac. Yes. Yes, I think that's right. I'm Isaac." He looks up, like finding his name has meant finding himself, filling his skin again where it was hollow a moment ago.

"Isaac," I say. "We're looking for Becca. For my sister. Where is she?"

He frowns. "She's—I'm sorry. It's hard to think. To remember. She wasn't with us. The us who came to the road together. We got to the fourth gate. Or was it the fifth? No, it was the fourth. We went through the Liar's Gate and the town and the marsh and we got to the mansion, and Grace—she wanted to keep going, but I needed to go back because—I was looking for Zoe. Zoe wasn't with us anymore, and I needed to find her, and Grace said we had to go to the lighthouse, but I couldn't go without Zoe."

"The gates. You mean the seven gates, the ones we're supposed to get through?"

"Yes. No," he says. He shakes his head. "Seven gates. Seven gates before the city, but the city is drowned. The Liar's Gate is first. If you're here, you went through it. You're here. You're Becca's Sara. Or are you Sara's Becca? Which you are you?"

"I'm Sara," I say. "We came through a gate. We came through the darkness."

"Did you?" he asks. He looks between us, peering into our faces. "Are you sure you're you? Sometimes you're someone else instead. I think I'm Isaac, but I might be Bryan, but Bryan met the bramble man. Or maybe I met the bramble man, and Bryan is here, and I'm somewhere else." He laughs. He sobs. He covers his eyes with his hands.

I look at the others, dread and pity curdling together in my gut. This is worse than the dark. This is worse than the crow. "Seven gates," I say. "You said there are seven gates. What are they? Please, Isaac. We need your help to find my sister."

He nods. "The Liar's Gate. The town. The mist in the marsh. The manor. We didn't know the rest except the lighthouse. The lighthouse is sixth. Or maybe fifth. Go through the gates. Don't break the rules. Bad things happen when you break the rules. I came back for Zoe, but I couldn't find her. I waited. I waited and she never came, but Becca, she came. With a boy. She told me things. Stories. She told me she had a sister. She tried to help me remember, but there's nowhere for memory to live anymore."

"How long have you been here, Isaac?" I ask. He doesn't answer. Maybe he can't answer. "You should come with us," I say. "You can help us find Becca."

He shakes his head, a whine in the back of his throat. "No. No, I have to stay. If I'm Isaac, I have to stay. I'm waiting for Zoe."

"You can't stay. Come on," I say, holding out my hand to him.

"Sara," Anthony says, shaking his head. He points his flashlight at Isaac's back, where it presses against the iron bars, which don't rise straight into the air but curve and branch. Branch into him. Through him. Puncturing his sides bloodlessly. Punching through his spine, his shoulder blades. One sharp end curling up just below his clavicle like a picture hook, almost invisible against his dark sweatshirt.

"I'm waiting for Zoe," he says. He smiles at me. "You're Sara."

"Yeah," I say. "I'm Sara."

"Good. She said you'd come. She said she left you a map."

His head droops. His eyes close. His breath settles back into that rhythm, in-out, in-out, like a wounded thing.

"A map?" I say. "What do you mean, Becca left me a map?" But he doesn't answer.

The notebook.

"We should go," Anthony says. I nod. We need to look at the notebook but I don't want to do it here, standing right next to Isaac. Poor Isaac, with the gate growing through him and his own name slippery in his grasp.

"Who wants to open it?" Jeremy asks. No one volunteers. "Let's see if Toyota does the trick." He pulls a car key from his pocket and steps up to the gate, giving Isaac as wide a berth as he can. The key slots in perfectly. He pushes the creaking gate open wide. No darkness this time. Just the road. We start to trail through. I wait as the others pass. I want to be last. I want to stay with Isaac as long as possible.

Trina gives him a pinched, sorrowful look as she approaches the gate.

His head whips up. His eyes open. They're empty. Not white, not black, just voids, an absence the mind refuses to read.

"They'll smell the blood on you," he says, and then his head drops, eyes closing, and it's like he never spoke at all.

Trina stares at him. She's trembling. Then she lets out something like a sigh, but harder, and she walks through the gate.

I stay with him another moment, waiting for him to open his eyes, to speak. I watch him breathe. In-out. In-out. He's alive, he's real. He's part of this place. Until now we have been separate from the road; it has been a dream unfolding around us. On some level it felt like we were real, that it wasn't, and the gap between real and unreal was a protection of sorts.

But now I see that gap can vanish. Is vanishing.

"Sara," Anthony says. They're all on the other side now.

I step through, and the gate shuts behind me, leaving Isaac behind.

EXHIBIT F

Page torn from a notebook belonging to Becca Donoghue

Text is written in blue ballpoint pen. Some text adheres to the lines of the page. Some is crooked or written sideways across the page. Approximately one-third of the page is filled with a rough sketch of a wrought-iron gate.

THE LIAR'S GATE

Darkness/Thirteen steps (the game // the Game)

Lie/deception/disguise

RULE NUMBER TWO don't let go

The town (BG?)—#2 (SINNER'S GATE)

It's never empty

Don't talk to them

What do the words mean?

DAHUT

Guilt / confession

"the toll"

Pass through seven times, and you'll be free.

I can hear her more clearly now.

I can almost tell what she's saying.

10

WE WAIT UNTIL we're out of sight of Isaac before we stop. The trees are dense around us, their leaves silvery and shuddering faintly in the breeze, making the woods seethe and whisper with conspiratorial sound. It smells of damp and rot—the smells of late fall with leaves moldering on the ground, not springtime like it should be.

I get out Becca's notebook, and we cluster around it as I page through, turning our backs on the trees as if to hide the notebook from them.

Some of what Becca wrote makes more sense now. Most of it is still hints and riddles, like seeing the shadow of something you don't know the shape of yet.

"'It's never empty. Don't talk to them,'" Trina reads over my shoulder, turning her head this way and that. "More rules?"

"I don't think they're rules. More like—tips," I say.

"We don't know where she was getting this information," Vanessa pipes up. "She doesn't exactly cite her sources."

"I don't think we're going to know what any of this means until we get farther in," Anthony says. "We don't have the context."

"What about what already happened?" Jeremy asks. "You heard

that guy. He said bad things happen when you break the rules."

"And?" I ask.

"And you broke the rules, didn't you? You let go," Jeremy says.

"I know. But whatever was going to happen, it didn't. I found my way back," I say.

"You also said there were seven gates," Jeremy says. "What seven gates?"

"On the road. There are seven gates before you can get to the end and get off."

"And you didn't think to mention that?" Jeremy demands.

"I—it's just part of the legend. I didn't—"

"Jesus! How do we know you're not hiding other stuff? Did you know this place was here? Did you know about the gates and the freaky screaming birds and the guy with iron growing through him? Did you know we were going to get stuck here?"

"Who says we're stuck?" Vanessa asks. She chews at her lower lip, the picture of shyness. "We don't actually know that. Maybe we c-can just go back." Her arms are folded over her middle, her head bowed, like she's ashamed to mention it. I fight a stab of anger, reminding myself that she didn't know Becca. She's only here because—because—

For a moment I can't remember, and panic crawls over me with centipede legs before an explanation clicks into place. She was curious. She's here because she was curious about local history, and nothing stands between Vanessa and her curiosity. But curiosity is getting ready to kill the cat. No wonder she's freaked.

"I don't think that's a good idea," I say softly. "Isaac tried to go back. You heard him."

"We don't know what happened to him. We can't be sure there isn't a way back off the road," Vanessa says. "We should try."

"I'm with V on this one," Jeremy says, nodding toward Vanessa. "I know your sister's out there. But it sounds like something bad happened to her. And to a lot of other people. I don't think we should *Saving Private Ryan* this thing."

"I've never seen it," Trina says.

"Spoilers: everybody dies saving Matt Damon," Jeremy says. "Great movie, though. You could come watch it at my place. After we go back, and don't die."

Trina gives him a flat look. "I'm not touching that. But I see your point. We all came for Becca—well, a lot of us came for Becca. But that was before we knew the whole situation. I think it's fair to give people a chance to reconsider before we go any farther."

"I'm not going back," Mel says immediately.

"You didn't want to come in the first place," Trina points out.

"Because I thought it was all fake," Mel says. "I didn't think we could actually get Becca back. But now we can. And Sara's not turning back. Are you, Sara?"

I shake my head. It isn't even a question.

"Then I'm staying. Going. Whatever," Mel says.

Thank you, I mouth. She shrugs, looking down at her feet.

"Should we split up, then?" Jeremy asks. "Or, like, vote?"

"I don't care how anyone votes, I'm not going back," I say.

"But the rest of us," Vanessa says, voice tentative. "We should at least make sure that the groups are even, right? You and Mel could go, and the rest of us—"

"No one goes back," Miranda says. We all jump, like we've forgotten she's there. She stands apart from us, as usual, the moonlight making her dark hair gleam like an oil slick.

"What, are you giving orders?" Jeremy asks.

"No. I'm just telling you what happens," Miranda says. "No one goes back. Sara won't go back without her sister. Mel and Anthony won't go back without her. Trina won't go back unless Kyle does, and Kyle doesn't want to keep going, but he doesn't want to go back, either. And Jeremy can't go back alone."

"You left out yourself. And Vanessa," Jeremy points out. "Vanessa and I can go back together."

"But you won't," Miranda says. "And we're wasting time. Seven gates, and we've only gone through two. We haven't even seen what's past this one yet."

"She's right," I say. "We're wasting time. I'm going. Anyone who wants to turn back can, but I don't recommend it. Everything we know tells me it's not that easy to get back home; you can't just turn back. Look what happened to Isaac. We have to keep going. Then we'll find a way off."

Miranda nods. Vanessa looks like she's going to argue, and so does Jeremy, but I don't wait for them to try to convince me. I just start walking. Mel's quick behind me, Anthony slower but only because he's talking to Jeremy; I know he'll follow.

Eventually, they all do. Jeremy with his jaw set, Vanessa lagging at the rear, but all of them trudging along.

"That was badass," Mel says, nudging me with her shoulder. She flashes me a smile that makes my belly twinge and my cheeks flame. I'm glad the darkness hides it.

I'm still listening to the steps behind me when we come across the first gravestone.

It sticks out of the ground like a broken tooth in a rotted gum, the soil lumpy around it. It might have been a classic tombstone shape once, but the top is cracked off and weathered. Even with our flashlights fixed on it, it's impossible to make out what might be carved on the surface—is that an eight or a nine? A *T* or an *R*?

It's a few feet off the road. I edge up close to the edge but don't stick so much as a fingertip over.

"If we get attacked by zombies, I'm out," Jeremy mutters. Trina hushes him.

"There's another one up there," Anthony says, pointing his flashlight. We traipse along. Sure enough, another tombstone juts out of the soil, leaning slantwise. Still unreadable. As we walk, more appear. Some farther out, some so close you could almost stretch out and touch them from the road, though no one tries. A stone angel hovers over a cluster of three headstones, her hands and face worn away, her wings broken.

"Spooky," Anthony says as we pass a double headstone. Husband and wife, maybe.

"I don't know. It seems almost normal," I say.

A tumbled-down stone wall intersects the road up ahead. A sign, wooden and rotten, sticks half out of the dirt just beyond, no more legible than the tombstones.

"This must be the town," Trina says. "Lots of towns used to have a cemetery just outside, right?"

It sure seems like she's right. As we keep walking, our flashlights sweep over the remnants of foundations—stones still stacked into the corner of a house, hip high, or a lintel and stairs still persisting amid root, vine, and mud. The road widens, and then the stones peter out. For a moment that panics me, but the road is still obvious. It's just dirt instead of stone. We walk through what might have once been the town square, skirting the open maw of a ruined well, padding silently past a huge, toppled building that might have been a town hall or something.

"Hey, look," Trina says. "Burn marks. They're on all the buildings."

We pause, our beams branching out as we confirm the finding. Sure enough, every building has some black scar—scorched beams lodged in the earth, mortar turned black and crumbling between the stones, metal soot-stained and pocked.

"Oh, crap," Kyle says, sounding excited. "You know what this is? Briar Glen. BG. It's right in the notebook. This is the old Briar Glen, the one that burned down."

"Could be," Anthony says. "No way to know for sure."

"We're in the Briar Glen Woods, aren't we?" Kyle says, and from the look on his face, he immediately regrets the question.

"I have no idea," Anthony says. "None of us do."

"But it could be," Kyle says. "Right, Vanessa? You're the history expert. Does this look like Briar Glen?"

Vanessa bites her lip, eyes widening as we all look at her. "I d-d-d—" She cuts off and looks apologetic as the word fails to come. I frown slightly, not sure why that bothers me. "S-sorry. I d-don't know," she continues. "It could be. I would need to look at a map."

"I don't think you're going to find a map of this place, V," Jeremy says. "Are we done sightseeing? Can we go?"

"We can go," I say, trying to decide just how much of a problem he's going to be.

We come to the edge of town quickly, and then the stone road picks up again, rolling along like it was never interrupted.

"Was that it?" Jeremy asks. "That was the town? I thought it would be a bigger deal. Like the darkness."

The Liar's Gate, I remember from Becca's notebook. It fits with that thing in the dark. Pretending to be Anthony. I shudder. And the notebook called this the Sinner's Gate. So what's waiting for us?

"There's another tombstone," Trina says. She's stopped, holding her flashlight in both hands close to her chest.

This tombstone is shattered, like the other one. The same sort of broken-tooth shape. Or is it *exactly* the same? But it can't be the same stone, because I can make out the text carved on this one.

MAURA O'MALLEY

LOVING MOTHER

D. 1856

"Another cemetery. Great," Anthony says.

"It's gonna be zombies," Jeremy says. "Guarantee it. Just you fucking wait." He stomps out ahead, tension in every line of his body.

There are more tombstones than before, but they're in nearly the same arrangement. There is the same cluster of three, the angel perched atop the center one whole this time, wings outstretched, only the ends of the feathers snapped off.

The same double headstone. Exactly the same. And there, standing at the edge of the cemetery, is the sign. Upright.

BRIAR GLEN

The sky is a foreboding shade of gray, the first hints of reflected light filtering to us, and we can see the shape of the town beyond our flashlights. Walls stand; roofs remain. But it's the same town. I'm sure of it.

"Everyone stay close," I say, fighting to make my voice louder than a whisper. It's not an instruction I need to give. We bunch up as we walk through the center of the town, our footsteps the only sound, tramp and scrape.

The buildings show no signs of fire, but they have a neglected look about them. Vines whispering up toward windowsills. Roofs beginning to sag. A broom discarded at the base of a wall, collecting spiders and dust. No sign of anyone, either a visitor like us or—

Or whoever might *belong* on the road.

"Look at that," Trina says, shining her flashlight on the lintel of a house. There's graffiti scrawled in what looks like chalk, there and elsewhere.

DAHUT, it reads. And then: THE GATE IS OPEN

WHERE TRAVEL WE

YS AWAITS

THE TOLL IS BLOOD

The words aren't like spray-paint tags, stylized, jagged, or loopy. They're written in a steady, blocky hand. Almost formal.

"It says that in the notebook, too. 'Dahut,'" I say. "Sound familiar to anyone?" A round of shaking heads. Is it a name? A place? A magic word? We creep along, the sound of my voice seeming to linger, waiting for something to drown it out.

There's more writing around the well. Lowercase letters, cursive, looping around the rim. The stones break up the words, and they continue in a circle, as if there is no beginning, no ending.

the sea rushes in her lover rushes in her lover is the sea she unlocks the gate he floods her salt her lips salt her thighs salt her tongue we are drowned the sea rushes in

My eye tracks it around and around and around, as if I'm caught in the loop of it, as if I'll never break free. I realize I'm reading it aloud, the words on my lips like a puzzle, like a riddle, and the others are listening, transfixed as I am. I can't stop.

"Dahut," Miranda says suddenly, clearly, and I stutter to a stop. We flinch back from the well, looking at each other wildly. The light on the horizon has a bruised quality. How long have we been standing here? "Sunrise soon. We should move," she says. As if sunrise means something to her that it doesn't to me, but Miranda seems to have a handle on this place the way none of the rest of us do, so I nod like it makes sense.

Perhaps the words are the trap the road set for us. And if we walk away from the well, we'll be free. The next gate will be waiting.

We find the grave again instead.

"Maura O'Malley," Vanessa says. We barely break stride this

time. Some part of us has expected this. No echo comes only once. "I wonder how she died. By fire or by flood or—"

"Stop," Trina whispers. "Just stop."

The angel, the double headstone, the sign: BRIAR GLEN.

The paint is fresh. There are flowers planted at the base. They have bright yellow centers and thick, fleshy purple petals. Dark crimson veins spider over them. Their leaves are blunted spades, splayed out over the dirt in a way that makes it look like the flowers are pulling, pushing themselves free of the soil.

"What *is* this?" Trina asks.

"Seven times through," Kyle says, and I nod. He continues. "The notebook said seven times through, then you're free. So we have to walk through the town seven times before we get to the next gate."

"That . . . sounds right," Anthony says. "In a twisted logic sort of way."

"Easy enough," I say, trying to stay upbeat. It doesn't exactly come naturally to me, and Anthony gives me a skeptical look. "That's twice. This is the third time. Four more after. We can do that." Becca used to be the one who talked everyone into things. I was her second-in-command. I'm not used to playing leader, but I know we need one. "Stick together, don't dawdle, and watch each other's backs."

"You got it, boss," Anthony says. Mel snorts, but she's bouncing on the balls of her feet, ready to move, and when I start out, the others follow.

The light is dim but strengthening. We don't need our flashlights to see the buildings up ahead anymore. The stone is whitewashed; the wood painted. Flower beds grow in front of all the houses, the same purple flowers, the same bright yellow centers.

"It looks nice," Trina says. "It doesn't—it doesn't look dangerous."

"I think everything here is dangerous," Anthony says.

We're passing the first house when I see her: a girl in the window, framed between two crisp white curtains. She stands as if she's watching us—except her back is turned, a brown plait running straight down between her shoulder blades, a blue ribbon at the end. Her hands are lifted to her face, cupped gently, covering her eyes, her nose, her mouth, so that I can't see anything but the curve of her jaw, the pink shell of her ear.

I grab Anthony's hand. My voice crouches at the back of my mouth, but I force it out. "There's someone there," I whisper.

"They're in all the buildings," Mel says. She's right. Every building has at least one figure. Men. Women. Children. Three in one window, a mother and two children. Hands over their faces. Turned away from us. Their clothes are old-fashioned, white and gray. Wide sleeves for the women, button-up shirts or suit jackets for the men. They don't move as we pass. Don't turn to look or leave the windows. I count seven. Twelve. Seventeen. And still more. Yet the silence of the place remains, as if we are the only things breathing here.

"Who are they?" Trina asks. "Are they the people that—are they ghosts?"

"Only two people died in the fire that destroyed Briar Glen," Vanessa says, almost contemptuous.

"They can't be people like us," Trina says. "People like Isaac."

"No," I say. "I don't think so."

"I'm not sure they're people at all," Mel says, and no one disagrees.

There is writing on the well again. Crammed together, almost illegible. I make out DAHUT and BLOOD and GATE and little else, because none of us want to stop, and I don't want to start reading again and leave us spellbound with those silent, still people all around us.

"Hurry," Miranda whispers. She's watching the horizon. I don't know if she's talking to me or whispering to herself.

The edge of town. The empty road. The cemetery. Trina moans, a sound of frustration and fear and foreboding, but we keep going, entering the town once more.

They aren't in the houses any longer. They're outside them. Some of them stand on their porches. Or between the houses. Standing with their hands over their faces, their backs to us. Farther off, among the trees, I see a woman standing, her hair blowing in the wind. Her ribbon has come loose; it dances away. She makes no move to capture it.

A crow caws. We seize into stillness, startled like a herd of deer. The bird flaps into sight, stoops in the air, and lands on the broad shoulder of a bearded man. It cocks its head at us, tilting its beak aside to fix us with one black, canny eye. And then it plunges its beak into the man's neck.

It stabs, and stabs again, the way a shorebird spears a fish on its beak. The man doesn't move. Doesn't even flinch. Blood and bits of skin fly out as the bird shakes its beak and drives it in again, making a gurgling, cawing noise.

"Oh God," Trina whispers. "Oh God."

The crow gets hold of something long and stringy and red. It pulls and pulls and the thing—the tendon, the ligament, the bit of flesh—stretches, pulling away, dripping blood, until it comes free with a sucking, tearing sound, and blood gushes from the wound, pours down the man's neck and his shoulder and seeps into his gray shirt, and still he doesn't move, he doesn't scream. The bird tips its head, and the meat slides down its gullet.

We run. I don't know who moves first. It doesn't matter. We run together, away from the man and away from the crow, past the others standing, faces hidden. We run through the center of the town.

The words are spilling down the sides of the well, tangling up with each other. I don't look at them. We just have to get out of here.

And then we stumble to a stop, grabbing at each other, heaving for breath.

A man stands at the edge of town, square in the middle of the road just a stone's throw away from us. His clothes are black. He looks like a priest, but the book clasped under his arm is not a Bible. The symbol etched on the cover shows concentric circles, thin, one inside the other inside the other. I can't count them from here, but I have a guess at their number. The wind catches the ribbons that thread between the pages of the book, making them flutter.

"They haven't done anything to us," I whisper. "They haven't hurt us. They just stand there. Let's—let's keep going."

Jeremy lets out a strangled sound as we edge forward, skirting to the very limit of the road. The preacher's hands aren't covering his face, I realize, because they're holding the book. It's tucked under one arm, and the opposite hand rests on its spine. He stares straight ahead and makes no move to intercept us.

He has no eyes.

They aren't empty sockets. They aren't a flat expanse of flesh, or caved-in lids, or simply closed. They are the nothing-void that Isaac's were for that split second, but the nothingness persists. It belongs. It is impossible to describe the sensation of *not* seeing, of perceiving nonexistence. I want to describe it as gray, I want to remember it as gray, but it is not. It is emptiness, filling him. It is hollowness, made solid.

He stares at me, and I stare back. I don't know how he can see without eyes, but he *sees* me. Knows me. The others are edging past. Trina looks away. Mel nearly walks backward, trying to keep her eyes on him. Jeremy gets past him and then stands as if to block any approach, if he decides to lunge. Anthony grabs at my hand.

"Let's get out of here," he says.

The man's mouth opens, his lips cracking like dried mud as they move. "The gate is not a gate of iron. The Liar's Gate is darkness and deceit. The Sinner's Gate is guilt, and it is judgment. The toll is blood, Sara Donoghue. The toll is blood, and the wicked among you must pay."

The crow caws. It flies to him, lands on his shoulder. A stringy gob of gore hangs from its beak. Its feathers ruffle out.

"Sunrise is coming," he says, but this time he tilts his head toward Miranda.

"Sara, let's go." Anthony is pulling at me. I let him drag me along. The crow calls, and it sounds like it's laughing. We stumble-run our way out of the town, onto the empty road. As soon as we're out of sight, we stop. We all know what we'll find, if we keep going. The same town, over and over again.

"There has to be a way to make this stop," Trina says. We've been standing, waiting to be shaken from this terrible inertia, for at least two solid minutes. "A trick or something. A way to make it stop repeating."

Vanessa shivers, fingertips playing with the ends of her sleeves. "The Sinner's Gate. That's what he said. The Sinner's Gate and—and guilt, and judgment. And the toll is blood, and one of us has to pay."

"It can't mean—he can't mean that one of us has to die. No way. That's—that's not fair," Mel says, shaking her head.

Jeremy snorts. "Fair? You think this place cares about *fair*?"

"He didn't say one of us. He said the wicked among us." Trina's voice is soft, almost vanishing in the dark.

Mel chuckles. "Guess you're safe, then." Trina doesn't look at her, eyes dropping to the ground. "Hey. It was a joke, Miss Valedictorian, Never-Missed-a-Curfew. I'm just saying, if anyone in this group is wicked, it's got to be me."

Anthony rolls his eyes. "Yeah, underage drinking is so cutting-edge."

"I've done worse things."

"Like?"

"I dunno. Old-timey preacher man probably wouldn't like the whole lesbian thing."

Trina interrupts, voice sharp and almost angry. "You aren't wicked, Mel."

Mel's eyes spark. An argument's easier than fear, but if we start sniping at each other, we'll have to waste our energy patching up self-inflicted wounds. I'm rusty at playing peacemaker. It's like an atrophied muscle, but I used to know the Wildcats so well I could stop an argument three syllables in.

"We just have to get through," I say. "Seven times, that's what the book says. They haven't done anything to us."

"*Yet,*" Vanessa points out. "*Yet.* They're going to turn on us, can't you see that? But he said there was a toll. Maybe we can pay it, and get through without—without whatever's waiting."

"Nothing in the town has tried to hurt us," I remind them. I know how to keep the Wildcats together, but Vanessa I don't know as well. She's a classmate, not a friend. "I say we keep going. If something does go wrong, then we can run."

Vanessa shakes her head. "I'm telling you, it's not going to be that easy. He said the wicked among us. I think we have to consider who that might be."

"We should have investigated more," Kyle says. "Gone in the houses, or—"

"No!" I say, in unison with Trina and Anthony. We all exchange a half-amused, half-horrified look. "We don't leave the road," I finish.

Kyle's cheeks redden. "Right. Dumb idea. But it's still four times through and all we've seen is some graffiti that doesn't make any sense. Hey, Miranda. When we were all hypnotized, or whatever happened, you said *Dahut*. How did you know that would snap us out of it?"

I've almost forgotten she's there—I'm half-convinced that she *wasn't*, that she's here now because we've remembered she is, but that doesn't make any sense. "I didn't," Miranda says. "It was just the first thing I thought of."

"Why does it matter if sunrise comes?" I ask.

"Does it?" Miranda replies.

"Didn't you say something about . . . ?" I shake my head. We're getting distracted. "Never mind. Okay. We're going. And no one's paying any toll. Agreed?"

Vanessa huffs loudly, but no one objects. When I set out, the others follow—but I can feel their nervousness behind me. Fear is beginning to truly set in. And we have a long way to go yet.

INTERVIEW

MELANIE WHITTAKER

May 9, 2017

Melanie Whittaker sits with her hands pressed together in her lap, leaning forward. Where the other room appears to be a converted storage room, this was clearly an office, a window on one wall overlooking what appears to be a warehouse interior, and a desk shoved in the corner. Mel sits in a faded blue swivel chair, the cushion split and fraying.

Mel jumps when the door opens. Abigail Ryder enters. She wears black gloves and carries a file folder under one arm, thick with papers.

ABBY: Sorry about that. I had to help Dr. Ashford with something.

She takes a seat across from Mel.

MEL: It's fine. You're talking to Sara, right? She's here?

ABBY: Yeah. You can talk to her when we're done, if you want.

MEL: I don't know if that's a good idea.

ABBY: It's your call. But for now we should keep going.

MEL: You want to know about Miranda, right?

Abby hesitates. Then she shakes her head.

ABBY: We'll get to that. Right now we should talk about the town.

MEL: I don't know if I should talk about this part.

ABBY: Because of the situation with the Jeffries family? I don't think anything you tell me is going to matter, honestly.

MEL: Should I—should I talk to a lawyer first, or . . . ?

ABBY: Look. No one is going to ask us about any of this. Dr. Ashford's been stripped of tenure and no university will even look at his résumé. They think he's crazy. So even if the police or anyone else *did* bother to ask us, they wouldn't believe us.

Abby sits back a bit. She glances at the camera, frowns.

ABBY: We don't have to record this part. If it would make you feel more comfortable. Less . . .

MEL: Disloyal?

Mel's voice is a whisper. She thinks, then shakes her head slowly.

MEL: Maybe it would be a good thing, if the truth got out there.

ABBY: That's more or less Dr. Ashford's philosophy in a nutshell.

MEL: Not yours?

ABBY: I'm a little less attached to the moral high ground than he is. Personally, I would have picked the tenure over the lifelong quest to prove the unprovable.

Mel laughs a little, starting to relax. Abby leans in.

ABBY: Now. We'd gotten to your fifth visit to the town.

MEL: Right. We were still in the Sinner's Gate, and it was starting to feel like we'd never get out.

11

THE FLOWERS HAVE spread when we get to the sign. They are no longer contained in tidy beds; they thrust up from the grass and the weeds, spilling in every direction, even pushing their way between the stones of the road. I crush one beneath my foot as I walk, and a smell like spices and cut grass fills the air—but with something else beneath it. Something rotten, like meat just beginning to turn.

When we come in sight of the town, Jeremy lets loose a long, quiet string of swearing, and I don't blame him.

The people are still here, still facing away from us. They are near the road, all of them, standing with an orderly quiet that makes you expect to find them lined up neatly in rows, but they're more scattered than that. As if they were all walking in a crowd, jostling each other, some walking together, some striking out on their own. And they all just suddenly stopped. Their hands don't cover their faces anymore; they hang at their sides, loose and relaxed.

At their feet, a thousand flowers bloom.

"Just . . . try not to touch them." I know that no one else will move until I do, so I stride forward.

The moment I reach the first of them, a woman with long, dark hair, the whispering begins. She turns her face to me. Her eyes—I don't have to tell you, do I? Their eyes are all like the preacher's.

"*Don't leave the road,*" she whispers, and it passes through the townspeople like a fever, repeated until the sounds dissolve into formless rustling.

"*When it's dark, don't let go,*" whispers a girl no older than nine, and this, too, dissolves among the crowd like ink into water.

"*There are other roads. Don't follow them,*" whispers the girl's mother.

I know, I want to tell them. *Tell me something I haven't heard yet.* But I remember the notebook. *Don't talk to them.*

I keep my mouth shut. I look at the others quickly, making sure they do the same, and catch Mel's eye. Her lips are clamped shut, her eyes wide. We hold each other's gaze for a moment, steadying each other, until she nods once and I turn my focus back to the path in front of me.

The whispers start to blend together. I try to pick them out as we inch along, try to move slowly, but it's hard not to hurry. Not to run.

the sea rushes in her lover rushes in the sea rushes—

He's gone to meet the bramble man

You're going to the gallows, girl

The gates are open

I smell the blood on you.

I whip around. It's the man, the bearded man the crow attacked. His shirt is clean, no sign of blood. Where the crow's beak ripped its hole, a curl of vine grows, grasping its way along his

throat, spade-like leaves lying flat against his skin. He isn't looking at me. He's looking at Trina, and she is transfixed.

"I smell the blood on you, girl," he whispers. *"And so will he."*

"The toll is blood," they whisper, until the sentence shreds
apart. *"The wicked among you must pay. I smell the blood on
you."*

Trina's eyes are wide. She takes a step toward the man, toward
the edge of the road, and she starts to open her mouth. I lunge,
but Jeremy is faster. His hand is over her mouth before she can
make a sound.

"Don't talk to them," he hisses. "And don't listen to them, either. Come on."

He lets her go, but takes her hand instead, and she follows
mutely, footsteps stumbling. Kyle watches her go, a puzzled expression on his face. Like he's almost begun to realize something,
but he hasn't figured out what yet.

The whispers swell. There are more people than the last time
through the town, hundreds of them, and they are crowded close
together at the center of the town, making the whispers an impossible rush of sound, as incomprehensible as wind through long
grass.

The words around the well have devolved into chaos even
more immune to interpretation. Letters layered on top of letters in
the same white chalk, so that only the frayed edge, three feet out
from the well, can be read.

*the gate of sin lies shut until the wicked are bled they bleed the
wicked they take them they are given the toll is blood DAHUT
OPENS THE GATES THE SEA RUSHES IN*

And that's all I can make out. The wind-in-rushes sound around me rises in a cacophony. And then every whisper turns to silence, like they've been gathered in one fist and cut through with a knife.

The preacher is walking toward us. He carries the book against his chest. With every second step he raises his other hand and it strikes the leather cover—*thump*. One step, another, *thump*. The ribbons in the book are fat and fleshy like the petals of the flowers. He stops at the edge of the town square, in the middle of the road we have to follow.

"The toll is blood," he says. "And the wicked must pay. It is your choice which of the wicked bleed, but bleed they must. Sunrise is nearly come, and the light lays bare many truths." He stands, his hands folded over the thick book.

Their ranks close behind him. Fingers graze my wrist—a boy, maybe seven years old, reaching for me. I yank away. The crowd doesn't move, but they seem closer than before.

"We push through," I say.

"We'll never make it," Vanessa says. "They want one of us. One of us must have done something. One of us must be wicked, or they wouldn't be asking." Her voice is high and fearful, and I can feel that fear infecting the others, skittering over them. Trina's eyes are wide, her whole body tensed.

"No," I say. "We make a break for it and—"

"Seven times. That's two more. And it's getting worse every time," Vanessa presses. She looks around between us, panicky. "Which of you is it? Which of you does he want? They're going to kill all of us if you don't—"

"Stop," I say, at the same instant as Trina stumbles back a step. Away from Vanessa and what she's saying.

Vanessa's eyes snap to her. "Trina?" she says softly. Around us is the silence of a still forest. A silence of waiting.

"No," Trina says. "No."

"What did you do?" Vanessa asks. She steps forward. So do the townspeople, crowding us. Jeremy snarls as one gets too close.

"I didn't—I don't—" Trina's voice is barely a whisper.

"Stop," I say. They're all watching her. Listening intently. "Trina, don't say anything." I look at Anthony, but he looks lost. We have to run. We have to make everyone run.

"They want you," Vanessa says softly. "Don't they?"

"Why would they want you?" asks Mel.

"Trina, don't—" I say, but it's too late.

"Chris," she says.

"What are you talking about?" Kyle asks, panicky.

"Your stepdad?" I ask, bafflement in my voice as fresh whispers swell and break and swell around us.

"What did you do?" Kyle asks, his voice rising.

"Can we not talk about this here?" Jeremy says.

"It's only going to get worse," Vanessa says. "If we keep going, it will get worse."

"No, stop, we'll be fine," I say. I'll say anything to quiet the panic in Trina's eyes. *I did this*, I think, not knowing what part of *this* I mean. "None of them have hurt us. We don't have to—"

"He tried to stop me," Trina says. Vanessa lets out a sharp hiss of breath between her teeth. "He tried to stop me from going."

"Trina, *what are you talking about*?" Anthony demands.

"They smell the blood on her," Vanessa says. "*They smell the blood*. What did you *do*, Trina?"

"I think I killed him," she whispers.

A hundred bodies surge. Kyle screams. Jeremy grabs him around the waist to hold him back from his sister as hands seize her, handing her to the next person and the next so that she's carried away from us like being snatched by a riptide.

I thrash my way forward. They won't die for me. They came for me, for Becca, and I won't let any of them die for it. It burns in me, bright, a brilliant truth that I believe utterly, with the whole of my being. I must save them. I can. I will.

I do not understand yet that I am so small, next to the thing that has swallowed us. I do not understand yet how much we will lose.

They have brought her to the edge of town. The flowers have grown over the road, bursting greedily between the cracks in the stones, thrusting their fleshy petals high on nodding stalks. Our feet trample them as we race to get to Trina, and the air is filled with their spice-grass-rot scent.

They push her to her knees, her hands behind her back. The preacher stands in front of her, thumb thumping the cover of his leather-bound book. Trina struggles, teeth bared in terror. She lunges forward, one arm breaking free, but the preacher closes a hand around her throat. She claws at him, her nails scraping across the book in his other hand.

I try to push my way to her, but there are endless bodies between us, and they have all the give and mercy of stone. Jeremy still grapples with Kyle, trying to hold him back from charging after his sister to help her, but Miranda and Mel and Vanessa are here. Vanessa is breathless, eyes wide, watching the scene with an expression I can't read. Mel has her hands pressed against her mouth.

I struggle to force myself between two women, but they don't budge. I fall back a step. I can't get to Trina. I can't stop them. I can't save her. I am going to watch her die. I look around frantically, searching for some way through the crowd, and instead I see Miranda. She's staring at the horizon as it bleeds light with the coming dawn. There is something odd about the shadows on her skin. Something too deep in the blacks of her eyes.

"They'll take their toll," she says. Tension streaks her voice. "Sara, listen. They'll take their toll. There's no way around it now. They want the wicked, but Sara—Sara, *who was holding Vanessa's hand*?"

Vanessa's gaze turns toward Miranda, and her expression is clotted up with such hatred, such venom, such raw rage that I flinch away.

One of the townspeople is stepping forward. A child. A girl. A red ribbon is tied at the end of each of her braids, and she's humming a song I almost recognize. She holds a knife in her hand. A kitchen knife, with a wooden handle and a spot of rust near the edge. The sort of knife you use to cut onions.

"I was with Anthony. Trina was with Kyle. Jeremy was with Mel and Miranda," I say. "Who were you with, Vanessa?"

Vanessa looks at me, and if I hadn't seen her face when she turned toward Miranda, I would believe the confusion, the fear in it now. "What?"

"You don't stutter anymore," I say.

"I d-don't know what y-you're talking about," she says.

"You've done it a couple times. Like you had to remember," I say. "And you were ashamed. You apologized. I've known Vanessa almost my whole life. She doesn't apologize for stuttering. She's got no reason to."

"Y-you're scaring me," she says. Shrinking back, in a way I've never seen Vanessa shrink from anything.

The girl lifts the knife. Kyle is screaming his sister's name. Trina shuts her eyes. The whispers swell.

Her lover rushes in
The sea rushes in
The gates are open

The moment is suspended. Unformed and undecided, but that decision is rapidly being made without me. I see it as clearly as if it were labeled and laid out neatly in front of me. The toll is blood. And someone has to pay.

I step forward, and lift my hands, and shove Vanessa in the chest.

Her arms pinwheel. For an instant she is balanced, her body a slash canted away from me, mouth open in an O of surprise. The light of the sunrise slashes down and glints on the blade of the knife, and Vanessa loses her balance. She falls back. Into the crowd, which is already turning to meet her. To seize her. To bear her down.

I see the knife flash twice more, above the press of bodies. The first time it is silver. The second time it is crimson. Jeremy is trying to fight his way through—to Vanessa, to Trina, I can't tell. Anthony is grabbing me, shaking me, demanding to know what I've done.

And then the people seethe back, like water withdrawing from a shore. Trina kneels at the place where the dirt road of the town turns back to stone. She is whole. She is breathing.

Vanessa is gone. Where I saw her fall, the ground is covered in a thick carpet of flowers, their petals purple pulsed with red, their centers bright and yellow as the sun washes over them. The preacher stands beside Trina, the book in his left hand, his right tight on Trina's shoulder.

"The toll is paid," he says. "The gate is open. The road wends on. To Ys. To the sea."

Trina screams, a sound of rage and fear and relief all at once, and springs to her feet. She whips around to face the preacher, but he only smiles at her. He whispers something, too softly to hear, and presses the book into her hands. I step forward, not sure what I intend to do—and then Jeremy shouts.

"Guys!" he cries, and points behind us.

The sea rushes in, the whispers say, but it isn't the sea rushing in behind us. It's the darkness.

Anthony seizes my hand. We run.

PART III

THE BEAST

EXHIBIT G

Post on Akrou & Bone *video game fan forum*

"Off Topic: Urban Legends & Paranormal
Activity" sub-forum

March 22, 2014

Subject: Lucy Gallows and the Ghost Road—Primary
Docs?

Things have been a little quiet on the Lucy front
lately, but I stumbled across an interesting
account in an old paranormal zine (found
somewhere very bad for my asthma and let's leave
it at that). This guy claims that he and his wife
traveled a "ghost road" and he mentions Lucy
Gallows. This account is from the 1970s (!!) which
makes it one of the earlier first-person accounts
we've found (if it's true, of course).

The zine had a bunch of water damage and
it's totally falling apart, but I did manage to
scan this part before it turned to brown mush:

to the end, barely. What we experienced along that road would fill volumes, and I don't know if I can bring myself to write about much of it. We found evidence that we weren't the first to travel along it. Eventually, we reached the end—or an end, at least. And there we met a girl. She said her name was Lucy. She asked us for help. She said she'd been stuck on the road for some time and couldn't escape on her own. I was eager to find a way to help her. At that point, any other human contact was welcome. But my wife became distressed.

She pulled me aside and told me that she knew the girl—or knew her voice, at least. She kept referring to "whispers that scratch at the inside of my skull" and called her "the gallows girl." She insisted that we had to get away from her. That we couldn't trust her.

I'm not proud of what we did, but by that point we had learned that the only way to survive was to trust one another's instincts absolutely. And so when we had the opportunity, we ran together, and left young Lucy behind.

[*Illegible*] ended her own life less than a year later. [*Illegible*] still dreamed of her. [*Illegible*] journals, they were filled with Lucy's name, along with two words, scrawled randomly through normal entries: Find her.

The one really incongruous thing is that this couple is from Missouri. They hitched a ride on the ghost road just outside of St. Louis, which might be why none of us have found this particular bit of Lucy lore.

—mnemosyne_amnesiac

12

WE CAN'T OUTRUN the darkness. It crashes over us, and it's all I can do to keep hold of Anthony's hand. This time there aren't thirteen steps, only one, staggering, before the darkness rips away as quickly as it found us. It rolls past, tearing itself apart as it moves. Scraps of pure shadow wrench themselves into small shapes—birds. Crows. Hundreds of them, thousands, as the tide of darkness breaks apart in a cacophony of caws and beating wings. For a few chaotic seconds they darken the sky, blocking the slanting light of the rising sun, and then they stream out over the forest to the west.

For a moment I think I see something in the direction they're flying, something that looms above the trees—maybe a tree itself, with branches jutting up to either side of its peak. But they look more like antlers, and then whatever gray shadow I saw is lost in the mist and the swarm of crows.

Four birds remain, wheeling above us in a tilting sort of dance; the rest are gone. The trees are sparser here, their branches mostly bare, letting the sunlight slant through. Water drips from them as if it's just finished raining, but the sky is clear.

"What did you do?" Jeremy demands, dropping Trina's hand and taking a menacing step toward me. Trina holds the preacher's book against her chest, both hands crossed over it.

"I—" I don't know what to say. How to explain.

"You killed her," Mel says, horror in her voice. Kyle edges toward Trina.

"Hold on," Anthony says, holding out his palms and stepping between me and Jeremy.

"She just murdered Vanessa," Jeremy says.

"And you're going to do what, exactly?" Anthony asks. Jeremy's jaw tenses, his hands balling up into fists, but he sets his weight back, done advancing.

"I don't think she *was* Vanessa," I say. "She didn't stutter anymore. And she was—she was different. And I couldn't remember—I don't think she was holding anyone's hand when we came through the Liar's Gate. Were any of you holding her hand?"

They glance at each other, unease breaking over them.

"That doesn't mean . . ." Jeremy trails off. "People don't stutter all the time."

"But the other stuff—she was acting different. I think," Mel says softly. "I don't know her that well, though."

"Sara didn't know her that well, either. Did you?" Jeremy asks.

I shake my head. "We weren't close, but we've been in school together for years. Vanessa wasn't Vanessa. Trust me."

"Vanessa wasn't Vanessa? Does that makes sense to any of you?" Jeremy presses.

"Here? Kind of," Anthony says.

"Am I the only one that thinks that murdering someone should require better than *kind of*?" Jeremy asks.

"No," I say. "You're not." I fist my hand against my stomach, feeling sick.

"You should have let them take me," Trina says. Her cheeks are streaked with tears and dirt, her eyes puffy and red. "I'm the one they wanted."

"Because you hurt Chris?" I ask. It doesn't make any sense. Trina's the girl who carries spiders outside under a glass. But here she is, shaking so much that I catch her hand in mine and I can feel her trembling through it. The other still curls protectively around the book. She's spent all her tears, but her breath hitches, a catch that makes me think of a fishhook in her throat, snagging every shuddering sigh. I try to think of how she's been acting tonight, but all I can remember is my own need, my own longing. My own fear. "It's going to be okay," I say, beginning at last to understand that it isn't.

She hauls her eyes up to mine. Her lips part, like she is waiting for words to arrive. And then they do. "Chris tried to stop me from coming tonight," she says.

Her stepdad has always been an asshole. The kind of guy who thinks that because he is a cop, he is the law in his house as well, an unimpeachable and righteous force before which there is no option but to yield.

"We got into a fight. I—" She swallows. She looks at Kyle, whose face is contorted, fear and confusion making it into a puzzle with the pieces all scattered. "I grabbed a bat and—I think I might have killed him. I'm not sure." Her eyes have no remorse in them, not exactly—only a kind of grief, a grief I understand. Grief for the person you were the instant before you acted.

"You killed your stepdad because he wouldn't let you come out here?" Jeremy asks.

She glares at him. "No, Jeremy. Not because he wouldn't let me come out here."

"I—" He stops. "He—he hurt you?"

"He was . . ." She stops. She glances toward Kyle but stops herself, takes a deep breath. "He was violent," she says. "I—I confronted him, and he came at me. I was defending myself."

Kyle has tightened in on himself. He looks ready to fracture. "You didn't have to do that," he says. "I could take it."

Because of course Chris wouldn't hit Trina—wouldn't hit the one who would fight back. Kyle, though? He's always been small, always delicate. Asthma and a smart-aleck attitude, eager to entertain, to please. He's an easy target, and Chris is the kind of coward who could see that.

Her hand is still in mine, warming under my skin, and I grip it tight like I can hold her together through my touch alone. But she pulls away, turns toward her brother, and the moment shifts and closes in until it belongs only to the two of them.

"You should have told me," Trina whispers. "I told him that I knew. He wasn't even sorry, he—" She stops. "I didn't know, before. Or I would have done something sooner."

"He's dead?" Kyle asks, disbelief strangling his voice. "You really killed him?"

"I didn't mean to." She stops. "No. I did. He said there was nothing I could do. No one would believe me. He laughed. And then he grabbed me, and . . . And I grabbed the bat. I hit him until he couldn't hit me. That's what they meant. They smelled the blood on me. It's my blood we needed to open the gate. Because I'm a sinner. A murderer."

"It was self-defense," I say. "You had to."

She shudders. She bends over and vomits. She staggers and I catch her, holding her. Mel has her arms around Kyle, protective. I have an image of him, towheaded and gangly, wrapped in Mel's bear hug as she tried to throw him into the pool—the two of them went in together, both of them shrieking with laughter while Trina and I rolled our eyes in the shade. He was ten, I think. Before Chris. Just before.

I help Trina up. I hug her, wrapping my arms around her the way I have wanted to be held for the past year, the way I wouldn't let anyone hold me. Her skin smells sour. I can feel the knobs of her vertebrae beneath my fingers. The book presses between us.

"I can't go back," she whispers. "I can never go back."

"Yes, you can," I say. "You don't know that he's dead. And you were protecting yourself. We'll figure it out. Okay?" I smooth her hair back and tuck the blonde waves behind her ears where they've come loose from her ponytail. She nods.

"Okay," she says.

"I'm glad you did it," Kyle says. "He deserved it."

"I'm glad I did it, too," she says, soft and fierce, and Kyle nods. Mel lets him go, reluctantly. He jams his hands in his pockets. The guys don't meet his eyes, and everyone looks like they don't know what expressions they're supposed to be wearing.

"Hey, so. Sara. Wanna make a club? Trauma Kids? You can be president," Kyle says to me.

"I don't get to be president?" Trina asks, swiping her nose with the back of her hand.

"Nah. You want to be treasurer. Admit it," Kyle says, and Trina laughs through a new spate of tears. He's not okay. She's not okay. But in that moment they find an equilibrium.

"Are we just not going to talk about the fact that Sara killed Vanessa?" Jeremy asks. "I mean, I'm sorry. I know this is a heavy moment. But Vanessa—"

"It wasn't Vanessa," I say.

"Are you sure?" he asks.

"If she says it's true, it's true," Trina says. I wish I felt as sure as she sounds.

"I—I don't know," I say. "Miranda asked who was holding her hand, and they were about to kill Trina, and—" I swallow. And then my stomach lurches. "Wait. Where is Miranda?"

We all look around like we'll find her lurking behind a tree, like she'll walk up behind us, fine and unhurt. But she's nowhere.

"I grabbed Kyle's hand," Mel says. "Miranda was near you." The hint of an accusation sharpens her tone.

"I just grabbed Anthony's hand and ran," I say.

"I was focused on getting Trina on her feet," Jeremy says. "Oh, *fuck*." Mel clamps a hand over her mouth, choking back a sob.

"She's gone," I say, because someone has to say it out loud.

"She must have—the darkness must have taken her. Somehow."

"Then we've lost two people in fifteen minutes," Jeremy says, his anger snapping out squarely at me.

"But we got through," Mel says. "Which means that either Vanessa was a secret ax murderer, or Sara was right. That wasn't Vanessa."

"Or they didn't care who they killed," Jeremy says.

"We can check," Kyle says suddenly. We look at him. He pulls out his phone, the movement and the downward tilt of his face a poor effort to conceal the tears on his cheeks. "I was recording when Trina and I went into the dark. I kept the video going. It should have caught Vanessa coming through."

A shudder of mingled relief and dread goes through me. And then Kyle's face crumples into despair.

"Crap. The battery's dead," he says.

"You've got to be kidding me," Jeremy says.

"I've been taking videos and stuff on and off for like six hours," Kyle says. "It was already in the red when we went into the town the first time. I'm sorry."

"Hold on," Mel says. "I have a portable charger. Give it to me." She rummages in her backpack, pulling out the battery pack, and takes Kyle's phone from him. Too eagerly—everyone desperate for some action to focus on to bleed off our despair. And then she swears. "Do you have the charger cord? With a USB?"

"No, I left it at home," Kyle says.

She sighs. "Then we're fucked. Mine has a different jack."

"Then all we have is Sara's hunch," Jeremy says.

"Does it matter if she was right or not?" Trina asks, voice flat. "Either way, she's gone. Miranda is gone. It's just the six of us now. Knowing what happened wouldn't change that. It wouldn't change anything."

"She's right," Anthony says. Jeremy looks at me, and I stare back. Because the two of us know it isn't true. Of course it changes things.

Either I'm a murderer, or I'm not. And now I might never know.

Mel holds the dead phone out to Kyle, but he's wandered over to Trina, who is staring down at the book in her hands as if she's not sure what to do with it. Mel tucks the phone and charger into her bag instead.

"What did he say to you?" I ask Trina. "Why did he give you the book?" It seems like such a trivial question, after what's just happened.

"'Arm yourself, child, for there are trials yet to come,'" she recites. She opens the book to the first page. The writing is spidery, the ink brown. *The words to unmake*, it reads at the top, and then a spill of cramped script, growing like thorns across the page. Trina turns the page, then another, her lips just barely moving as she reads.

"What does it say?" Anthony asks.

"It's talking about the ocean," she says, sounding distant, almost dreamy. "And Ys, and Dahut, and the gates. The stars, and something behind the stars. The earth and what's below. Things waiting. Things unseen. It—" She stops. Snaps it shut. "It's just

a bunch of nonsense," she says. She looks around as if she's trying to decide on a place to discard it. Finally she tucks it under
her arm, shrugs. "Maybe it'll have something useful in it."

"But for now we should keep moving," Anthony says. "Right?
I know I don't want to hang around in one place too long."

I hesitate. The book bothers me. This isn't a place to go trust-
ing gifts.

"Gate number three," Mel says. "Let's go find out what's going
to try to kill us next."

I don't object. Trina keeps the book. It's another mistake, but
it will be a long time before I realize the extent of it.

INTERVIEW

SARA DONOGHUE

May 9, 2017

ASHFORD: What made you decide to push Vanessa into the crowd?

SARA: I'm not sure I can explain it completely. It's not like I was thinking everything through logically. I was terrified. We all were. It was happening so fast, and Miranda was talking, and . . . I didn't want Trina to die.

ASHFORD: And you didn't know Vanessa as well.

SARA: That's not why I did it. I don't think it is.

She pauses. Her voice drops until the microphone can barely pick it up.

SARA: I hope it isn't.

ASHFORD: Miss Donoghue, I think you've been through a great deal. More than any person should bear. Perhaps I can help with this small portion of it.

SARA: What do you mean?

ASHFORD: As Miss Whittaker still had Kyle's phone, we were able to recover all of the video Kyle Jeffries took on the road. Nearly two hours of footage between your arrival in the woods and when the battery died. I can show you the video of the exit from the Liar's Gate, and the events that transpired after.

SARA: After? You mean—the crow? The one that was screaming?

Ashford's look is one of pity.

ASHFORD: Yes. It does involve the crow. I should warn you that this video is quite upsetting. But it should clarify the . . . omissions in your memories. Would you like to see it now?

SARA: Yes. Yes, please. I—I just want to know.

Ashford nods, and reaches into a bag beside his chair, pulling out a laptop.

ASHFORD: Just a moment, then.

He glances toward the door, which opens on Abby. Her hand is in her jacket pocket; just visible, protruding from that pocket, is the plunger of a syringe. She nods. Ashford opens the laptop.

VIDEO EVIDENCE

Retrieved from the cell phone of Kyle Jeffries

Recorded April 19, 2017, 12:51 a.m.

The group ahead of Kyle moves cautiously, bunched together.

JEREMY: Do you hear anything? Is she still there?

SARA: I can't tell.

MEL: I don't like this.

NICK: Oh, come on. What's not to like? It's just a nice walk out in the woods.

Mel giggles nervously. Vanessa shoots Nick an irritated glance.

VANESSA: Maybe we should—

MIRANDA: Shh. Listen.

A scream splits the air. The teens flinch at the sound, and Mel cuts off her own scream with a hand clamped over her mouth. They whip their flashlights up into the trees, illuminating a crow perched on a branch.

ANTHONY: Is that . . . ?

TRINA: It was just a bird?

NICK: Oh, man. There's more of them. Look.

He points his flashlight farther in among the trees. Birds' eyes flash. Dozens of crows fill the branches, eerily silent.

SARA: The birds come after the dark. That's what it said in Becca's notebook.

ANTHONY: Are they dangerous?

SARA: I have no idea.

TRINA: Oh God. Oh God, what is that?

Her flashlight points among the trees. Not at the branches this time, but at the ground, where a figure staggers. Its hair hangs bedraggled around its face. Its gait is uneven, knock-kneed, as if some vital thing has been broken in its legs, twisted. Its clothes are torn and muddy. It grasps at the nearest tree to pull itself forward with one hand; the other is missing. Its arm ends in a ragged black stump that sheds black, oily smoke, which seems to eat at the remaining flesh.

If it weren't for the brightly patterned leggings she wears, visible even under the muck, it would be nearly impossible to recognize Vanessa Han.

The camera whips around, focusing on the other Vanessa Han standing on the road as she clucks her tongue, a gentle tsking sound.

VANESSA: Oh dear. How did you get all the way out here?

Nick looks at the Vanessa on the road, and then at the girl dragging herself toward them through the trees, her mouth opening and closing like a gasping fish. Her glasses sit crookedly on her face. Nick takes a step back from the Vanessa on the road, eyes wide in uncomprehending horror.

NICK: Vanessa? What—what's going on?

She cocks her head in a movement reminiscent of a bird getting a better look at the grub it's about to eat.

VANESSA: Shouldn't have let go, Nicky.

TRINA: Oh my God.

JEREMY: We have to help her.

He steps toward the edge of the road. Anthony catches him, holds him back.

JEREMY: We can't just leave her out there.

ANTHONY: The rules—

JEREMY: Fuck the rules!

VANESSA: Yes. Fuck the rules. Go help her, Jeremy. I'll come with you.

She smiles. Nick is shaking his head, a moan in the back of his throat. He whirls toward the Vanessa struggling toward them. She is perhaps fifteen feet away now, but she falls to her knees, her remaining hand braced against the ground.

NICK: Vanessa! Come on. Get up. Keep moving. Vanessa, come on.

He reaches out toward her. She looks up, dazed, and for a moment she doesn't seem to see him. Then her eyes focus.

VANESSA: There's no point. She's not strong enough.

JEREMY: Shut up!

The Vanessa on the road smiles blandly. No one seems willing to move any closer to her, even Jeremy, his whole body alive with fury. The injured girl lets out a wordless scream and pushes herself back up to her feet, stumbling faster now, her hand outstretched for Nick's.

VANESSA: Oh? That won't do.

The imposter strides toward the edge of the road, heading for the injured girl. Nick shouts and lunges to intercept her. The camera swings away and misses the moment of contact. We

*have only the screams and shouts of the others to guess at
what happens next.*

JEREMY: Damn it!

ANTHONY: Grab her!

MIRANDA: No!

*The camera stabilizes as silence falls. The scene is so still it
could be a tableau. Nick stands stock-still at the edge of the
road. Beside the road, a few inches from the safety of the
stone path. His outline wavers, black smoke curling from it.*

*The injured Vanessa is huddled at the base of a tree just out
of reach, arm still stretched out toward him. The imposter
stands between them, clear of the others where they gather
at the edge of the road.*

MEL: Nick?

SARA: Pull him back on!

*Mel grabs Nick's arm—or tries to. Her fingers close around
his upper arm and keep closing, cloth and flesh and bone
crumpling under her touch like ash still holding the shape of
a log. Mel screams, snatching her hand back.*

MEL: Oh fuck oh fuck oh—

SARA: What did she do to him? Nick! Talk to me. Come on.
You have to get back on the road.

VANESSA: He can't answer. But don't worry. You won't have
long to be upset. In a few minutes, you won't remember
him at all. Or any of this.

*She bends down, and gently removes the glasses from the in-
jured Vanessa's face.*

VANESSA: You're distressingly flawed, you know.

She slips the glasses on. And then she grips the girl's face in one hand, covering it with her palm, fingertips sinking into her skin. Vanessa bucks, screaming, as black rot spreads from her double's fingers, crawling over her skin, eating away at her with incredible speed. One moment she is arching off the ground, her entire body and voice united in terror and pain, and then she seems to crumble in on herself, turning to ash that scatters on an unseen wind.

The girl is gone; her double remains.

JEREMY: I'm going to kill you.

VANESSA: You're not. You're already forgetting why you're angry.

Jeremy's expression spasms. The others have oddly vacant looks on their faces, fear giving way to consternation. Nick's outline blurs more, wavering; he is being undone. More slowly than Vanessa, but steadily, without mercy.

SARA: She's making us forget.

Her tone is deadened. She blinks.

SARA: She's making us forget. We're not going to remember she's not really Vanessa. We have to—

She can't seem to finish the thought. She rakes at her hair, slaps herself. Vanessa laughs. Mel whimpers, holding her head in both hands.

SARA: We have to do something!

She yanks open the zipper on her bag and shoves the flashlight into it, pulling out a camera instead. She turns it on with shaking hands, focuses it on Nick. His head turns toward her, the movement barely perceptible. He mouths something. It might be her name. The flash goes off.

The darkness crawls over Nick's skin. Vanessa steps up to him. She puts a hand on his chest, rises to her tiptoes, and kisses him on the cheek.

He dissolves. She steps through the flurry of ash as every crow in the forest takes off in a storm of wings. No one moves. They stare, unfocused, into the forest. Except for Miranda, who watches the imposter, her anger electric. But she doesn't interfere as Vanessa steps back onto the road and points.

VANESSA: Look, a crow.

They raise their flashlights, illuminating the last remaining crow.

CROW: Oh God. Oh God, what is that?

The crow screams again, and then flings itself into the air.

MEL: This is fucked up.

VANESSA: It was just a bird.

At the edge of the frame, Vanessa looks at Miranda, and presses a finger to her lips.

The phone swings as Kyle lowers it. The video ends.

INTERVIEW

SARA DONOGHUE

May 9, 2017

Sara's hand is pressed to her mouth so hard that the skin around it blanches. Ashford closes the laptop.

ASHFORD: Miss Donoghue?

SARA: No. No, that can't be—no, that's not—

Her words devolve into incoherence, and she moans, rocking forward. Then she shoves back from the table, shooting to her feet. Her chair clatters to the ground. The table skids five inches, feet screeching on the concrete floor, and Ashford jerks out of his chair to avoid being struck. Abby steps forward, drawing the syringe from her pocket, but Ashford holds out a restraining hand and she stops, eyes fixed on Sara.

Sara covers her face with her hands and huddles with one shoulder against the wall, her breathing ragged.

SARA: We left him.

ASHFORD: Nick Dessen?

SARA: Nick. We left—we forgot him. We . . . how did we forget him?

ASHFORD: Do you remember him now?

Sara's hands drop. She frowns, looking past Ashford, eyes un-focused.

SARA: I—no. Yes. I'm not sure. I remember something, but . . . She took him from us. And Vanessa—oh God. Poor Vanessa.

She scrubs tears from her cheeks. Then she sees Abby, still with the syringe out, though her arm hangs relaxed at her side.

SARA: What the hell is that?

ASHFORD: Just a mild sedative. We weren't certain how you would respond. Sometimes this sort of thing provokes . . . adverse reactions.

SARA: What kind of adverse reactions?

ASHFORD: Seizures. Self-harm. Sudden violence.

Sara laughs nervously. She picks her chair up and takes her seat, sneaking another glance at Abby.

ABBY: We good?

ASHFORD: Yes, Miss Ryder, I believe that will be all.

She nods and exits, shutting the door behind her with a click.

SARA: So I was right. About Vanessa.

ASHFORD: It would seem so. Whatever she was, it was not your friend. Miss Donoghue, if you'd like to take a break . . .

SARA: No. I want to keep going. I want to get this over with.

ASHFORD: If you're sure.

13

WE WALK THROUGH a thick mass of trees. They crowd each other and the road, and the morning light barely filters down to dapple the ground. Something feels off about the forest. False and thin. It takes me a few minutes of walking to realize that the morning has brought no burst of birdsong, no movement among the trees. As if every breathing thing has been snuffed out, or fled.

Water glints between the trees up ahead, silvery and sharp. An iron gate blocks our way.

"Whose turn?" Anthony asks.

"Does it matter?" Mel replies. She steps forward, rummaging in her pocket, and shoves her key into the lock. "Gate number three," she says in a game-show-host voice. "Step right in, ladies and gentlefolk."

We step through the gate and past a thick stand of the evergreens. They thin so suddenly it makes me lurch. Only a few feet in front of us the road stops. Or rather, it vanishes— disappearing beneath the impossibly smooth surface of the water, which stretches as far as I can see in every direction. A few scattered trees stand here and there; the water must not be very deep, then, but it's impossible to be sure. The light hits it and reflects everything—sky and trees and the six of us standing at its edge—a perfect mirror.

"That can't be right," Anthony says. He gives me a bewildered look. "It can't just end. How can we keep going?"

A flutter of panic passes from Anthony to the others, like a ripple in the air. If we tip over into it now, I don't know if we can recover. I don't have time to think or consider or debate; someone needs to act, now, while we still can. So I step forward, into the water.

My feet sink ankle deep, and the surface of the road is waiting for me. When I slide my foot back I can feel the short slope, dipping below the surface of the reflective water, but after that initial drop it feels level. I take another sloshing step. The water laps against my ankles, cool but not cold, its mirrored surface opaque. I can't even see my own feet, or anything below the surface, even where my shadow blocks the sun.

"The road's still here," I say, trying not to sound *too* relieved.

Jeremy sits down at the edge of the water and starts pulling his shoes off. I raise an eyebrow. "What? I don't want to walk the rest of the way in wet shoes," he says. "Besides, it'll be easier to feel where the road is with bare feet. Unless you want to accidentally step off the edge, and find out what happens when you break the rules."

I shudder, a feeling like guilt and grief snaking through me. "Good idea," I say, regretting my soggy hiking boots already. I splash back to dry land and join the others in stripping to my bare feet, rolling my wet jeans up to mid-calf.

We set out in pairs—instinct by now, to stay within arm's reach of each other. I find myself glancing behind us, checking for the tide of shadow that took Miranda. But there is only the forest behind us, and the trees scattered here and there in the water, spikes of dark green against the silver blue. In the distance—it's hard to be certain exactly how far—the air fills with a pale mist, obscuring the horizon and any sense of how far we have to go. Instead of making the water seem smaller, it makes it feel as if it stretches for an eternity.

We inch along, taking tentative steps, feeling for solid ground before we move forward. Once my foot lands on nothing, just deep water, and only Anthony's grip on my elbow, hauling me back, saves me from pitching forward into the unnaturally still water.

After that, we take shifts at the front. It's safer to follow along behind, in the footsteps of the two in front. For a long time, we are silent—yet every noise we make seems amplified, echoing off the lake. The slosh of the water, every inhale and exhale. The road isn't wide here, and Anthony's shoulder bumps against mine from time to time.

"I know why you did it," he says quietly. In the silence, it's like a shout, but while Trina's shoulders stiffen, and Kyle stumbles a step, no one turns around. Jeremy, up at the front with Mel, probably doesn't hear—and he's the one most likely to argue. I keep my eyes fixed on the back of Mel's wild curls, the curve of her neck.

"Why do you think I did it?" I ask.

"I mean that I get why you thought that Vanessa might be . . . I don't know. Bad," he says. "I noticed it, too. I should have said something. I was trying to keep track to make sure everyone had a partner, and that's when I realized that she didn't, at the first gate. But I didn't say anything, because I didn't want us turning on each other. Not when . . ." He looks uncomfortable.

"When I'm the one we *know* was alone in the dark," I say. Or rather, not alone—which was worse.

"I was alone, too," Anthony points out. "Hasn't it occurred to you that if Vanessa was—compromised, somehow—that I could be, too?"

"Or me. Or all of us," I say, refusing to consider it. Becca might have been the brightest star in our constellation, but Anthony was the most constant.

"I don't know if you did the right thing. But I *think* you did," Anthony says. "And I've got your back." He smiles crookedly at me as we wade through the water.

"Thanks," I say, my heart giving a double beat. "That means a lot to me."

"Hey, guys?" Mel calls back. She and Jeremy have halted. "Look." She points. In the distance, near where the mist swallows up the water, is a woman. Long red-brown hair hangs tangled around her shoulders, a red-and-black plaid shirt is tied around her hips. She shuffles and lurches as she walks, dragging a water-logged messenger bag behind her. She's coming toward us. Not directly, but if we keep walking, her path will intersect with ours. She gives no sign that she's seen us.

"What do we do?" Mel asks.

There it is again. Panic. So many ways we haven't even discovered yet that this road could destroy us, but that one worries me the most. "It's okay," I say first, trying to come up with a reason why that's true. "She doesn't look . . ." I pause. "She looks more like Isaac. Like us."

She's still moving toward us. Lurch and drag. What happens if she reaches us? Is she even on the road? Is she going to come straight toward us, and if she does, do we run? Do we move aside? Or is she just another traveler like us?

"Let's get closer," I say. "Get a better look. If we have to run, we run, but if we can go forward instead of back—"

"Yeah. Not sure we want to try backtracking," Anthony agrees. Even Jeremy nods.

"I'll take lead," Jeremy says.

"Me, too," Anthony chimes in.

"Our brave protectors," Trina says, but with only a hint of sarcasm.

We reshuffle. Mel and I are in the middle, but I press forward ahead of her—still in reach if we have to grab hold of each other, but closer to Jeremy and Anthony. For a while there's only sloshing. The young woman's features grow clearer as she approaches. She has a long nose and prominent cheekbones dusted liberally with freckles. She wears glasses with black rims and a T-shirt that hangs oddly on her. Her mouth gapes open slightly, like she's breathing hard.

"Hey," I say. She's twenty feet away now, and the angle of the road has shifted so that we're facing each other. She'll reach us soon. Anthony and Jeremy have stopped. At my back I can feel the tension of the others deciding whether to run.

It'll be hard to get past her, if it comes to that. The road's too narrow. But I don't want to find out what happens if we try to go back.

She's closer, and closer still. She's going to walk right into us, and still she stares straight through us, her drag-shuffle steps never breaking their stilted rhythm.

"Hey!" I say again, loudly this time. "Who are you? Do you need help? Are you—"

Suddenly she veers to the side, her body canting as she follows the curve of the road.

Not *the* road. Her road. She walks parallel to us, feet slushing and sloshing through the water, and as she draws level with us, Mel lets out a scream.

Most of her back is gone. Huge furrows rip through her flesh, gouging through skin and bone and tissue from the side of her ribs to the gleaming, exposed column of her spine. There's no blood. No blood—but her organs glisten inside the cavity of her torso, obscenely exposed. Another gash rakes along the base of her skull.

She cannot be alive. And yet she's breathing. I can hear it, a labored but steady sound. And still she's walking, one foot in front of the other, the bag dragging along behind her.

"She must be one of the others," Kyle says, voice too loud and too fast. "One of the ones who was with Isaac, right? She must—"

"One way to find out," Jeremy says, and before I can stop him, before anyone can stop him, he pushes past me, drawing up beside the shuffling woman, and steps out to her.

One foot. The other still planted firmly on the road, and Mel and Trina and I all grab for him, wrapping our hands around his arm as if we expect him to be wrenched away. But his other foot hits solid ground, and he leans out, snags the strap of her bag, and yanks.

The strap catches. She swings around at the tug and stands swaying, arm extended. Jeremy swears and unwinds the strap from her wrist. It comes free and we jerk him back. He holds the messenger bag to his chest, panting, wide-eyed, like he can't believe what he just did.

Neither can the rest of us.

The woman hasn't moved. Her hand is still outstretched, not quite pointing. Her eyes focus. It's a slow process, her pupils contracting, her gaze lifting centimeter by centimeter until she's staring at Jeremy. She gives a tiny gasp, a hiccup of sound. Her index finger rises, pointing straight at him. And then she whispers, sharp and urgent, "It's coming."

Crows burst from the trees. Dozens, hundreds hidden within the shadowed limbs of each one, and now they stream screaming into the sky. And thundering through that cacophony is a sound, a horrendous, bone-shaking sound like boulders being sheared apart.

"Go," I say, but I didn't have to. We're already moving, a stuttering, stumbling run as we push forward as fast as we can, our feet greedy for the unseen road beneath our feet. The crows wheel and clamor in the sky, and that sound comes again. Did I say it is like stone? It's more like metal, steel girders twisting out of shape.

I look back. She stands where we left her, hand outstretched, eyes tracking nothing.

Behind her, in the mist, something moves.

At first I don't understand what I'm seeing. A tree, I think, but it looms above the trees. A man, a giant shrouded in mist—but there is something about the shape of it that is wrong, arms too long, fingers too sharp, a tangle of shadows above where its head must be. It's still lost in the mist, still indistinct, but it's coming toward us.

In the rear, Jeremy halts. He looks at the thing. And then at the girl.

"What are you doing?" Anthony calls. But Jeremy is already sprinting back, throwing the bag's strap over his shoulder. He skids to a halt across from the girl, lunges, and grabs her wrist. It almost unbalances him, but then he's found his footing, pulling her toward him. He stoops to lift her as the giant thing grows closer still.

"Jeremy, *run*!" I scream, and he finally listens. Anthony grabs my arm, pulling me along. We can't help. We can only hope he's fast enough.

"Up ahead," Mel calls.

A shore trembles indistinctly at the edge of the mist. A shore and a gate, the iron bars solid and black even with the mist curling over them. Three crows perch atop the gate, immune to whatever has flung the others skyward, watching our approach.

We move at a lurching run. Almost to the shore. I don't look back. I won't look back.

Kyle skids to a halt in the front, pivots. "There's a seam at the edge of the road," he says. "Just a tiny gap, and then there's another road, but the real one turns. You have to feel your way—" He catches sight of the thing behind us, and his eyes go wide. "What the f—"

"Just *go!*" I yell, before anyone else can waste time gawking. Jeremy puts his head down and bulls forward, dragged down by the girl's weight, lagging farther and farther behind. The road slews to the left, then the right, and then we're barreling straight for the shore. And then we're *on* the shore, muddy ground squelching, grasping at our heels. The crows on the gate finally take flight, an eruption of movement. Anthony already has his key out. It scrapes against the lock as he fumbles with it.

I turn. The mist is closer, folding in toward us. And with it comes that *thing.*

The beast.

I can see the shape of it more clearly now, its long arms, the three hooked claws on each hand. Claws that could carve through a person as easy as tissue paper. The mist blurs its details, but it must be forty feet tall. Fifty. And its head isn't the head of a person, but triangular, and above it antlers branch and twist and tangle.

It's the creature from Becca's notebook.

"Sara," Anthony says. The gate is open. I'm the only one on this side. Me and Jeremy. His eyes meet mine. *Go,* he mouths, not sparing the breath to voice it, and I do.

I dash through. Jeremy is still far behind us. Too far.

Anthony hesitates—and then slams the gate shut behind us.

The mist collapses, like the barrier holding it back has given way. In an instant everything behind the gate is shrouded, bleached to gray-white.

"He could still make it," I whisper. I find myself reaching into my bag, pulling out the camera. Training it on the mist. On the gate. As if by looking through the camera, I can make the scene less terrible, less terrifying.

We wait, breath ragged, to see what comes through.

EXHIBIT H

Photos retrieved from the camera
of Becca Donoghue

1. *Anthony Beck, his hands white-knuckled, pale against the gritty black of the gate as he waits to open it again, if his friend should appear.*

2. *Trina Jeffries, standing with her arms crossed over the preacher's book, her head tipped back, eyes shut as if to feel the rain that falls in a light haze. Pinpricks of light, like the sun reflecting off dust motes, hover in the air around her. At the upper corner, a gnarled black tree slashes like a wound across the frame. The tree is out of focus; it is impossible to discern whether the figure at its base is a person, or simply a shadow.*

3. *The gate. The mist. A blur to the iron bars, betraying the unsteady hand of the photographer.*

4. *Anthony Beck, crouched, fingers laced behind his bowed head. The gate, the mist, the featureless gray.*

5. *A shadow in the mist.*

6. *Jeremy Polk, stepping out of the mist, a body in his arms. He carries her as if she weighs nothing, as if her substance has been carved away with her flesh. Her*

eyes are open. One can almost see the faint movement of her lips, the murmur slipping between them.

7. Jeremy Polk, through the gate, lowering the girl to the ground. Her extremities blur, break apart, dissolve, the undoing already reaching her wrists, her ankles.

8. Jeremy Polk, the gate closed behind him, leaning close to the vanishing girl, as if she is whispering in his ear.

9. Jeremy Polk, his jacket discarded before him, no sign that the young woman was ever there.

10. The gate. The mist. And in the mist, the beast, four amber eyes glowing, ink-slash antlers branching up to impossible heights. Crows wheel around its antlers, like bits of its shadow fraying free, wheeling, diving back to merge again. It stands oddly. Swaybacked, as if it must lean backward to balance.

11. The beast, one long, long arm stretched out. The hand ends in craggy, matte-black spikes, not proper claws but more like burnt wood hacked into points, that tear free of the mist. It's pointing—like the girl pointed—straight at Jeremy. As if it knows him. As if it is not done with him.

12. The beast, turning away. The crows dive and swoop in its wake, and the mist follows, seething back from the shore, the water, the dark and lonely trees.

13. The gate. The mist. And nothing else at all.

14

JEREMY KNEELS WHERE he set the woman down, his hand braced against the stone. His jaw is clenched in anger, but the anger isn't directed at anyone. At the road, maybe, the thing that has devoured her—made her vanish into a cloud of black ash, into nothing.

"What did she say?" I ask. He blinks, looks up at me. I repeat it so he can see my lips, and he shakes his head.

"I couldn't hear," he says. He stands, rubbing the palm of his hand with his opposite thumb as if to clean it, though no ash remains. "She was too quiet. I couldn't hear."

"That was stupid," Anthony says loudly, standing a few feet back still. Nearer the gate.

"I couldn't let her wander out there forever," Jeremy says.

"What happened to following the rules?" Anthony demands. He strides forward and shoves Jeremy in the chest. Jeremy stumbles back a step, then snarls and shoves Anthony right back.

"Back off," he says. "I knew what I was doing."

"How?" Anthony demands. His palms find Jeremy's shoulders again, a staccato impact that sends them both stumbling another step away from the gate. "How the fuck do you know what you're doing when none of us know a fucking *thing* about what we're doing?" Another shove. This time Jeremy doesn't raise his hand, doesn't defend himself at all, just falls back under the blow.

The rest of us pull back to the edge of the road, Mel casting me a helpless look, Trina just setting her jaw, eyes bright with anger.

"How do you just—do that"—two more shoves—"when you could have fucking *died*?" This time Anthony doesn't shove Jeremy. He grabs him by the shirt and yanks him forward, throwing one arm around his shoulders in a halfway bear hug, a sound like a growl in his chest. "Don't fucking *do* that, man!"

"I'm sorry," Jeremy says. "That was stupid. Worse than stupid. I'm sorry." He pulls free of Anthony, who scrubs both hands over his scalp and gives a strangled yell of frustration.

I will never understand guys. But it looks like the fight, if that's what you'd call it, is over. Jeremy's shaking his head, like he can't believe what he did. Or like he can't believe he survived it.

Anthony's face is red and he looks like he's trying to avoid a less masculine display of emotion, so instead of making him feel worse by staring at him, I take stock of the road beyond this gate.

The forest is gone. The land to either side of the road is covered in knee-high grass, summer-gold and whispering as a light rain patters down. The road leads up a hill, and from there it must drop down the other side; the only thing I can make out at the crest is a gnarled old tree with bare branches like needles jabbing up from thicker, twisting limbs, the sort that in any other context would seem spooky.

Here, it's almost quaint.

The Liar's Gate, Isaac said, and then the town, and then the marsh. He must have meant the water. Which means the mansion's next, if Isaac was right, but all I see is the grass, and the tree at the top of the hill. We've a ways to go yet. Maybe we've got a little room to breathe, here in the shadow of the gate.

"We all made it through," I say. "And nothing's coming at us. So we should rest. Anyone hungry?" I start to unzip my bag, but everyone's shaking their heads. "Me neither," I say. Nerves? No, I don't think so. Because I'm not tired, either. Oh, there's a kind of exhaustion in me, the kind that lies in your bones and works its way outward, but the thought of sleep is foreign. "Okay. Maybe just . . . maybe just a break," I say.

"We should look in the bag," Mel says. She juts her chin toward the wet messenger bag, which Jeremy has picked up again. "You risked your life for it. And probably the rest of our lives, too. So let's find out if it was worth it."

Jeremy looks down as if he's forgotten what he's carrying. Then he nods and sinks into a crouch. He fumbles with the buckles on the bag for a moment, but it comes open. He sits the bag on its side and jiggles it until the contents slide free. I suppose I wouldn't want to reach inside blindly, either.

A pair of ballpoint pens roll out, along with a spiral notebook so waterlogged it's falling apart. A few granola bars, a water bottle, two containers of prescription pills, the labels unreadable, a wallet—and a video camera, sealed in a plastic bag.

I expect Jeremy to reach for the camera first, but he flips open the wallet and prys out a driver's license. "Zoe Alcott," he reads.

"It's her." I'm standing closest, and I'm the one he hands the ID to. Our eyes meet for a moment, and his lips go thin before his gaze drops.

I busy myself with the ID. It's definitely the same girl. In the photo she's smiling, looking a little embarrassed, like she knows that the photo's going to look terrible before it's taken. It's a Virginia license. Her address is in Roanoke. She's twenty-six years old.

Was twenty-six years old? Or was she younger when she died, and . . . ? I shake my head. There's no point chasing that logic down. It's someone else's tragedy.

Jeremy pulls the camera out of the bag. There's a bit of condensation on it, but it doesn't look damaged. He tries the power button. Nothing happens. "Batteries, maybe?" he mutters, flipping it over. He opens the battery compartment and shakes out two AAs. "Don't suppose anyone brought spares," he says.

"Sure we did," I say. "In the flashlights. Here."

We crack three flashlights open before we find one with AAs. Eager now, Jeremy swaps out the batteries and tries the power button again. It lights up.

"All right. Let's see what's on this thing," he says.

"I'm not sure I want to know," Trina says, but she leans in with the rest of us as he opens the viewfinder and toggles to recorded video.

"Most recent first?" he asks. I grunt an affirmative, leaning so close that my hair brushes the side of his head. He doesn't seem to notice as he presses play.

VIDEO EVIDENCE

Retrieved from the camera of Zoe Alcott

Time and date unknown

ZOE: Oh shit. Oh shit. Okay. Camera's on, here's—

The camera swings up, the view clarifying from an indistinct mass of shadows to an expanse of brackish water, so murky it's nearly black. Gnarled trees hunch here and there, damp and rotting leaves clinging to their branches. The view is limited, shrouded in mist.

ZOE: Okay. So. The others—the others are gone. I only stopped for a minute and when I looked up, they—and so I kept going, and now I'm here all by myself, and that *thing* is—

She takes a deep breath and gives a desperate kind of laugh. The shape in the fog lets out a sound, a mix between a deep lowing and the crash of rocks. It strides to the right of the camera's field of view. It's close enough that the water at Zoe's feet ripples with the wake of it.

ZOE: None of this was supposed to be real.

Just through the mist, voices sound.

GRACE: Zoe! Zoe![5]

ISAAC: I only turned around for a moment.

....

5 Voice indentified as Grace Winters.

Zoe pauses, but she doesn't call to them.

ZOE: I thought . . . I thought I heard something, but the sound's all weird here. Everything's weird here. Even my thoughts seem like they're echoing. Like the inside of me is hollow. I think . . .

Zoe hums softly, and then she begins to speak in an odd, distant tone.

ZOE: Where does the road lead? Down to the shore, but there's nothing there anymore. She let her lover in, and then the ocean drowned her. She opened the gate, and now all of us are salt and bone, are coral deep. Still the road leads. Still the road needs. Travelers and wanderers. Salt and bone.

The camera slowly dips, as if her arm is growing weary but she doesn't quite notice it. She begins to walk, the water shushing at her ankles. The light shines down between the trees, through the mist, and for a moment flings back the dark reflection of Zoe Alcott.

Little detail can be discerned in the shadowed image. It's mostly silhouette, but that silhouette is wrong. Torn. Flesh is simply missing in great gashes from the side of her ribs, her back. The shape of her skull is deformed where it meets her neck.

ZOE: I'm so tired. I think I'll keep . . . I . . .

A shadow falls across the water, obliterating her reflection. The water rises in a wave, then settles, leaving her soaked to the knees. Something massive is breathing, a hollow sound like wind between rocks. She hums again.

ZOE: The road is—the gate is—I see it now. Grace was wrong. I have to tell her. It isn't about the city, it's what's beyond. I . . . I'm so tired . . . I should . . . I should put the camera away . . .

<Recording ends.>

15

I TAKE THE camera from Jeremy and watch the recording twice more. What Isaac said makes more sense now. The water was a marsh—at least when Zoe and the others were in it. Which means that the road isn't the same for us as it was for them. Not exactly the same.

"She's dead," Mel says. "But she sounds—she's practically lucid. Does that mean . . ." Mel swallows. "What about Miranda? Is she still out there?"

I shake my head. "I don't know." No one mentions Vanessa. But I know we're all wondering. Did she die? Can you die, out here, or is everyone trapped, like Zoe? Like Isaac?

Jeremy's jaw is set. He rubs the skin behind his hearing aid.

"You did everything you could," I say.

"I know," he says angrily.

I tuck Zoe's camera into my bag. I itch to watch the rest of the videos, but I want to know what's up ahead first. "It was brave, Jeremy. It's good she's not lost out there. If it was Becca—"

"Yeah. Whatever," Jeremy says. His voice holds a vicious edge that sends me a step back on instinct, alarm in the deep recesses of my mind. I try to tame it. I've always thought Jeremy was a jerk.

And okay, he is—no getting around that. But he just put himself into danger to put a lost girl to rest, and you can grow out of dumb jokes but it's a lot harder to grow into that kind of courage. "What's next?" he asks me, quieter now, as if he's realized how angry he sounded.

"The mansion," I say. I pull Becca's notebook from my bag. "That's what Isaac said, right? They got to the mansion and Zoe was missing, so he went back for her. So that must be what's next." I flip through. So many fragments, notes that don't make any sense, others that seem to have snapped into focus, nestling in among the strands of warped logic in this place.

In the house in the town in the woods on the road are the halls that breathe. The singing will lure you the smoke will infest you the words will unmake you the woman will hate you.

The spiral of words catches my eye. The spiral trails outward, the last of the words reaching the edge of the page. I flip it over. The handwriting is different on this page. Sloppy, careening over the lines, letters crammed together or tumbling apart. *Watch for her light. Stay to the shadows. Listen for the spider's singing. Step softly when it comes. Keep on the move. The words are a weapon. If things look wrong, THEY ARE.*

"That's a lot," Anthony says as I read it out loud. "Watch for the light? Listen for its singing?"

"I guess we'll know what it means soon enough," I say. "We should pick partners. Make sure nobody gets left behind." *Again,* I don't say, Miranda's name a prickle across my skin.

I guess I'm not surprised when Anthony nods to Jeremy. They bump fists. Bro version of kiss and make up, I guess.

"Mel?" Kyle says.

"I got you, kid," Mel says, and that leaves me with Trina, who is distracted, flipping through the pages of the preacher's book again. I clear my throat. She looks up, startled, and sees Kyle with Mel. A faint frown traces her lips before she steps close to me.

"Too cool for his big sister, I guess," she says with a flip of a smile, closing the book gingerly.

That I don't get. I never wanted to be apart from Becca. The more she drew away, the more I wanted to press myself into her life. I used to pretend we were twins, real twins, never mind the obvious difference in ethnicity. I wanted to dress like her, act like her, but I never had her talent or her poise. I imagined we were matched, but I was only a mirror held up, reflecting a bit of her shine.

But I only say, "It's a younger sibling requirement. Making sure you don't get complacent." Her smile stabilizes for a moment.

The rain has cleared, and the sky is an utterly normal shade of blue. We could be anywhere, under a sky like that. We could be home.

Except there is an odd substance to it. A thickness. Dimensionality. What my eyes read at first as clouds is—folds. Wrinkles and creases, striations, so faint they nearly vanish against the blue. And for a moment—for a moment—I think it moves, seething like the skin of an animal when it's been pricked. And then the movement and the folds and the thickness of the sky are gone, the blink of my eyelids clearing them back to vast and empty blue.

"Did you see that?" I whisper, but when Trina doesn't hear me, I let the question drown in silence.

We pause long enough to put on our shoes again—mine uncomfortably wet—and climb the hill. Up to the gnarled tree. It's so twisted and lumpy it looks like puddled wax; its branches stab out of it in crazed directions. Its roots have grown beneath the stones of the road, buckling them into a hazardous ripple.

A knife, a short switchblade, is stabbed into the trunk of the tree at the point nearest the road, pinning a torn sheet of lined paper in place.

If anyone comes after us—we made it this far. Going to try to make it to the end. Thought someone ought to know.

—*Becca Donoghue & Zachary Kent*

I snatch the page from the tree, tearing it free of the knife. The ink looks practically fresh, though I know that doesn't make sense. Any more than it made sense that Zoe was still wandering, dead, or that Isaac lingered so long in his tangle of iron and misery.

Anthony takes the note and runs his fingertips over the words as he reads them to the others. A faint smudge of blue comes off on the pad of his middle finger. He rubs it clean with his thumb. Then he carefully folds the note and tucks it into his jacket pocket. I have the urge to grab his hand. I want this moment to belong to him and me, but the others are tense, nerves thrumming, and I know we have to keep moving before someone snaps. A few more steps to the brutish head of the hill, and I take them at a loping jog.

At the top, I halt. The hill spills away, steep but not alarmingly so, and at the bottom is nestled a town. Or something like a town, at least. Houses with roofs and windows and paths between them, dirt paths that lead from the road like veins and arteries. But the borders are wrong. Grass growing a foot up the side of one house, the pattern of wood spreading flat on the ground at the base of another. And something wrong with the windows, too—no emptiness behind them, but a kind of fleshy *presence* that reminds me of what I saw in the sky.

Planted in the middle of the town stands a massive house—the mansion. Its surface is a pale, gray-toned, off-white, too smooth for stone. I can see veins running along it, but not the veins of a human body. More like the veins of a plant. Beneath the eaves of the roof are gills like beneath a mushroom cap, black and withered, though the roof itself is shingled and firm. A pair of crows hunker in the eaves, feathers ruffled against the chill air.

"This is fine," Kyle says. "This is all fine."

The road leads straight to the door of the house. The stone continues, flowing from road to steps and in through the door that stands open like a surprised mouth. Or a hungry one. There is no way around. Only through.

So through it is.

The slant of the hill makes it seem as if we're being pulled forward, pulled down, steps too heavy and too loud against the stone. Sometimes I think I see a quiver in the sky, hear something not quite like wind.

We pause at the bottom of the steps. At the top of them, the stones fuse, then meld seamlessly into wooden flooring in the same constant gray. It flows down a hallway and into a wide foyer. Through the dust and shadows I can make out twin staircases, flanking a pair of double doors.

"I guess we go in," Anthony says.

"Keep an eye on the floor," I say. "We don't know if all of it counts as the road. Make sure you don't step off accidentally." And then, more boldly than I feel, I march up the front steps, Trina right behind me, and into the shadowed house.

[*Note: The remaining text of this section has been torn from legal pad. Contents recovered at later date and appended. Text is scribbled out. Paper is crumpled, torn. Reconstruction was difficult.*] I pause just inside a moment to let my eyes adjust. In that instant, before I can properly see anything, I see *her*.

She stands in the foyer, hands at her sides, staring straight at me. A shaft of sunlight cuts through the dust-choked air—and through her, too, turning the curve of bone to gold beneath her skin. Just for an instant, and then she's gone.

Miranda.

INTERVIEW

SARA DONOGHUE

May 9, 2017

ASHFORD: Miss Donoghue. I think it's time we talk about Miranda.

SARA: What about her?

ASHFORD: You tore a page out of your written statement before you gave it to us.

Sara chews on her lip, looks away.

SARA: I just—made some mistakes.

ASHFORD: We have the page, Sara.

Sara looks up. At first her expression is startled, and then it shifts into something else—anger, jagged and raw.

SARA: Who gave it to you?

ASHFORD: Sara—

SARA: Who was it? It was in my room. In my private things. No one should have been in there.

ASHFORD: It's not important right now. What is important—

SARA: It is important. I don't want to do this anymore. I'm done talking.

Sara stands.

ASHFORD: Sara . . .

She walks to the door. Grabs the knob. It doesn't turn.

SARA: I want to leave.

ASHFORD: Sara, you need to sit down.

SARA: I want to leave. You can't keep me here.

ASHFORD: We need to talk about Miranda.

SARA: Miranda is dead.

ASHFORD: I know.

SARA: She died in the dark.

ASHFORD: No. She didn't. And you know that, Sara. What I want to know is why you're lying about it.

Facing the door, Sara presses her fingertips against her face, digging them against her cheekbones. She whispers to herself, almost too quietly for the microphone to pick up.

SARA: Miranda died in the dark. She died in the dark. She died—

ASHFORD: All right. That's enough for now. Please sit down.

SARA: Why is the door locked, Dr. Ashford?

ASHFORD: Don't worry about that right now. Let's move on.

Sara walks slowly back to her chair, sinks into it. Her eyes are red-rimmed. She licks her lips, and her fingers start their tapping. Ashford watches, mouth pressed in a straight line, until her fingers curl under.

SARA: You want to hear about Becca. That's why we're here, right?

ASHFORD: I'm here to listen to whatever you want to tell me, Sara.

Sara laughs.

SARA: And a few things I don't. Okay. The house. It was . . .

ASHFORD: Take your time.

Sara closes her eyes and draws a deep breath through her nose, lets it out.

SARA: The house is where we found Becca. And where I started to think coming for her was a mistake.

16

THE FLOOR CREAKS beneath me. Not a hollow sound; more organic, like the wheeze of an animal. I brush a hand against the wall. Firm plaster, but where I expect it to be cold, it has a faint warmth, and a slickness to it like condensation. My steps disturb a thick layer of dust. It's an inch deep where it heaps against the walls, and bits of dried leaves and other detritus have blown in and tumbled their way around the room.

Windows to either side of the foyer let in golden light, but the chandelier that hangs above us, glittering with crystals, is dark. Double doors stand ahead. The stairs, the same continuous color as the floor, lead up to a balcony, beyond which are more doors and hallways leading deeper into the house.

The double doors are huge and ornate, carved with scenes that have worn with age until they're almost indistinguishable. I run my fingertips over the blunted shapes, trying to identify them. A city, maybe? And there the curl of waves. A lower panel is more intricate, with contorted bodies, limbs twisting with limbs, faces stretched in agony and ecstasy. They give way to vines and thorns, and at the edges waves crash in, every gasping form suspended moments from drowning.

"That's . . . intense," I offer. No one answers. I turn, heart leaping. I'm alone.

"Guys?" I call. No answer but my own echo, faint and crumbling. "Trina? Mel? Anthony?" Nothing and nothing and nothing. Were they with me when I stepped inside? I don't remember their footsteps.

I feel it. Panic. It's a wet, slippery creature forcing its way up my throat. I clamp my teeth down and dig my fingernails into my palms. I will not panic. I will not scream. I will not run.

I am still on the road—the floor the same uniform gray. I haven't broken any rules. And neither have the others. *Not recently, at least*. I shove that thought away. If we haven't broken the rules, I think, then maybe this is just what's supposed to happen.

Is there a *supposed to* here?

Yes. If there are rules, there's a way things ought to be.

I force myself to take steady breaths and look around. No sign of the others. And no sign of the front door—it's swallowed up in ink black. And I have no one's hand to hold.

"So how do I find the others?" I ask aloud, voice soft, brushing against the quiet like a hand trailing over cobwebs.

And then something *does* touch my hand. Grabs it. I yelp and yank away, but it comes again, groping at me. There's nothing there, no one. I scramble away. The darkness in the doorway seems to shudder, stretch. My fear is not a locked door. It stands open, and panic floods out. The memory of the hand that grabbed mine at the Liar's Gate comes flashing back.

I scramble away from the touch, the unseen *thing*. I stumble toward the stairs and up them, slap a hand against the step, keep moving. I hit the top of the stairs and freeze. Hallways stretch to either direction, darkness pierced at intervals by shafts of light from narrow windows.

A stair creaks behind me.

I dive for the nearest door and stagger through.

VIDEO EVIDENCE

Retrieved from the cell phone of Melanie Whittaker

Recorded April 19, 2017, 12:52 a.m.

The view is chaotic as the phone sweeps around the room, catching only shadows before stabilizing to the front-facing camera, showing Melanie Whittaker, eyes wide with panic.

MEL: What the fuck. What the *fuck* is—everyone just vanished. We were all standing here and then it was just me. Okay, Mel, stay calm. Stay calm. I'm going to—I don't know what I'm going to do.

She looks around, breathing fast.

MEL: Okay. I need to figure out—find the others. There's nothing here except a creepy-ass chandelier. And I'm talking to myself. Or my phone. Whatever, makes me feel less like I'm about to get ax-murdered. Okay. Let's look around.

She flips the camera around, focusing it on the room.

MEL: Nothing too spooky around—*What the FUCK?!*

Someone walks into frame. Sara Donoghue, turning as she takes in the room.

MEL: Sara?

Sara doesn't respond or seem to react in any way. A second person walks into her path. Anthony Beck. They step around each other neatly, not seeming to notice their own movements.

MEL: Oh my God. Okay, so I can see them on the camera, but I can't see them or hear them myself. So where's—

She swings the camera around, locating the others. Jeremy is stalking around the room, head swiveling to and fro. Kyle stands near double doors, hand hovering hesitantly over the nearest handle. Trina, her phone out and the book clamped between her elbow and ribs, stands behind him, yelling soundlessly and waving an arm.

MEL: Oh, thank God. Hold on.

She runs across the floor and moves around until she's partly in front of Trina. She waves. Trina jerks around to face her, eyes fixed on the phone in her hand. She looks up, then back at the screen.

MEL: I see you. Can you see me?

The flickers of movement at the edge of the screen suggest she's signing, though clumsily. Trina signs back.

TRINA: *I see you, but I can't hear you.*

MEL: Me neither. What do we do? Ah, can't remember half this stuff but you know what I mean.

TRINA: *The others are splitting up. Hold on, can you—*

She reaches out. Mel hesitates, then seems to get it. She puts her hand out, and their palms press against each other.

MEL: I can feel that. Okay, so we can perceive touch?

TRINA: *Get the others. Make them stop. Stick together.*

MEL: I'll go to the—out there, you get these guys.

Trina nods sharply and turns to grab Kyle's wrist as he finally

*takes hold of the knob. His reaction is cut off as Mel sprints
for the foyer. Jeremy and Sara stand facing each other, awkwardly close and utterly unaware of each other.*

MEL: Ew, you look like you're going to kiss. Of all the injus-
tices this place has flung at us . . .

*She strides forward and grabs Sara's hand. Sara jerks out of
her grasp and runs.*

MEL: Damn it!

*Mel chases, dodging around Jeremy, who stands oblivious to
the chaos. Sara bolts up a staircase. Mel follows, but her
foot catches. The phone flies out of her hand. The screen
goes dark for two full seconds, then the view springs back
as Mel grabs it.*

*Sara's shoulder flashes into view, then out again. Mel swings
the camera as Sara dives through a door. The door slams
shut behind her.*

MEL: No, don't!

*She's steps behind. She yanks open the door, but there's nothing
beyond but an empty hallway.*

MEL: Do I follow? I don't—Okay. No. Don't go running down
a creepy empty hallway by yourself. Get the others. Then
go after her. That's the smart thing. Do the smart thing
for once in your life, Mel.

*She pulls herself away from the door. Without her hand hold-
ing it open, it swings shut with a click. She trudges back
down the stairs. The others are clustered in the foyer. Kyle's
hand grips Trina's upper arm, and he stares blindly into the
room, but the others all have phones out, cameras on.*

TRINA: *Where's Sara?*

MEL: She ran off. Ran—how are you not getting this. She's gone.

JEREMY: *She says Sara ran off.*

MEL: Man, I knew I should have taken ASL instead of Latin. Probably better if you read my lips and translate.

JEREMY: *Yeah, I can get like 80 percent of what you're saying instead of 20 percent and a bunch of nonsense.*

MEL: And I got enough of that to know the proper response is my favorite sign.

Jeremy laughs; it isn't difficult to guess what gesture Mel is making.

TRINA: *Can you guys not fight right now?*

ANTHONY: *Seriously. Focus.*

Mel at least understands his exasperated expression.

MEL: Sorry. Punchy. Imminent death. Sara disappeared. I mean really disappeared. Couldn't see her in the phone anymore.

ANTHONY: *It was trying to separate us.*

TRINA: *Seems likely.*

Kyle tugs on Trina's arm, mouths, "What's going on?"

TRINA: *We have to find a way to see each other properly. My phone's dying.*

ANTHONY: *Mine's not much better. Ideas?*

He finger-spells the last word for Mel.

MEL: A dumb one.

Everyone but Kyle looks at her expectantly.

MEL: If it's trying to separate us . . . There are a bunch of doors. If we could see each other, we'd all pick the same one. The only way we'd go through different doors is if we weren't together. So let's all go through the same door, and maybe that'll be enough.

JEREMY: *I think I got most of that.*

ANTHONY: *I get what you're saying. We should try it.*

TRINA: *Same door as Sara?*

MEL: We should use the same door as Sara.

JEREMY: *Yup, she's got the same idea. Let's move. Mel, grab . . .*

He offers her his arm. Mel grabs hold. He grips Anthony's other hand with his, leaving each of them one hand free for a phone. Trina puts a hand on Anthony's shoulder, bringing up the rear with Kyle as Mel twists to train the camera on them briefly.

They trudge up the steps at an uneven, jerky gait, Mel nominally leading the way as she takes them to the door Sara disappeared through. She opens it with the hand holding the phone, takes a breath, and guides them all through.

The door slams shut behind them, leaving them in near darkness.

MEL: I can see you all again. It worked.

TRINA: Sara's not here.

ANTHONY: Maybe she's farther ahead.

JEREMY: Maybe—

??: Quiet.[6]

---

6 Voice is nearly identical to that observed in the first Donoghue interview, but distortion is less extreme. Comparison to confirmed recordings of Miranda R. are inconclusive but promising.

17

THE DOOR SHUTS behind me, and I am in darkness. There's a panic in my chest like a bird beating its wings against glass before I realize that this is the darkness of shadows, not the impenetrable dark that swallowed Miranda.

~~Miranda~~[7]

Whatever was chasing me is gone now, or I hope it is. I stretch my fingers out, ball them into fists, stretch them again, trying to get feeling back into my extremities. The hall is narrow and featureless. Only one way to go.

I haven't gone far when I reach an intersection, other hallways leading left and right. An arrow is carved in the wall in a dozen frantic lines, pointing left. They look like old lines carved on a tree trunk, swelling shut. As if the house is healing over them.

Do I trust it?

I touch my fingers to the gouges. They don't belong. Made by someone who didn't belong. I turn left.

I pass a door to my right and don't stop. The hallway hooks, hooks again. More doors. No windows, no source of light, but I can see through the gloom—not well, but a bit. The hallway branches

....
7 Word is scribbled out.

again. Three directions this time, and something scratched in the floor itself, but the head of the arrow is gone. Only a few narrow, broken lines remain, and those are scabbing over. Left or right? I'll have to guess.

I turn right. Down another hall, just like the rest. Three doors. A turn. And then—

An intersection up ahead, but that's not what stops me. Light, gold-yellow, creeps along the floor and along the walls. The source of it is moving toward the intersection from the left-hand hall. And with it, footsteps and a soft, gentle chiming. I take a tentative step forward, then halt.

Watch for her light. Warning? Or instruction?

There has been nothing kind in this place.

The light is drawing closer. I turn, ready to hurry back the way I came. I just stepped around the corner, and yet behind me the hall stretches straight and narrow until it vanishes into the dark. No corner to duck behind. Nowhere to run, except the doors to either side of me.

I hesitate. The light spills farther toward me, oozing across the floor. Where it touches the walls, gouges appear, deep rents in the plaster and something meaty and soft behind it, pale as milk.

I can't stay. I reach for the nearest door, my hand closing around the handle—

And it's already open, and opening wider.

She stares at me, mouth agape. Becca. Hair tumble-wild around her face, skin streaked with dust, pupils blown wide. And then her eyes dart past me, and she hisses between her teeth.

"Get in!"

She yanks me through the door, shuts it fast—halting just shy of the frame, so it makes no noise. She leaves it open a slit and peers into the crack. My heart hammering, I look past her as the light swings around the corner and into view.

It's a woman, carrying a candle in an old-fashioned holder, the kind with a loop on one side. She wears a mushroom-colored dress, Victorian, high-collared and formal, and her hair is pinned up on her head.

She has no face. The shapes of a face are hinted at, but no eyes, no mouth, no nostrils. Only a pattern like bark. Like the striations in the sky. She walks on slippered feet, steady and deliberate, the flame never flickering. With every step, something chimes softly. She draws close. Draws even with our door.

Becca reaches back and grabs my hand, squeezing tight. *Quiet*, the touch seems to say, but I can't even breathe; I couldn't make a sound if I wanted to.

Across the hall, behind the other door, something makes a muffled flapping. The woman pauses. Becca's grip tightens. The woman half turns, away from us.

Her back is hollow. No spine, no flesh, no organs. Only a smooth cavity from her shoulder blades to her hips, and five tiny, silver bells hanging from silvery thread, chiming softly as she moves.

She opens the door across the hall. The light spills in, but all I can make out is a frantic flutter of movement. A quick *thump-thump-thump*. She strides in with sudden purpose, and I lose sight of her. Another sound, a keening, begins but cuts off quickly, and then she returns with brisk steps. She shuts the door and returns to her position in the center of the hall, bells ringing *clink-clink-clink*.

She rolls her neck from side to side, smooths her skirts with one hand, and resumes her walk. One deliberate step after another. The light draws past, draws away. The chiming of bells fades.

Becca turns to me. I expect—joy, perhaps. Relief. Anything of what I'm feeling, this overwhelming crash of emotion that steals every word from me.

But her face is crumpled. She puts a hand to my cheek, shaking her head. "Oh, Sara," she says. "You shouldn't have come."

INTERVIEW

MELANIE WHITTAKER

May 9, 2017

Mel sits idly drumming her fingers on the table when Abigail Ryder returns. Abby gives a tight smile, a poor attempt at seeming personable, before taking her seat opposite once more.

MEL: You keep leaving like that, I'm going to think you don't like me. Which, by the way, sorry about punching you.

ABBY: It's really not the worst reaction I've seen to that kind of thing.

MEL: I still can't believe we just forgot about Nick.

ABBY: You remember now, though?

MEL: Pieces. He was my best friend, but I only know that because you told me. And people have been asking me where he went, but I didn't even remember *that* until just now.

ABBY: You might never fully remember.

MEL: Great.

She rubs her eyes; they're puffy, as if she's been crying. She clears her throat, seeming uncomfortable with this display of emotion, and gives Abby a forced smile.

MEL: So. What's the weirdest thing you've seen, doing this?

Abby considers. Her answer, when it comes, has the cadence of a lie.

ABBY: I have to be honest, I think you've seen much stranger things than I have. Ask Ashford, maybe, but he tends to share exactly zero things of substance from his past. Won't even let me look at most of his files. Most of what I've done is standard spook stuff— ghosts. Hauntings.

MEL: But you do believe in all of this.

ABBY: Yeah, you don't have to worry about either of us pulling the skeptic card on you. I mean, skeptical about details, maybe. But we both know what's out there.

MEL: Then you're not just here because . . .

ABBY: Because what?

Mel hesitates.

MEL: It's just. I heard you talking to Dr. Ashford, before. You said you wanted to ask us about Miranda, and he told you to wait. And I thought you must have—it seemed like you knew her.

ABBY: I did.

MEL: I'm sorry.

ABBY: You don't need to be.

MEL: We lost her.

ABBY: You really didn't.

MEL: If we'd been paying more attention, one of us could have grabbed her hand, and—

ABBY: Melanie, Miranda died months ago.

MEL: What?

Abby slides a file across the table to Mel, who opens it hesitantly. The angle of the camera offers no glimpse of its contents.

ABBY: Autopsy report. Look at the date. And the location.

MEL: It says Jane Doe.

ABBY: There's a photo, but I don't recommend—

Mel turns the page and lets out a small cry, pressing a hand to her mouth.

MEL: Oh my God. What—what happened to her?

ABBY: It's not . . . that isn't relevant right now. But it's not your fault. It happened long before you met her.

MEL: But she was there. She was with us.

ABBY: I know. And I don't think she left you when the dark came. There's a voice in the video, right before the phones shut off. I've listened to it a few times. It's her, Mel.

MEL: I . . . I wasn't sure. I thought so, but then I decided it wasn't possible.

ABBY: What happened?

MEL: She said *quiet*. And we all went quiet. And we heard this sound. It was like—a sort of singing. Humming. And a scuttling. And then someone whispered *this way*, and the door next to me opened. I went through. I don't know if I trusted the voice or if I was just more afraid of whatever was making that sound, but the others followed.

Abby nods.

MEL: You really think it was Miranda?

ABBY: Sara never told you?

MEL: Wait. Sara knew? Why wouldn't she—

Her brow furrows.

ABBY: That is a big part of what we're trying to piece together.

VIDEO EVIDENCE

Retrieved from the cell phone of Melanie Whittaker

Recorded April 19, 2017, 12:52 a.m.

*Mel, Trina, Jeremy, Kyle, and Anthony move swiftly down the
    hall, their footsteps echoing. The scuttling and the singing
    follow them. The hallways are a tangle; they make little
    sense. They approach a T-intersection.*

TRINA: It's getting closer.

MEL: Then hurry!

*Her voice is too loud in the quiet hall. The humming sound
    swells, and the camera spins around as Mel whirls to face
    the thing that's following them.*

*It could almost be called a spider. Thick black legs spike around
    the corner, spanning the hallway, with their hooked ends
    gouging holes in the wall to either side. It glistens, even in the
    shadows. Then comes the head: almost human, but eyeless,
    desiccated flesh pulled tight over the contours of a skull. Its lips
    pull back from black, jagged teeth, and a long, papery tongue,
    pointed at the end, slithers between them, tasting the air.*

*Its shoulders emerge next—withered skin, protruding bones.
    No arms, only nubs, puckered flesh at their ends. A thin
    chest and then a rib cage, exposed, blackened. But more
    disturbing than that, something is inside the ribs. Barely*

visible as more than the faintest silhouette—and fingers,
threading through the ribs, like hands about to part curtains
and peer through. It is from behind the ribs that the piping,
singing sound comes.

Where the humanoid torso's legs should be, it connects clumsily
to an arachnid's body. It approaches steadily as its tongue
lashes the air.

GRACE: Hey. This way.[8]

The voice is a whisper. Mel sucks in a startled breath as a
white woman peers out from one of the sides of the hall-
way intersection ahead, beckoning. She wears a T-shirt with
a cartoon fox and a grungy gray sweatshirt. Her hair is
buzzed short at the temples and longer on top, sections of it
dyed blue. Midthirties, perhaps, though weariness ages her.

GRACE: Come here. And whatever you do, don't run.

The teens glance at each other, and then at the creature. It's
nearly on them. They dart down the spur of hallway the
woman occupies, and she waves them into stillness and si-
lence as the spider advances.

It moves on, past them. It doesn't seem to realize that they're
there, and soon it vanishes down the hall in the distance.

TRINA: What *was* that?

GRACE: Keep your voice down. Something's always listening, and everything's always hungry. There's worse
things than the spider in here.

MEL: Uh, sorry—who are you?

GRACE: I'm Grace. Winters. And don't worry. I'm going to
get you out of here.

....
8 Identified as Grace Winters, reported as missing along with husband Bryan in April of
2014.

18

"YOU SHOULDN'T HAVE come," Becca says, and my throat feels closed up. "Are you—you're alone? But you couldn't have gotten this far without—"

"Shut up," I say, desperate with emotions too immense to have names, and pull her close. She's stiff against me for the first moment. In the second, one of her hands creeps up my back with the fluttering step of a cautious insect, and then flattens between my shoulder blades, a pressure that is as much disbelief as love. Then she wrenches away.

"You can't have come this far alone," she says, gaze dropping from mine and shifting toward the dark corner of the room like she can't bear to meet my eye. She stands like she's resisting the urge to scrape the sensation of my touch from her skin. I want to ask her what happened to her, but I don't need to know to understand.

A year in this place? I must be stranger than any monster.

"The others are with me," I say, and she flashes me a look of relief at the chance to retreat into practicality and fact. Feeling is too dangerous. "Anthony and Trina and Mel. Kyle and Jeremy Polk, too, and Vanessa Han was with us, but—"

She holds up a hand. "Wait. They're all here? In the house?"

"I don't know. They were, and then I was alone," I say. I'm babbling. Still not sure I believe what I see—my sister, standing right in front of me.

"It does that," Becca says. "They're probably in the halls some-where by now, though." She cocks her head, listening. "We have to move. It's not good to stay in one place too long. Come on."

She takes my hand again and leads me out into the hall. She's not wearing shoes, I realize. Her bare feet are filthy, but they make hardly any sound on the floorboards as she hurries forward. I'm not so graceful. She takes a practiced series of turns, then ducks inside another room—an office, maybe, with a desk piled with books and old papers sitting in the middle of the room, a wide book like a ledger open and covered in dust at the middle. The pages are covered in spidery writing, familiar—*in the town in the woods on the road are the halls that breathe*, I make out, and then Becca shuts the door almost all the way and turns back to me.

"Tell me again who you brought with you," she says. "How many have you lost?"

"Two," I tell her. "A girl you don't know and Vanessa." I name the others quickly, and she shuts her eyes, lips moving as if she's speaking to herself. When they open again, they're shiny with tears.

"You shouldn't have come. None of you should have come," she says.

"We came to find you."

"And it's no good," she says. "Two by two. You can only get out two by two, and there's an even number of you."

"What?"

"The exit to this place. It's darkness," Becca says. "The kind you need a partner to get through. Like the Liar's Gate—the first one?"

"I know its name. It was in the notebook. What—what happened to Zach?" I ask.

"Zach's dead," she says flatly. "I've been by myself for . . . I don't know how long."

"You've been gone a year," I say. And however long we've been on the road now. A day? I can't be sure.

"A year?" she asks. Laughs, half-wild. "So you're older than me now." I make a confused sound, and she waves a hand. "You don't change in this place. No getting hungry. No sleep. You get tired, but I don't think you age. So you're older than me. Big sister." She smiles, crooked. I keep wanting to touch her, reassure myself that she's real.

"We thought you were dead," I say. "We looked for you. The police—they thought you ran away with Zachary, and—"

"I didn't mean to leave. I thought—I thought we could get through, and find her, and it would be all right. She promised it would be all right."

"Who?" I ask.

"Lucy," she says, as if it's the most obvious thing in the world. "She called us here, to save her. She's trapped. Can't you hear her?"

I stare at her. Lick my lips, the answer inexplicably impossible to get out. "No," I say at last. "I don't hear her."

I cannot tell if I am lying.

Becca tells me we have to keep moving. She leads me through halls, through rooms, somehow seeming to keep track of the endless turns. It's all the road, she assures me, every plank in this house. There's no danger of wandering off.

I tell her everything that's happened so far. The darkness and the town, Vanessa and Trina.

"Echoes," she tells me. "When they replace you, they're called echoes. Zach found this book by someone who said he'd been on the road. He talked about them. It helped, the book. Told us what to expect. But the monsters aren't the only thing you have to be afraid of here."

"What happened to you?" I ask.

She gives me a hollow look. "I try not to think about it much," she says. "I'd been having these dreams. Dreams about the road. About Lucy Gallows. About the beast. They were just nightmares, but Zach went looking online. He helped me put it all together. He's the one that found out about Ys."

"Ys?" I echo, pinging against a scrap of memory. The words in the town.

"It's a city. Or was. It's where the road goes—used to go. It was destroyed a long time ago by a woman named Dahut. She was a princess, or something. There was a gate in the city that held back the sea, and she left it open, to let her lover sneak in to see her. But she forgot to close it, and the tide came in and drowned the whole city. That's the story, anyway. And it's all that death that made the road. If you can get all the way to Ys, you can escape it. But most people get trapped. Lucy did. She's been stuck on the road for all these years, but she's found a way to—she sort of whispers. Only to certain people. Sensitive people. And I guess I'm one of them."

Every so often she stops, listening. Sometimes she pulls us in a new direction, but I can never hear what she does.

"I've got your notebook," I say after a while of silence, because I need to hear her speak again. "It's hard to understand, but it helped us, too."

"My notebook?" she says, face screwing up in confusion. "What notebook?"

"I—this one," I say, unzipping my bag. I pull out the journal and she snatches it from me, paging through. Something like fear sketches across her face.

"How did you get this?" she demands.

"What do you mean?" I ask. "It was in your room. Under your bed."

"No," she says. "I brought it with me. I had it here. I lost it—I don't know. A long time ago now. But here in the house. Most of those notes I took on the road."

"That doesn't make sense," I say. Anything can happen on the road. But back home? There's a threshold between this world and the one we came from, and the inexplicable isn't supposed to cross it. Until this moment, the road has felt contained. A separate world that couldn't encroach on ours; we could only enter the road's world. This is different.

"Something wants us here," she whispers. Her fingertips spider up my arm, her eyes fixed on my shoulder, on nothing at all. "Something brings us. The road. Or something on it." Her finger-

RULES FOR VANISHING   213

tips pause, set sharp against the hollow of my collarbone. She's trembling. And then she buries her face against my shoulder, burrowing in. Not crying. Pressing herself against me, as if ravenous for any kind of touch, any contact. It lasts a furious moment, and then she's dragging me down the hall again. Around one more corner, and—

"Becca."

She stops. Turns back to me, eyes shining. "Let's go," she says.

The hall beyond is dark. Clotted and thick with darkness, impenetrable.

"We can't leave," I say.

"We can't stay. I can't keep you alive in here," she says.

"The others—"

"They'll find their way out," she says. "Or they won't. But we can't stay."

"Becca," I say gently, but her eyes are feverish.

"Everything here rots," she whispers. "Turns to ruin. Turns to hate. I don't remember half the time why I'm bothering to stay alive. We can't stay. We can't."

Behind her, something moves at the edge of the darkness, sliding out, pale and sharp. My mind offers up *thorn* and *claw* until the length of it brushes both words away, and another long, sharp thing—*leg*—emerges, the color of bone. It pierces the wall halfway up, spanning the hallway. And then, pushing through the dark, a face. Eyeless, gaping, purpled tongue lolling between split and bleeding lips.

I hiss a warning. Becca turns, and her whole body goes still, the kind of stillness only the dead achieve.

The head withdraws. Then the legs, leaving only one needle-thin point protruding from the dark. Becca falls back a step on the balls of her feet. She draws me away. One step. Two. She doesn't even breathe. She eases open a door, glances inside, and pulls us in. Shuts the door. Opens it.

A new hallway stretches in front of us. On the wall opposite is an arrow, scratched deep but fading. She frowns and crosses to it, pulling a knife from her jeans pocket to gouge new lines as she mutters to herself.

"Becca, what was that?" I ask.

"Spider," she says. Doesn't look at me. "I thought that one got out somehow. Died. There's two. One white, one black. There used to be other things in here, but the spiders killed them. Except the woman. They don't bother her. Can't get past the light." She stops. Lets out a shuddering sigh. "If it's hiding in the dark, we can't hurt it with light. Can't get past it."

"We will," I say. "Let's find the others. We'll figure something out. Together."

She looks down at her knife blade. Her tongue wets her lips. She rolls her sleeve up, slowly, and I suck in a startled breath.

There are words inked on her arm. Some dark black, others smeared and faded into illegibility. The letters overlap and spill over one another until the skin beneath looks less real than the ink.

Don't speak

Don't move

Listen

She fumbles in her pockets, muttering, and pulls out a pen.

She squints at it, assessing the ink in the clear barrel, throws it aside. Searches again. The actions are manic, so focused she seems to have forgotten I'm there at all. She swears suddenly, dives for the discarded pen, and, kneeling on the floor, sets the tip to her skin, raking it back and forth to coax out a pale gray, broken line of ink.

"Running out. Last one. Can't be the last one," she's whispering. The pen scratches at her skin. It starts to redden.

I catch her wrist, catch her eye. It takes a long time before I'm sure it's my sister looking back at me.

"We'll get out of here," I tell her. I take the pen from her and slide it into my pocket, out of sight.

Slowly, she nods.

"How do we find the others?" I ask.

She touches two fingers to the last word written on her arm. *Listen.*

"We need to get my things," she says. "Then we'll find them."

VIDEO EVIDENCE

Retrieved from the cell phone of Melanie Whittaker

Recorded April 19, 2017, 12:52 a.m.

The group hunkers in an empty room. The wallpaper is covered in flowers, the same sort that filled the old Briar Glen. Trina sits cross-legged on the floor, idly paging through the preacher's book, her lips shaping indecipherable words. Kyle leans against the wall; the rest stand uneasily as Grace keeps watch at the door.

MEL: You said that you could get us out of here. We've been wandering around for hours.

GRACE: The thing you have to know about the road is that it's not the thing that's going to kill you. Three rules. Simple. Follow those and you can just work your way along the road, no problem.

MEL: No problem? I told you, we've already lost two people.

GRACE: You've done better than us. By the time I got here, I was the only one left. But the thing is, most of the time it's *not* the road that kills you. It's the things on it.

MEL: What's the difference?

Grace grunts, as if this should be obvious.

GRACE: They're not *from* the road. It doesn't want them here. It wants people to walk it. That's what a road needs.

Travelers, going from point A to point B. The trouble is, this road's got no point A. No point B. You kill a person by stopping their heart. You kill a road by stopping its purpose.

Her voice rasps and rattles as she whispers, the words slushing into each other. Trina looks back at Mel and the camera, mouth pursed a little, uncertain.

MEL: Okay. Well. We need to find our friend.

GRACE: Right. Six of you. Two by two by two. That's the way through. Here's the thing—as long as you follow the rules, the road's not that dangerous. Breaking the rules hurts it. It's like a cut. A cut can get infected. Bacteria. Parasites. They want to feed. Break the rules, and you let them in. Let them in, and they can hurt you.

MEL: Solid advice. But again, we need to find our friend. Sara. And Becca—she was here, too.

Grace gives her a flat, unreadable look.

GRACE: Becca? No. No, I don't know anyone named Becca. No one in here. Listen, you won't find your friend. Safer to go. We have the numbers. Two and two and two.

JEREMY: She has a point. We have to be smart about this.

Grace grunts again, this time amused.

GRACE: Smart? You've been careless. Let the beast get your scent. You think the gates will protect you, but the beast strides between. Step one inch out of line and it'll find you in a blink. Cut you to ribbons.

Jeremy swallows, eyes wide.

ANTHONY: Look, we're not leaving without Sara. Right?

MEL: Right.

They look at Trina. It takes her a moment to realize they're waiting for her to speak. She looks up from the book. There is something strange about the light against her eyes.

TRINA: What? Right. Sara. No, we can't leave without Sara.

Grace is silent for several seconds, then she nods.

GRACE: Right. Loyalty. That's good, that's a good thing. All right. We'll look for her. Don't worry, I've been here a long time. I know the tricks. You're safe with me.

Mel drops back from Grace. She mutters under her breath.

MEL: Yeah, I definitely feel safe . . .

ANTHONY: Just stick close to each other. We'll be fine.

He doesn't sound convinced.

19

BECCA LEADS ME through what feels like an endless sequence of corridors before we find the room she's looking for. The smell reaches me first. Decay and rot, but not the unpleasant, sour stink of putrefying flesh. It's earthy. Wood and leaves collapsing into soil; wet, dark places traced over with the delicate script of beetle tracks and lacy roots. The smell does not belong to these walls, but it seeps from behind a door like any other. The door hangs open a crack. Something has been stuffed into the frame to keep it from closing.

"Good," Becca whispers. She braces the fingertips of one hand against the door. "The house tries to shut it. Move it. When it can. I try to keep track of it." She pushes the door open lightly. It swings inward with a not-quite silence like a bow settling against the strings of a violin. The body lies in the middle of the floor.

I met Zachary once, and I have looked at his picture a hundred times and more, but still I wouldn't recognize him if I didn't know he died here. All that is left of his face is one eye, a bare inch of cheekbone, a stretch of brow I could cover with one cupped hand. The rest is covered in roots, thin milk-white things that weave a net over him. A quintet of bell-capped mushrooms grow elegantly from the roof of his mouth. Thick, flat plates of fungus sprout in layers like ridges down his neck, shoulder, ribs. His torso is a constellation of tiny white mushrooms, flecked here and there at the extremities—hips, collarbone— but clustering closer and closer together, framing the wound that lays him open above the navel.

From the body, the roots and fungi spread and splay, spilling to the walls, up them. A chandelier of gilled mushrooms and twining stalks hangs above us—off-white, bone-white, shot through with veins of scarlet and blue.

You would think my shock would be used up by now, but I stand with my knuckles crushing my lips to my teeth, holding back a moan. "How long?" I ask. I feel like I am dredging my voice up my throat. "How long has he been—"

"Dead?" she asks. "A while. It was early. I don't think we were in here more than a day or two. She said that it was the spider. It killed him. But . . ."

"Who?" I ask. "Who else was here?"

"Grace," she says. She worries at her bottom lip with her teeth. "We met her here, in the house. She was the last survivor in her group. She couldn't get out of the mansion on her own. The only exit is through the darkness. She said she'd help us, but then . . ."

She steps across the floor. Practiced steps on the tips of her toes, picking her way between the roots. She bends at the waist, hair falling in front of her face. One fingertip touches the belled cap of a mushroom, and the net of roots seizes, a ripple of movement that turns into a rustle that turns into a whisper, emanating from the fungal growths themselves.

When it fades, I find my teeth clenched, anger in me like a lash of thorns. I take out my phone. I've kept it off. No point draining the battery. Now I turn it on as Becca watches me, head cocked.

"What are you doing?" she asks.

"Recording it. So there's proof," I say.

"Proof?" She makes an odd gesture, her hand turning over, thumb pressing to middle finger. "For—for when we get back."

"Exactly," I say.

"You think we're going to get back," she says. Like she hasn't considered it. Not really.

"Of course," I say. "That's why we came. To find you. And get home. Don't you—you were talking about getting out. I thought . . ."

"Out of this house," she says. "I don't know. I guess I haven't thought about what comes after that for a long time. It's easier not to. Safer. And all of that . . . Home? The world we came from? It feels less real than this place. It was easier, knowing that I would always be here."

"But if you were always going to be stuck here, why stay alive?" I ask. "Why survive so long?"

She laughs. Quiet, like everything she does now, a flat spiral of sound. "Because I wanted to outlive that bitch," she says, and that hard glint in her eye is the first I've really seen of my sister since I found her. "Make the recording. People should know. Whatever happens."

VIDEO EVIDENCE

Retrieved from the cell phone of Sara Donoghue

Recorded April 19, 2017, 12:49 a.m.

The phone's light casts the scene in harsh, blue-tinged tones.
Becca, hair a tangle, somehow gaunt though she is not one
ounce lighter than when she stepped onto the road, waits for
confirmation. She makes a soft sound, tongue against the
back of her teeth, and bends again, this time her fingertips
skimming the bared curve of Zachary's brow before a finger-
nail flicks once, lightly, against a mushroom cap.

The whispers spin themselves together like spider silk. The
voices are distorted but recognizable as Zachary Kent and
Grace Winters.

ZACH: . . . get back to Becca.

GRACE: We need to think this through.

ZACH: What's to think through? Separating is a bad idea.
We don't know what's in this place. That spider—

GRACE: Zach. You're a smart kid. Smart enough to divide
by two. There's three of us. That leaves a spare. Someone
with no way out.

ZACH: We'll find a way.

GRACE: Two of us are leaving here. And it will be easier if
we make the decision now.

ZACH: You think you should be one of them.

GRACE: An organism strives first for self-preservation. Understanding that is the key to understanding everything else, don't you see? There isn't room for morality in survival. The road wants to survive. That's why it calls us here. And we want to survive.

ZACH: I'm not leaving Becca behind. And she won't leave me behind.

GRACE: Are you sure about that, Zach?

ZACH: Yeah. I'm sure.

GRACE: You know she doesn't feel about you the way you feel about her. I've seen the way you look at her. You're in love with her. She's got none of that in her eyes for you.

ZACH: That's not—

GRACE: I know more about this road than anyone. If you want to survive, I'm your best bet. Or you can risk your neck for the girl who will leave you the moment she gets off the road. You don't think she will?

ZACH: I don't care.

GRACE: Of course you do. And you should.

ZACH: If Becca doesn't want to be with me . . . I'm not going to leave her to die just because she might break up with me. How psycho would I have to be to—

Zach grunts. Surprise and pain mingle. Judging by the location of the wound on the corpse, it is likely the blade has struck his lung, which explains why he makes little other sound. The edges of the wound are sloppy. One imagines the hand holding the knife working it up and down, sawing at the

vulnerable cavity below the ribs, inexpertly wreaking dam-
age. The whispers do not capture this, their silence merciful.
They offer instead the sound of a body striking the floor, and
the panting breath of the killer.

GRACE: Lost him. I don't know what happened. He was right next to me. He was right next to me. I don't know what happened. I don't know where Zach is. He was right next to me. No—she'll want to look for him. The spider. The spider took him. I don't know what happened. One minute he was right next to me, and the next second the spider was there.

The rehearsal grows more precise with repetition. Grace takes a long breath.

GRACE: There. It's better this way. Two of us now. No reason not to go.

The whispers fade.

VIDEO EVIDENCE

Retrieved from the cell phone of Melanie Whittaker

Recorded April 19, 2017, 12:52 a.m.

The camera trains on Grace, moving purposefully down the dim hallway. She mutters to herself as she moves, counting turns. Anthony and Mel walk in the back of the group, the others shuffling along ahead.

MEL: I feel like she's leading us in circles.

ANTHONY: How would we know if she was? We can't even tell what hall we're in. There's no guarantee a hall is the same every time you look at it. [*Pause*] Is it just me, or is she . . .

MEL: Kind of nuts? Sure, but after God knows how long in a place like this, you'd have to be. Why, you don't trust her?

ANTHONY: I didn't say that.

MEL: Because I sure as shit don't.

ANTHONY: So it's not just me.

MEL: No, and I . . . Hold on. I know things keep shifting—okay, this sounds weird, but I'm really good with spatial stuff, right? And I think we're not just following a route, we're making it by making certain turns. I think the changes are predictable. And I think she knows it, too.

ANTHONY: Meaning what, exactly?

MEL: I can't be sure. But I think the way we've been turning, it's making the house into almost a loop. If she turns
up there . . . Yeah. If she turns right, we'll walk right up
behind ourselves.

ANTHONY: Is that possible?

MEL: Here?

ANTHONY: Good point. What does that mean?

MEL: I don't know. Except—

*Grace halts. The others follow suit, confusion and alarm evi-
dent. Grace stands just past a dark hallway—deeply dark,
a dark immune to light. Kyle stands right behind her, a
frown creasing his features.*

Grace stomps on the ground twice.

*It's like knocking on a door, and the answer comes quickly. The
spider erupts from the dark: milk-pale, legs like blades.
Eyeless face twisting, jaw working side to side as the tongue
lashes. It dives for Grace and Kyle, but she grabs hold of
Kyle and freezes, and Jeremy doesn't, the others don't, stumbling back on instinct.*

*The spider moves in stutter-step, joints clicking, clattering into
the hall and dividing Grace and Kyle from the others. It
turns on the older teens. They do the only thing they can—
they run.*

20

I STOP THE recording and turn the phone off, not yet willing to break the silence the whispers have left in their wake. "She's still in here. Grace," Becca says. "She's still trying to find someone to leave with her, because I wouldn't. She's dangerous."

"What do we do? How do we fight that spider? How do we fight Grace?"

Becca shakes her head. "I don't know. I don't know. I don't—"

I touch her arm, stopping her. "We'll figure it out," I promise. "You said you needed to get your things. Let's get them, and find the others, and figure it out from there."

She crosses to the corner, where the shadows have concealed a black backpack. The one she vanished with. She opens it and pulls things out. There's a phone, probably long dead, and a flashlight, which she tests pressed against her palm so her skin takes on a glow but the light spills no farther. She puts everything back in the bag and settles it over one shoulder.

And then we hear the scream.

It seems to live in the walls. As if it is not echoing down the hallways but has been consumed by the thing that holds us, the walls themselves vibrating out the sound. The moment splits us in two, our instincts sending us arrowing in different directions before we correct—Becca away from the sound, survival the only truth in her blood, and me toward it. We stop steps from each other. Our eyes meet.

There are moments when the world realigns itself. The words for it are too grand—revelation, epiphany. This moment is more subtle. Pieces that fit one way find a new arrangement. Becca bends her course. She follows me.

We race toward the scream. We are not the only things drawn to it. We hear the clattering, the skittering, deep somewhere behind us, and the echoing clip of swift and steady footsteps. Everything that hungers hears prey.

But we're closer. We nearly crash into them—Trina, Mel, Jeremy, Anthony. *Where's Kyle?* I think, and then the spider-thing comes around the corner, too. There's no time for stillness or silence. Too late for that. No time for reunions, either, and the skittering and singing behind us says there's no place to run. Not down the halls.

The doors, maybe. I lunge for the nearest. We rush and tumble through. I try to slam it shut, but a leg stabs through, pierces the floorboards at my feet. I shriek and stumble. Someone catches me, hauls me upright—Anthony, face pale in the dark. Another door on the far side gives us an exit, but only the narrowness of the doorways is keeping us ahead of the creature.

"Scatter," Becca says. "Find a place to hide."

"No," I say. There it is again: that shift, things fitting in a new way. She listens. "You said it hates the light. The woman—"

We can hear her steps. The faintest clamor of bells.

"We can lure them together," Mel says. "I know how."

No time for more than that. We closed the second door behind us, but the skittering drawing near says the spider has a fix on us—or its friend found us. Either way, we need to move.

Mel points. Four of us move, unthinking, to obey. Becca trails. Trina's limping—ankle twisted. Jeremy gets a shoulder under her arm, helps her along. We shuttle left-left-right-straight-left, Mel tapping her fingertips against her thumb.

The skittering, the footsteps—they're coming from opposite directions now. And they're close.

"Hide," I say. Through one last door, not quite closed behind us. We've dropped into stillness, though none so still as Becca, who stands apart from the rest, watching us with her head cocked to the side a little.

The spider—the pale one—stalks down the hall. The woman comes in the opposite direction, swift and angry. The light sweeps along with her. The spider rushes into it.

Through the narrow crack of the door, I can't make out much. The woman makes that horrible shrieking sound. The spider screams. The hands in its chest scrabble at the ribs that cage them, and it rears back, blade-like legs slashing down.

Becca reaches past me. She puts her palm against the door and shuts it. Shakes her head. "Don't look," she says. "It's safer not to look."

She waits, then opens the door again. An empty hallway, the sound of inhuman screaming far away. She slips across the hall, and we follow. This door she leaves cracked. She turns. "You're lucky. That shouldn't have worked," she says. She looks at the others. "What happened to you guys?"

"Grace," Mel says, and Becca nods, as if unsurprised.

"Becca," Anthony says. "Is it—are you really . . . ?"

"I'm me," she says, smiling, face softening in a way it didn't for me. "I'm alive." And then she steps forward and kisses him.

I don't want to tell you about what I feel in that moment, the jealousy that steals over me—the anger that she would go to him when she could hardly look at me. I don't want to tell you about the kiss, either, the way her hands creep up behind his neck, the way his run up her back as if he has to feel the curve of it to believe she is real.

So I will tell you instead about the way her weight settles back, her heels lowering to the floor again, and the way that the simple movement brings her back to her center of gravity and brings *Becca* back. It's as if she began waking up when she saved me and is finished now, free of the unceasing dream she has been trapped in for months.

I will not tell you about how I feel my ribs are twigs, snapping one by one, but instead about the way he leans his forehead against hers and lets out a sigh like he's been holding his breath for a year.

"I told you that you shouldn't have gone off with him," Anthony says.

"Okay, great," Mel says. Snaps. "So that's new and weird and I'm so not going to get into it. Grace took Kyle. We need to get him back."

"What?" Becca says, startled, eyes flicking over us. She didn't notice. Eyes only for Anthony.

"Grace took him? Then he was still with you?" I ask.

"We were by—I think it was the exit," Trina says. "She made noise to make the spider come. We couldn't get to him." I expect her to crumble, but she's angry instead. Sharp steel.

"She'd made the halls into a loop," Mel said. "I think she could have just gotten right back behind us. If she was dragging Kyle with her—"

"Then she could get out," I finish.

"You shouldn't have trusted her," Becca says.

"We didn't have much choice," Mel shoots back. She still sounds angry—angry at Becca? Why?

"There's no point in arguing. We can't let them get too far ahead," I say. "We're even, at least. We can all get through. Fast. Catch up. Get Kyle back."

"What about that thing?" Anthony asks. "What if the spider's back there?"

"I can stop it," Trina says. We all look at her in surprise. She holds the book tight against her ribs, her knuckles white where she grips it. "The book is a weapon—or the words in it are. The words to unmake."

"Where did you get that?" Becca asks, voice a hiss of breath between her teeth.

"He gave it to me," Trina says defensively.

"The preacher in the town," I explain.

"You can't read the words," Becca says. "They're dangerous."

"They can destroy the spider, can't they?" Trina says. "I can feel the power in them. They want me to read them. They want me to speak them."

"You shouldn't," Becca insists.

"How would you know?" Trina asks. "Have you even seen them?"

"I've been here a long time," Becca says. "And I'm not the first. Neither was Grace. The people who came before wrote their stories on the walls. Whispered them in the shadows, and the shadows sometimes whisper them back. Some of them say the words are a weapon. Some of them say they're a trap."

"I don't care," Trina says. "We need to get Kyle back. I'll take any chance we have. We're getting past the spider, and we're getting through the dark."

"We don't know what's out there," Becca says. Desperation makes her voice brittle.

"She's right," Anthony says, but I set my jaw.

"We do know what's out there," I say, meeting Trina's eyes. "Kyle is out there. We have to go. And we're wasting time."

I step past Becca—between her and Anthony, really. I grab Mel's hand. The motion has more meaning than I intend—or maybe I do intend it. Either way, we walk into the hall together. Trina follows. She's limping but her lips are pressed in a determined line, the book gripped in one hand.

I realize I don't know where I'm going. I glance at Mel. She shrugs.

"Not sure where we are anymore," she says. "We need to do some wandering for me to figure it out again."

"It's this way," Becca says, and my gesture of defiance loses some of its power as she and Anthony edge toward the head of the group, their hands entwined. He can't look anywhere but her, it seems.

When we get to the exit, it isn't the spider—either of them—waiting for us. It's the woman.

She stands in the hall, still as stone, the candle guttering and the circle of light making wild judders around her. Something litters the floor at her feet. It takes me a moment to realize that it's what's left of the spider. Divided neatly. Sorted. Stacked. An eyeless head framed by six slender sections of rib. A leg, disarticulated at each joint and then arranged again in its proper shape. The spider, deconstructed, stretches the length of the hall.

The edge of the woman's light touches the edge of the dark. There's no getting past her.

"You." The voice is the sound of insects crawling over each other. Of beetles spreading their wings, snapping them shut again. It comes from the woman, impossibly.

"You are a disruption. All of you. There must be silence, in this place. Or things will wake." *Or things will wake.* The echo comes from the air around us.

"Then let us go," I say, stepping forward. Becca claws at me but misses. I square myself in front of the woman, just shy of the light. "We'll leave. No more noise."

Her chest rises and falls as if with breath, though I don't see how she can breathe. The bells chime at her back.

"You're the one," she says. "You're the one she's calling. Little insect. Little rat. Vermin. Looking where you shouldn't. Talking when you shouldn't."

"Get out of the way," Trina says, advancing so we're shoulder to shoulder.

"You are not in charge here, girl," the woman says.

"Move," Trina demands.

The woman laughs. "The light will burn you hollow," she says, and lunges for Trina. I shove myself between them, trying to block the woman's progress. She bats me aside. She reaches greedily for Trina, but Trina stands her ground, feet planted, the book clutched in both hands.

The woman's grasping hand is half an inch from Trina's neck when she begins to read.

The words slide out of her, sinuous as a snake. I won't write them down. I won't write them down, even though they want me to. The book wasn't there to preserve them. It was there to contain them. Once your voice gives them form, they aren't so easy to leash.

The woman screams. Just as suddenly, the scream cuts off. Her head snaps back, the tendons of her neck standing out like cords. Her hands rake the air, fingers distending into needles, and the candle falls to the ground. The light pulses and heaves at her feet.

A writhing, twisting smoke spills from her skin, and rises from the pages of the book as well, and then the woman is becoming the smoke, evaporating into it, but the words won't stop spilling from Trina's mouth, an endless riptide of sound. The smoke flows into her mouth, her nose, and she gasps.

The candle gutters out.

The woman is gone.

Trina's eyes roil with smoke.

EXHIBIT I

*Text messages between Sara Donoghue
and Becca Donoghue*

Sara   **Becca**

7/6/16

I know you aren't there, but I'm going
to pretend you're going to read these someday.

I miss you. We all miss you.

7/28/16

Where did you go? Did you mean to leave?
Why didn't you take me?

Are you alive? Are you hurt?

I love you.

8/9/16

I've been having these dreams.

You're in them sometimes.

We're walking somewhere. On a road.
An old footpath. We're in the woods.

Except I'm not me, and you're not you.

9/2/16
More dreams. There's a girl in them.

9/5/16
It's Lucy Gallows. The girl I dream
about on the road.

Ridiculous, right? Getting obsessed
with old ghost stories.

Except it doesn't feel ridiculous.
It feels real.

11/7/16

Tttt[]ttt[]

Becca?

Ahcr.p-apsrchusrchu[][]

[*Photo: Blurred, dark. Barely
distinguishable as a road.*]

[*Photo: The same road. Clearer.*
A figure, shadowed. Female.]

Becca?

11/9/16
Lucy?

INTERVIEW

SARA DONOGHUE

May 9, 2017

Sara sits alone at the interview table, staring into the middle distance. She hums softly, a formless tune that collapses in on itself after a dozen notes. Her fingers tap against the table in that familiar, regular rhythm. Note: Camera was left rolling unintentionally between interviews. We do not believe she was aware she was being recorded.

SARA: You want to know about Miranda. I knew that Miranda was dead. I knew—

The tapping stops. She flattens her hand against the table, whimpers. She bends her head over the table, cupping her face in her hands.

SARA: The Liar's Gate, the Sinner's Gate, the Blind Man's Gate. The Gate of Many Doors. The field. The flood. The first in the dark. The second on the road. Then the beast and the field and then—

She slams her hand down on the table, whipping her head up.

SARA: You can't do this to me! You can't *do this*! You can't—

She falls suddenly silent. She walks to the door, tries it. Locked. When she speaks again, her voice is calm.

SARA: You can't keep me in here forever, you know.

Her hand drops from the knob. She turns. Sinks to the ground with a moan. Her fingers catch against the edge of her sleeve, pulling it up to reveal the words written there: RE-MEMBER YS.

And near the crook of her elbow, hash marks. Three clusters of lines, further grouped, each dash of ink perhaps an inch long. 1-5-1, 1-4-3, 2-5-2.

SARA: One and five and one. One and four and three. Two and five and two. One and five and one. One and four and three. Two and five and two.

Her fingertips probe the lines. Her breathing eases.

SARA: Little tricks. They don't change anything.

She lets her head fall back. After a few minutes, she pulls down her sleeve, hiding the writing once more. She stands and walks to the table. When Ashford enters several minutes later, she appears perfectly calm.

ASHFORD: Miss Donoghue. Can I get you anything before we get started again? Something to drink?

SARA: No, I just want to get started.

ASHFORD: All right. I believe we were just talking about your exit from the mansion.

SARA: Yes. And then—I think—I think I'd like to tell you about Miranda.

ASHFORD: Is that so?

SARA: It's hard to . . . There's a pattern to things. Like a map. You have to go in order.

ASHFORD: In order?

SARA: One and five and one. One and four and three. Two
     and five and two. We're almost there.

ASHFORD: I see.

He does not sound as if he sees at all, but Sara nods.

SARA: But first we have to talk about the field.

21

THIRTEEN STEPS. WE take them quickly, and the need to move forward, to catch up to Kyle, overwhelms the urge to let go. Trina and I come out of the dark with our hands firmly entwined and step through an open door at the back of the house.

Outside the sun slants down like a blade against our eyes. We flinch away from it. I have to shut my eyes against the onslaught. The afterimage on my eyelids supplies me with a flat expanse of scrub, and something beyond it—water? And the dark thorn of a shape on the shore, a tower. Lighthouse, maybe.

I force my eyes open again. The light hurts, but I begin to adjust. Trina is already running forward. The others emerge behind us—Jeremy and Mel, Anthony and Becca. I squint along the road. It snakes out through the grass, looping first to the left, then the right, a long switchback through the field. A dirt path has been beaten down between the ends of the switchback—a shortcut. A temptation. Another road, and one we can't follow.

Two people move awkwardly along the road just ahead.

"There they are," I say, and my eyes trace the length of road between us. They're not far. A hundred feet. But the road curves and twists, and it will take us an eternity to reach them.

"Kyle!" Trina screams. Smoke still rolls and folds behind her eyes.

"Trina!" Kyle flings himself back in Grace's grip, but she holds fast. He hits at her, flailing. Trina stutters at the edge of the road. Swears. Starts running down it, limping on her injured ankle. Anthony and Mel are quick behind, Becca flitting after.

Five crows make lazy circles in the sky above us, and I don't move. I watch the next three seconds' movement with a strange, analytical detachment.

First, Kyle's awkwardly closed fist finds the side of Grace's jaw.

Then her grip falters, and he flees. Then she lunges for him again, and they are falling, and the sun glints off something metal in her hand. A knife.

The others are hurtling down the road. A twisting mile to go. Jeremy stands at the edge of the road with me. A hundred feet to cross.

It isn't until afterward that I realize that in those three seconds, I decide I am ready to die to save them. Any of them. It isn't until even later that I realize that Jeremy had made that decision long before I did.

We don't speak. The decision is made. We take the footpath, the other road. In the distance, the beast bellows, the sound of metal shearing. The beast has Jeremy's scent once more; the hunt resumes.

Tufts of errant grass crunch under my feet, brittle and dry. Wind slices past me. Fifty feet, thirty, twenty. The knife glints. Kyle wraps his hands around Grace's wrist, but he's always been small, always been fragile. Mel would lift him up when he was twelve years old, old enough to be embarrassed by it, and spin him around with a whoop. The knife dips lower, toward his torso. I imagine his skin blooming with mushrooms.

Jeremy and I are matched step for step; we reach Grace at the same moment. I dive in low, grabbing her arm and pulling it away, pulling the knife off course. Jeremy grabs her by the shoulders and yanks her back.

The knife arcs through the air. It opens a line of pain across my chest. I raise a hand to ward her off as she swings wildly, throwing her weight toward me. Jeremy gets an arm around her neck, hauling her backward.

The beast bellows. It strides toward us from beyond the house. No mist to cloak it now—we can see its body, densely furred, dark sable at the head and shoulders fading to white. It has the torso of a man but the legs of a stag, and its hands end in jagged black claws. Its four amber eyes are open, and it strides toward us.

"I had no choice," Grace shouts, struggling in Jeremy's grip. "I had to reach her, don't you understand? Can't you hear it? Can't you hear her calling? I need to get to her. You have to let me go. You have to—" She's still straining to bring the knife to bear. Jeremy tries to control her arm, but her wild panic makes her strong. The knife bites across his palm; he yells.

The beast is two steps away. We can't outrun it. I meet Jeremy's eyes. We can't stop her. She'll kill us, and she'll convince herself she was in the right. We have to defend ourselves.

I step forward, grabbing hold of Grace's arm. Together, we throw her from the road.

She flails for balance. She keeps her feet under her, but her momentum carries her off the edge of the road. Onto the grass, the empty field, not even the false road to anchor her. She stands stock-still, mouth gaping open, then shut. Sooty blackness crawls over her skin like a slow frost, and smoke curls from her.

The beast reaches us. For a moment, it pauses. It looks down at us, and in its eyes is an intelligence, however alien, but no anger, no hostility. Only something akin to pity.

It reaches out a clawed hand. Everything on this road has found some cruel way to undo us. Our trust. Our perception. There is something merciful, something kind, in the swift flick of that claw as it carves through Grace's chest.

Zoe, wandering the false roads, persisted. Grace comes apart, as ash and soot. Not sated, the beast turns to me.

Someone is screaming my name. I never find out who. The tip of one black claw settles softly against my chest, where I am already bleeding. I shut my eyes and breathe out.

Something slams into me from the side. I hit the ground and roll. Jeremy stands over me, hands still out. "Run, damn it!" he shouts.

The creature bellows. The sound is heat and rage, shaking the air. It seizes him, claws closing around his lower body, and wrenches him into the air. And then it brings him down. Hard.

His body cracks against the road. His limbs flop. His head lolls, blood sheeting over his face—I can't tell from where. The beast tosses him. Casually, like you'd flick a bit of meat off the end of your knife. His body hits the ground, tumbles like a broken doll.

The beast turns again to me.

"*—and beneath it writhes and scrapes its bulk against the rocks, and there is no light, and in the sinner's hand the cup—*"

I tried not to write the words. I'm sorry.

It's Trina's voice, but not Trina's voice. The words slither out of her. Her smoke-shrouded eyes are fixed on the beast, her hands spread with palms up as she advances step by step. She doesn't even have the book anymore; it lies on the ground behind her.

Smoke pours from the flesh of the beast—and from Trina's palms. She is no longer shaping the words; they are shaping her tongue and lips and mouth to force themselves into being.

Black tendril-like bands detach from the beast's torso, its chest, dissolving into smoke as they peel free, as if the words are flensing the flesh from it, strip by strip. It staggers back, lowing, a sound that makes my joints ache with the vibration. Still the words come, a torrent, and still Trina advances.

The beast retreats again. Trina gulps, the flow of words stopping for a moment. She shakes with the effort of containing them—and the beast, recovering, advances.

"Stop," I yell at Trina, but she's already speaking again. The beast bellows as its skin writhes away from its torso, and this time it turns, fleeing—striding away with great steps as smoke coils and curls from its massive shoulders, its ravaged chest.

Trina stands, swaying, the words pouring out of her. Her eyes are clouded over completely with smoke. I grab her wrists; her skin scorches, but I hold fast.

"Trina, stop," I say, my words lost under hers. "Trina, it's gone. It's running."

She sucks in a ragged breath, and for a moment her eyes clear.

She looks at me, desperate and afraid, and shapes four words of her own. "I can't stop it," she whispers, and then they begin again. The rolling rhythm of the words, looping and repeating, her voice layered over with other voices, echoes and whispers. Her eyes fill up with smoke again, and her fingers begin to turn a sooty gray.

Kyle stands frozen, gape-mouthed, shaking his head in a movement so small it is almost a tremble, the fluttering wing of a dying bird.

"No. No, stop. Trina, please. Please, it's killing you," I say, knowing it's true, feeling the shift beneath my hands as her skin becomes insubstantial. "Stop! This was my choice! I decided! I was the one who chose! I was the one—"

She sucks in one final, sharp breath between her teeth. Her head kicks back, her gray-drowned eyes fixed on the empty sky—and she comes undone. It is as if she is unweaving, coming apart in strips, in ribbons, her face dissected cleanly, her body already hollow but for the smoke.

I try to hold on. But there is nothing to hold on to.

"I chose," I say. My hands are empty. The air is empty before me. I chose to run. I chose to die. But I'm still here. And she isn't.

Jeremy lies faceup, eyes staring. A crown of blood below his head. The geometry of his body is wrong. I cannot look too closely. I do not need more than a glance to know he's dead.

Footsteps behind me. Kyle. The others slow as they arrive, mute in the face of what's happened.

"How can she be gone?" he asks. I can't look at him. I can't look at Jeremy. I shut my eyes instead. "You saved her. In the village. You saved her yesterday, how can she be gone today?"

It's a child's logic, and neither of us is a child, but the wrongness of it lies open like a wound.

"She should have let me die," I say.

I can't stay here. I walk. Past Jeremy, down the road, toward the water that wrinkles beyond the shore.

"Sara," Mel calls.

"Let her go," Anthony says. He still knows me better than anyone, I think.

The ground drops away down a hill; I follow it, follow the road. More switchbacks, an easy descent. The gate lies halfway down the hill, and I walk until I reach it. I sit facing it, facing the setting sun over the water. It is already half-set, and the light that spills from it is red-hued.

Two crows land on the gate. They ruffle their feathers, watch me with dark and glinting eyes.

And then I'm not[9]

---

9 Section ends abruptly. Pen has dug through the paper on the next stroke, leaving a hole through to the next page.

INTERVIEW

SARA DONOGHUE

May 9, 2017

ASHFORD: Sara?

Sara idly traces the crook of her elbow with her fingers—the spot, hidden by her shirt, where the hash marks are written on her skin.

SARA: Mm.

ASHFORD: Sara, you said that you were going to tell us about Miranda.

SARA: That's right. I can write it down, if you like. I think it will be easier that way. Can I do that? Can you add it to the rest?

ASHFORD: We can do that.

SARA: Good. Good. I want to tell you, you know.

ASHFORD: I know. This isn't your fault, Sara.

SARA: Yes it is. Of course it is.

She reaches out for the pen and paper he offers, and begins to write. She writes only a few lines, and then she sits back. Ashford reaches out, a question on his face. She makes no objection, and he pulls the paper toward him. He looks down. His lips purse slightly, then flatten into a thin, hard line.

The door opens. Abby steps through.

ABBY: What did she say?

ASHFORD: We can discuss this outside.

She turns to Sara.

ABBY: What did she say to you?

She grabs the paper. Reads quickly. For an instant, she is completely still, eyes wide.

ASHFORD: Abby . . .

Abby lunges for Sara. Ashford is on his feet in an instant, catching her by the shoulder, holding her back as Sara first laughs, then lets out a sob and buries her face in her hands. He presses the page from the legal pad into Abby's hands.

ASHFORD: This is just another piece of evidence for the file. Go add it to the rest. And take a walk.

She seethes.

ASHFORD: Abby. You know what this is. Don't let it affect you like this.

She grabs the page and strides out, slamming the door behind her. Ashford rubs a hand across his jaw.

ASHFORD: I'm sorry about that.

Sara makes a noncommittal noise, straightening up. She looks, if anything, puzzled. She picks at her sleeve.

ASHFORD: I think we're all feeling the strain.

SARA: I'm okay.

ASHFORD: You've been through a lot today.

SARA: I've just been talking to you.

ASHFORD: That's right. We're just talking. And I think

we're most of the way there. Almost to the end of the road, as it were. Do you need anything?

SARA: I guess I'm pretty hungry. Dr. Ashford?

ASHFORD: Yes?

SARA: Are you ever going to tell me why the door is locked? If I wanted to leave, would you let me?

ASHFORD: What do you think, Sara? Why would I be keeping you in here against your will?

She frowns.

SARA: There's no reason. Is there?

ASHFORD: I'd like you to be able to answer that for yourself.

She bites her lip.

SARA: Dr. Ashford, where's my sister? Is Becca here? Is she with you?

Ashford hesitates.

ASHFORD: I don't think it's a good idea for you to see your sister right now, Sara.

SARA: Why not?

ASHFORD: As I said, I think it's better if you remember for yourself.

SARA: I did something, didn't I?

ASHFORD: That's what we're here to find out. Let's keep going, shall we?

SARA: Weren't you going to ask me about Miranda?

Ashford looks pained.

ASHFORD: Later. For now, just . . . walk us through the lighthouse.

EXHIBIT J

Note written by Sara Donoghue

Writing is barely recognizable as Sara Donoghue's handwriting. The note is sloppy, spilling over the lines on the page.

Miranda Ryder died choking on her own blood. She died alone and afraid and she knew that no one was coming for her and she knew that her sister was a useless, pathetic nobody who couldn't save her.

ShE DIeD BEcAuSE OF YoU

PART IV

THE GIRL

EXHIBIT K

Newspaper clipping from the Briar Glen Beacon

November 1, 1983

Satanic rituals or a prank gone wrong? The residents of Briar Glen were treated to quite the sight last night when a troop of girls dressed as the infamous Lucy Gallows cavorted through the town, leaving an odd litany of graffiti messages in their wake. With recent disappearances blamed on the popular "game" connected to the same legend, some residents were on edge, but the girls were identified as the cheerleading squad at our own Briar Glen High School. Senior Jenny Hudson organized the Halloween parade.

When asked what inspired the antics, Hudson said, "I've been having dreams about her. She's waiting at the end of the road. She's been waiting a long time. I hear her whispering. She's calling. More and more."

Junior Candace Thompson had a less dramatic take. "We just thought it would be fun and spooky. Halloween pranks are traditional, right?"

22

MEL AND KYLE come to get me. I have run ahead of the reality of what happened, but now I walk back with them to face it.

We cannot do anything to honor Jeremy. We can't bury him. We have no shroud to drape over his body, but Anthony has covered him as best he can with his coat. Becca sits cross-legged nearby, hands limp in her lap, staring at nothing. I force myself to walk to where Jeremy lies, where Anthony stands beside him.

He was never my friend. I didn't even like him—I thought he was a jerk. And he was. But he went with us onto the road, when he didn't have to. And Trina—maybe she was running from what she'd done, when she stepped onto the road. But I don't think so. I think if everyone else had run away, she would have been the last one there, ready to face anything to be a good friend.

"We should—we should say something," Anthony says. He stands with his hands tucked into his pockets, his head bowed.

"Why?" Kyle demands. "Is saying something going to change any of this?"

"Jeremy was a hero," Anthony says, pressing on regardless. "He was—he was a good person. Trina, too. They were both good people."

"Stop," I say. Anthony's head jerks up. His look is questioning, wounded. The air is brittle around us. "You can't make it matter by saying a few nice words."

"Sara—" Mel steps forward.

Kyle shakes his head. Tears well in his eyes and rake down his cheeks, but he doesn't seem to notice them. "She's right. Two people just died to save me. How does that math work?" he demands.

"It's not an equation," Mel snaps.

"Either one of them would have done it again. In a heartbeat." Anthony swallows. "And that *does* mean something."

"Only if we survive," Kyle says. His voice is bitter and without hope. "Only if we get home."

"You will." The words surprise me, coming from my own mouth. "You all will. I won't let anyone else die."

"*We* all will, you mean," Mel says. I don't answer.

"The road won't let us go easily," Becca says.

"I didn't say it would be easy, I said I would do it," I say. I walk back to the preacher's book, lying inert on the road. I pick it up. The cover is leather, softened with age. The words whisper to me, promise and pull.

I throw the book as far as I can into the field. It lands somewhere in the grass, far out of reach, and the whispers fade reluctantly. I shiver and turn away.

"Let's go," I say.

"Wait," Anthony says. "We can't just leave Jeremy. What if he—what if he ends up like Zoe?"

"We'll take him through the gate," I say. "That's what ended things for Zoe. We'll bring him through the next gate, and then we'll keep moving. Make it matter."

Becca stands. She brushes her hands off on her jeans and walks to me. Nods once. There could be a hundred layers of meaning in that nod, but I'm too tired to catch a single one of them.

I help wrap Jeremy's bloodied body in Anthony's coat, and between us and Mel, we carry him, slowly, toward the shore, leaving Trina—the memory of her—behind. There is nothing we can say to make what happened okay. There is nothing we can say to make it hurt less. We can only watch Jeremy's body turn to smoke and ash as we approach the next gate, and add their names to the litany of the dead.

I open the gate this time. I wait to see if there is any strange sensation as I push the key into the lock. Some tingle the others missed or didn't mention. But there is only the scrape of the key in the lock and faint resistance as it turns—and then, softly, a whisper, hardly more than a breath against my ear. *Find her.* I shiver.

Beyond the gate, the road turns to gravel, and then melds seamlessly with the rock and then sand of the shore. The whole beach is the road, I realize, and it curves like a hand clutching the water. The sea smells of salt and fish-rot. Ropy kelp clumps here and there at the edge of the water, shoved a few inches farther, then dragged back by the breaking of the swells. White specks and lines interrupt the gray sand: the skeletons of birds, delicate wings outstretched, ribs crushed down against the gray. Hundreds of them, as far as I can see in either direction, until the beach curls out of view behind black, toothy rocks.

A short walk to the left, a spit of land protrudes into the sea. The waves crash to either side of it, sending plumes of spray that meet over the highest point. If the tide rose, it might swallow the land and leave the nub at the end with its pale, narrow lighthouse an island—but I am not certain there is a tide here. There is no moon to replace the fading sun. We get our flashlights out again, though there's still enough light to navigate by. None of us want to be caught unawares by the dark.

"The lighthouse?" I ask. "Or—do we go down the beach?" I look to Becca. She bites her lip.

"I think the lighthouse," she says. She wrings her hands rhythmically, her gaze darting down and to the side. She's nervous with so many people around—even just the four of us. She's been alone so long. "The lighthouse. Yes. We should—we should go to the lighthouse."

We make our way single file down the spit of land. Salt-spray batters us and the delicate bones of birds crunch beneath our feet. With the sun down, it's getting cold. We might not need to sleep or eat, but the cold still bites its way in.

The door is painted red, or was—faded now to dull wood and a few scraps of paint.

I push it open. The whole structure gives a hollow groan. A desolate, empty sound. The room is round and largely featureless. A staircase winds up—narrow, no handrails, tightening with the shape of the tower until it reaches a hatch in the ceiling.

I am overcome suddenly with weariness. I shrug off my bag and set it inside the door. The others follow suit. Kyle sits with his back to the wall, and Mel walks to the stairs for a more comfortable perch.

"Look at that," Becca says. She points above the door. I twist to see. Carved in the rock are two words: *Final Refuge*.

"Does that mean we're safe here?" Mel asks. I laugh, louder than I mean to. She cracks a crooked smile. "Dumb question."

"Safer, maybe," I say. "I'm going to go check out the top."

"I'll go with you," Mel says immediately. I hesitate. I don't want to be alone with Mel, really. I don't have room right now to deal with what I feel when I'm around her. To grapple with what I want and can't have—Mel isn't interested in me, and even if she was, just thinking about it makes me feel selfish and shallow with so much horror around us.

"Okay," I force myself to say, and head for the stairs. Mel's footsteps echo behind me.

The trapdoor is heavy, but I manage to shoulder it open without Mel's assistance—which is good, since by the time we reach the top, the staircase is barely wide enough for one person, much less two. We clamber up through the hatch and into a round room with a single narrow window. A wooden ceiling stands above us, along with another trapdoor, this one accessible with a ladder.

The only furniture is a cot, a little table with an oil lamp resting on it, and a bookshelf. The books are swollen and discolored, their titles illegible.

"Did someone live here?" Mel wonders.

"Maybe. Or maybe it's just a prop. Like the houses around the mansion," I say. I crouch by the bookshelf and pull down a book. The text inside is readable on some of the pages—if I could read French. The illustrations need no translation, though. A young girl dangles a noose from one hand. A man's face is drawn in intricate detail, his eyes covered in clusters of fat, fleshy moths. A precise drawing, like a scientific illustration, depicts another man, this one composed of branches and thorns, with vines growing out from his shoulders like twisted wings.

"So," Mel says. Too casually. "Anthony and Becca."

I turn the pages, past a drawing of a snake twining through flowers. "Yeah," I say. "What about them?"

"Did you know?" she asks.

"That they're . . ." I wave my hand. They never really did define what they were. They just wanted each other. But he didn't believe her about the dreams, about Lucy. Just like me. And so she found someone who did. "I knew. I wasn't supposed to, but I did." She was my sister. He was my best friend. I spent too much time around them not to put it together—the secretive texts, the whispered conversations cut off when I entered the room, the way they took such precise care to never stand too close together.

Plus, I was always a nosy little sister. I snooped.

"And you're not upset?"

"I know that I can't be the only important person in my sister's life. It's just weird," I say, glossing over the selfish heart of my hurt. I have tried so hard to find her, and Anthony is the one who brought her peace by simply appearing.

"But you and Anthony," she says, and stops when I look up in surprise. "I mean, you've always . . ."

I give her a quizzical look. "What are you talking about?"

"You. Have a crush. On Anthony," she blurts out, brown cheeks reddening subtly.

I let out a sharp, startled bark of laughter and shut the book with a dull slap of sound. "Crushes are for twelve-year-olds," I say with a more genuine chuckle. "And that's the last time I had a crush on Anthony Beck."

Her blush deepens, and she stammers. "But you guys were always so close."

"He's my best friend," I say. "Or he was. But that was over long before he and Becca—you thought I still liked Anthony?"

"It would explain why you never dated anyone," she mutters, hands jammed in her pockets.

"Who's going to date the weird, sarcastic failed goth who never talks to anyone?" I ask. "Even before Becca. No one's asked me out since sixth grade. Besides . . ." I almost tell her. Can't. Crushes are for twelve-year-olds, and I should have shaken this one ages ago.

I put the book back on its shelf and walk to the ladder.

She looks like she wants to ask me more about it, but instead asks, "Where are you going?"

"Up," I say, and climb. I tell myself it's the responsible thing— exploring. Gathering information, definitely not running. I throw open the trapdoor at the top of the ladder and haul myself up. There's no room for awkward revelations and rejections on the road.

The top level is the same size as the one below, but instead of a round and empty room with stone walls, the walls are glass, and the center of the room is taken up with the lighthouse lamp and the lens surrounding it—thick glass, shaped to bend the light of the gas lamp that sits at the center. Carved in the glass is a familiar symbol—seven concentric rings. It's the same symbol from the preacher's book.

Mel emerges behind me. We look out over the water. "We need to get across," I say.

"How?" she asks. "The beach is part of the road. The water isn't. We need to follow the shore."

I shake my head. She's wrong. I can't explain how I know it; I just do. "We need to cross the water, like we did when we found Zoe. And look." I point downward, leaning out so I can see the base of the lighthouse, barely visible in the light of the stars. A boat is moored at the edge of the water, bobbing up and down, oars tucked inside.

"There's no way across without leaving the road," Mel insists.

I sigh because she's not wrong. I know there must be a solution, but I can't see it.

"You're really not mad at them? Becca and Anthony?" she asks.

I look her straight in the eye for the first time. "Sometimes I'm angry that Anthony wouldn't believe Becca. If he'd believed her, maybe she would have told me about all of this. If she'd told me, maybe I could have convinced her not to go. Or gone with her," I say. "I could have kept her safe. But no, I'm not mad that they're together."

She stands beside me in silence for a while. Up here, I feel almost safe. Nothing but the sea lurks outside, and thick glass stands between us and the waves. And it's the first time I've been alone, quietly, with Mel in who knows how long. Even when we were spending most of our time together, our friendship was never quiet. But this—this feels nice. A peace steals over me that I didn't think was possible here on the road. I'm not sure it *would* be possible if anyone but Mel was standing here. "Do you want to go back down?" Mel asks.

"Not really," I say. "I'd rather stay here with you. For a little while. If that's all right."

"Yeah," she says. Silence again—silence that I wish I could live in forever. And then, "Do you think we're going to die?"

"I don't know," I say. "I hope not. Obviously."

"If we do die . . ." She pauses. "If we do, or if we don't, it feels stupid not to say anything. So. I kind of like you, Sara. I came for you. Not for Becca. I came because I have . . . feelings. For you."

Surprise comes first, and almost in the same moment the smile, a spy sneaking through the city of dread within me. "Feelings. For me," I echo, in the same stilted tone, and she groans.

"How is there not a non-stupid way to say that?" she asks. "Look, I know that just because you're bi it doesn't mean ta-da, rainbows and unicorn farts, you must like me, too, and I don't want to make things awkward, and this is the worst fucking time to bring it up, but—"

"I like you, too," I say. She blinks. "I've liked you for a long time."

"Then why didn't you . . . ?"

"I didn't know if you . . ."

"I always thought you and Anthony . . ."

We break off, weary laughter chasing our words. "We're kind of slow on the uptake, I guess," I say.

"You're telling me—I just found out my information is off by about five years," she says. "And here I thought I was a keen observer of the human condition. But seriously, why didn't you say anything?"

"I guess I was scared," I admit.

She laughs. "Come on. You? Miss Nerves of Steel? You're the only one of us that's managed to keep it together in the face of doom, gloom, and six-story stag-men, and you're saying you were scared of me?"

"I was scared of losing you as a friend. I thought it would make things too awkward," I said. "Also, I'm completely terrified and I have been the entire time."

"You don't show it."

"It's not that hard to hide your emotions, once you get a little practice," I say.

"For you, maybe. I can't even fake being excited about my grandma's weird Christmas presents," Mel says with a shake of her head. A smile sneaks its way into the corner of her mouth. She tries to smooth it out and just ends up with a grin, as if to prove the point. Finally she clears her throat, shakes her head, and manufactures a neutral expression. "So what does this mean?"

"I don't know," I say. Part of me wants to ignore everything around us—hold her, kiss her, laugh with her up here and let the road wait. But the dark water lurks outside, and I can't bring myself to forget it. "I don't think I can sort through anything I'm feeling right now. I mean, Trina, and . . . It's all too much. But as impossible as it is to feel happy, I did. I do. So I think . . . I think in a while, when we're home, and we've had like a hundred years of therapy . . ."

"Dinner?" she suggests. "Movie?"

"That's a start," I say. I let my hand brush hers, and her fingers hook around mine as we look out over the dark ocean. However much we might wish otherwise, there isn't room, in the grief and the fear, for more than that.

But it's something.

"No therapist is going to believe this," Mel says.

"No one's going to believe this," I say.

"Someone will. If this is real, other things must be real," Mel says. "And other people must have encountered them. People who can help us. If we can even get home."

I frown, a memory faint at the back of my mind. My fingers tap out a rhythm on my thigh. "Count the crows," I whisper, almost to myself.

"What?" Mel asks.

"Nothing. I don't know." I rest my fingertips against the glass for a moment, frowning out at the water. "We're going to get home," I promise. She nods, and the look in her eyes is bright with faith. With hope. With, for maybe the first time, anticipation of what might be waiting for us, when we get back. Some scrap of joy at the end of the road. I try to mirror her expression, but it feels false.

I didn't slip up this time. *We*, I said, instead of *you*. But I haven't failed to notice—there are five of us.

Which means at least one of us won't be getting home.

SUPPLEMENT A

Text messages between Andrew Ashford and Abigail Ryder

May 9, 2017—Day of interviews

Ashford   **Abby**

Are you done reviewing Miss Donoghue's
written statements?

                                                                      Mostly.

You've had them for over a day.

                                                            She wrote a _lot_.

                                          I'm looking over your notes. Obviously the
                                                Nick Dessen thing is disturbing.

                                          I also think that given the messages from
                                    Jeremy Polk's phone, something's off about the
                                          bridge where she met up with Anthony.

Interesting that she doesn't
say anything about the dreams.

I would go as far as to say "key,"
not just interesting.

Yeah.

You don't trust her.

You do?

Not precisely. But I want you to be certain
that you are remaining objective.

Why wouldn't I be objective?
Because of Miranda?

You know Sara knows more about
her than she's saying.

I believe so, yes. But again, we do not
know the reasons why.

Sara Donoghue is a victim in all of this.
Our responsibility is to her well-being.

We'll see about that.

She is arriving in a few hours.
Please make sure that everything is prepared.

You're the boss.

I am not sure I am comfortable with
that classification of our relationship.

If you can think of a less sketchy version of
a teenage orphan hanging out with a balding
middle-aged disgraced professor, crossing state
lines and inappropriately involving ourselves in
ongoing criminal investigations, let me know.

I admit there does not seem
to be a suitable alternative.

I've been telling people I'm your intern.

Please . . . don't.

I could tell people you're my dad.

Abby.

You don't think we look alike?

Just get everything ready.

The syringes are in the glove box.

Sure thing, boss.

INTERVIEW

MELANIE WHITTAKER

May 9, 2017

Abigail Ryder sits across from Mel and flips through a legal pad of notes.

ABBY: Sorry. Just trying to make sure I've got everything fresh in my mind.

She rolls her neck and rubs one shoulder.

MEL: We've been at this awhile.

ABBY: Yup. We don't know how much time we'll have, so we want to get everything out of the way all at once. Are you holding up?

MEL: Yeah, I'm okay. I mean. Not really. I still feel like I'm going insane half the time.

ABBY: You're keeping it together pretty well. From everything I've seen, you were pretty much rock stars on the road. Most people fall apart when supernatural stuff starts happening. I did.

MEL: I was wondering how you ended up . . .

She waves a hand vaguely.

ABBY: It's kind of a long story.

MEL: I'm not going anywhere.

ABBY: The short version? Ashford saved my life. He saved both of us.

MEL: Us?

ABBY: Me and my sister. Something was after us. It killed our parents, but Professor Ashford helped us get away. For a while, at least. I've been traveling with him ever since.

MEL: What about your sister?

ABBY: She was with us for a while, too.

MEL: Where is she now?

ABBY: You saw her more recently than I did.

MEL: I did?

ABBY: Miranda. She's my sister. Or she was.

MEL: I—oh.

Abby nods, tries for a smile. It fractures.

ABBY: That's her. The thing that was hunting us caught up with us. I tried to protect her, but I couldn't. Not even Ashford could . . .

She stops and looks away for a moment to compose herself.

ABBY: I guess she decided to keep up the work, even after . . .

MEL: So that's why you're here.

ABBY: No. Or only sort of.

MEL: But you are trying to find her.

ABBY: Of course.

MEL: And what happens if you do?

ABBY: I have no idea. But I think that Sara knows something

that can help. And I think it might be the key to helping Sara, too.

MEL: You think she needs help?

ABBY: You don't?

MEL: I don't know. I haven't been around her like Becca has. If she knows something about your sister, why wouldn't she just tell you?

ABBY: That's another question we're trying to answer.

MEL: Got a theory?

ABBY: Yeah.

MEL: But you're not going to tell me.

ABBY: Not until we know for sure. I think that we have everything we need from you.

MEL: Does that mean I can go?

ABBY: Not yet. We'd rather keep everyone until everything is settled.

MEL: That sounds ominous.

ABBY: Yeah. I guess it is pretty ominous, isn't it?

MEL: Has anyone ever told you that you need to work on your people skills?

ABBY: Probably.

23

DOWNSTAIRS, BECCA AND Anthony stand in quiet commu-
nion. Becca's head is tilted in until it almost touches Anthony's,
her mouth moving in a murmur, but when we enter she straightens up and clears her throat. "We need to get across the water,"
she says.

"Sara said the same thing," Mel replies. "I still don't see how
that makes sense."

"I know because Lucy told me," Becca says. She fiddles with
her sleeves, picking at the seams. "I had dreams of her before I
got on the road, mostly. But now I can hear her. She tries to help,
because she needs help. She's trapped, here on the road. And she
says that we need to get across the water."

My mouth is dry, and my heart thuds in my chest. *Find me.*
My finger taps that odd rhythm against my thigh, and I think of
dark-feathered wings. There's an inexplicable ache in my chest,
and the persistent feeling I'm forgetting something.

"But how? The road definitely doesn't include the water,"
Anthony says.

Kyle is looking upward, as if he can stare through the ceiling to the room above. But there's nothing up there except the books—and the light.

"I have an idea," Kyle and I say at the same time.

"The light?" I ask.

"Yeah."

"What about the light?" Anthony asks.

I lift one shoulder. "This lighthouse is the obvious destination so far. And a lighthouse has basically one purpose. To keep the light going at night. So maybe that's the key, somehow."

"One way to check," Kyle says. He's already heading for the stairs, and this time I'm the one following. He trots up without any concern for the steep drop beside him. I take things a little more cautiously. Kyle might be skinny, but he shares Trina's athleticism and dexterity. I, on the other hand, do not.

The others troop after. By the time we reach the top, Mel is panting a little; she has the same allergy to sports as I do, and her most physical hobby is composing sarcastic hashtags, but she doesn't complain. The ladder takes us a little longer to negotiate, but then we're all crammed at the top level.

Kyle walks around to the back of the bulb of glass. The lantern at the center of it is clean, polished. Like everything else on this level, it looks perfectly preserved for its purpose. Even the five fingerprints I left on the glass walls are gone. I wonder what would happen if we died up here. Would anything be left? Or would it clear us away, as if we'd never existed?

I shiver and join Kyle. He's picked up a box of matches. Old-fashioned and thick, with bulbous ends, but still more modern than the lamp itself.

"So we turn on the gas, right?" Kyle says. I reach out and carefully twist the knob on the side of the brass lamp. The air in the glass flute above it shimmers, and there's a faint hissing sound. Kyle strikes a match. It flares to life with a startlingly long flame, and Kyle almost drops it. He clears his throat. "Then I guess we touch this . . . here . . ."

The gas catches almost at once. Easy. The flame elongates elegantly, filling the glass cylinder built to contain it. In front of the large glass case, Mel yelps. "Damn, that's bright!" she says, staggering around the side with her hand over her eyes.

"But look," Becca breathes, pointing.

The glass focuses the light. Not to a beam, shining out to warn ships, but to a narrow slice that cuts down to the water and across it as far as I can see. It's angled so that the light touches down precisely where the shore meets the water and continues in a strip along its surface. The light is golden, but it turns the water gray— the same gray as the road, as the shore, as the floorboards in the house.

"That's it," Becca says. "That's the road."

"That's our way forward," I say.

"And that's where something's going to go wrong," Kyle says. He looks grim. "It's too easy. It's a *puzzle*. And none of the gates have been easy. Whatever's waiting on that water, it's going to be bad."

"We'll deal with it," I say. "But we need to go now."

"Why?" Anthony asks.

"Because it's night. The light is strong enough now, but what about when the sun rises?"

"Good point," he concedes.

We head back down. At the bottom of the stairs, we collect our things, Becca hanging awkwardly back. She never let go of her bag. Probably smarter than the rest of us.

When I pick up my bag, it's ridiculously heavy. I start sorting through it, pulling out all the food and the extra clothing and the water bottles that now seem foolish. Becca's survived a year without food, and here I am lugging around enough protein bars to last a week. I take Becca's camera out and cradle it a moment before looking up at her. "I brought this," I say. "Do you want it?"

Her eyes light up. She reaches for it, and when I hold it out, she takes it gingerly, her fingers running over it like she's rediscovering its contours. "I didn't want to bring it out to the woods, so I just brought my point-and-shoot," she says. "And then I lost that in the house somewhere." She turns the camera on, fiddles with a few settings, and lifts it, snapping a photo of Anthony. He looks up, surprised, and she laughs. She turns it on me. I look away. I've never liked having my photo taken.

I've never liked having my photo taken, *except* by Becca. I hate how my cheeks bulge out when I smile, how I always look hunched, how every angle seems to capture the awkward bump at the top of my nose. Becca's photos are the only ones that I look at and see myself the way I look in the mirror. But still I turn away. In the moment I'm not sure why, but now I think I know.

I don't turn away because I am worried about the way I will look in the photo, about seeing *myself*. I turn away because the reason Becca has always been able to take my picture so well, the reason all her pictures are so good, is that they're how *she* sees. And for some reason, I don't want her to see me right now. As if there's something that only she might be able to discern— something I don't want revealed. But that thought skitters away into the dark like so many others I can't seem to keep hold of.

I get to my feet, throw the bag over my shoulder. It's lighter now, especially without the camera. The movement puts my shoulder to her, blocking her view of me.

"Let's go," I say.

We traipse down to the shore. The boat bobs in the water, bathed in the light. A thick, water-swollen rope lashes the boat to a metal ring bolted to the rocks. Anthony leans out to grab it, then hauls the boat in close enough that we can step onto it from the dry shore to the boat.

It's a rowboat. Not huge, but big enough for five people who don't mind bumping shoulders. Mel and Kyle crouch at the front together, Becca and I take the bench at the back, and Anthony, unsurprisingly, mans the oars at the center bench. It takes us a while to get the rope loose and cast off, and another few lurching tries for Anthony to figure out the rhythm of the oars. But then we're moving, and the boat, for all its apparent age, is surprisingly smooth and swift. The shore falls away; the path of light spills ahead.

"Let me know if I'm going off course," Anthony says, focused on the unfamiliar movement. I watch his shoulders as he rows, the coiling and uncoiling of his muscles. I feel oddly detached.

I want what I told Mel to be true. I want there to be a some- day we're reaching for, waiting for, when all of this is far enough behind us that I can care about crushes again. Think about being kissed and feel that thrill like fingers running up my spine.

I almost, almost let myself believe it for a moment. And then I see Anthony's eyes widen in horror, and twist around, half standing.

The road is vanishing. At first I think something is wrong with the lighthouse—and then I realize the lighthouse is gone, too. It isn't that the road is gone. It's that the darkness is coming.

"Dark," Anthony manages, a frantic warning. Kyle and Mel whirl, the boat rocking at the movement, their hands already clutching together.

Becca turns in the seat. Breath hisses between her teeth.

Five of us. One too many.

She looks at Anthony. She looks at me. Her hand hovers, indecisive, and I don't know which way I want her to reach. Who I want her to choose.

I never get the chance to find out. The darkness crashes over us, and the boat suddenly rocks, struck from beneath by some unseen force. I'm thrown from my awkward position. I scrabble blindly at the wood of the boat, but it slews, and my shoulder strikes the side hard the instant before I hit the water.

EXHIBIT L

Police interview of Rebecca Donoghue

April 19, 2017—Morning after disappearances

Becca sits hunched in a chair, her hands wrapped around a mug
of steaming liquid. She wears an overlarge sweatshirt, and
her hair is damp. A female officer sits across from her, a
woman with a broad frame and no-nonsense features.

OFFICER BAUER: Becca, my name is Linda. I'm here to talk
about what happened last night.

BECCA: I've already said I don't know anything.

OFFICER BAUER: Do you know where you've been for the
past year?

BECCA: Like I said. I ran away with Zachary Kent. He broke
up with me, so I came home.

It has a singsong, nursery-rhyme quality.

OFFICER BAUER: And where is Zachary Kent now?

BECCA: I don't know. I think he said something about LA.

OFFICER BAUER: All right, Becca. We'll look into that. But
things aren't as simple as you make them sound.

BECCA: Aren't they? It's exactly what everyone thought. I
lost my head for a boy and ran away. It's why none of you
looked for me, isn't it?

OFFICER BAUER: I have your file, Becca. Your family was distraught when you left.

BECCA: I know. I'm sorry.

OFFICER BAUER: And we're going to have to talk about the details of the last year, but we also need to know about last night. How well do you know Officer Chris Mauldin?

BECCA: I don't.

OFFICER BAUER: His stepdaughter is a good friend of yours, isn't she?

Becca flinches, pain and sorrow flashing across her features for a moment before she smooths her expression.

BECCA: Trina and I haven't talked since I left, so I don't know if you could call us friends. I don't know her step-dad. Never said more than hello to him.

OFFICER BAUER: Do you know where Trina is now?

BECCA: No. Like I said. I haven't seen her in a year.

OFFICER BAUER: Officer Mauldin is in the hospital right now, Becca.

BECCA: Oh. Um. Is he—what happened to him?

OFFICER BAUER: He was beaten last night. Badly.

BECCA: I'm sorry. Is he going to be okay?

OFFICER BAUER: We still don't know that.

Becca's gaze fixes on the tabletop.

BECCA: Where's my sister?

OFFICER BAUER: Your sister is with your family.

BECCA: Is she all right?

OFFICER BAUER: She's in shock, I think. Your whole family

is. The news that you're back is a lot to take in, after all this time.

Becca gives her a curious look.

BECCA: Where did you find her?

OFFICER BAUER: Find her? It's just past dawn, Becca. She was home in bed.

BECCA: But . . .

OFFICER BAUER: Becca, before you can see your family, there are things we need to know. There are a lot of missing pieces, here. Like where Trina Jeffries is. Or why you were out in the woods last night. Or why you were covered in blood.

BECCA: Ask Sara.

OFFICER BAUER: Becca . . .

BECCA: I'm not telling you anything until I see my sister.

24

THE WATER HITS me with a slap of sound and cold. Immediately, all sense of the boat is cut off. The creak of wood, the voices, the scrape and splash of the oars.

A curious sense of peace washes over me. It's all right, I realize. This is how I do it—how I make sure they make it. Someone was always going to die. This way, the rest of them survive.

Thirteen steps—maybe it will be thirteen strokes—and they'll have to manage with one hand apiece. But they'll manage. Becca will take charge. The way it's supposed to be.

I tread water, waiting. Waiting for what, I'm not sure. I should be afraid, but I think this is the first moment since we saw the road that I am completely, utterly calm. I have done all I can. It's not enough, of course. Nothing would ever be enough. But it's all I have to give.

And then something brushes past my leg. Then another, more constant pressure, like fingers probing the shape of my ankle. I kick out and connect with something that gives easily. I feel the passage of a dozen flurrying bodies around me, and I force myself to breathe evenly. Whatever is going to happen is going to happen. But my instincts kick in and I can't stay still and wait for it.

I kick off my shoes, try to gauge the direction of the road, and strike out. Swimming in clothing isn't exactly easy, but the water has a strange buoyancy that makes up for some of the drag, and years of swim lessons come back to me readily enough. A few strokes take me away from the questing touches, and then I pause, catching my breath.

I hear voices up ahead, and for an instant I think it's the others. But these voices are wrong. The *language* is wrong, something that chatters like a stream over rocks, and there are too many of them. I don't want to swim toward the sound, but I'm sure that's the way the road went. I take another few cautious strokes. How many is that? Seven, I think. Six more and—and there's no way I'll make it, not alone. The rules are the rules.

The voices draw closer. They're all around me now, but still I can't see or feel anything, anyone. They whisper in my ear, babble behind me. A hand grabs my arm. I yank away. Another seizes my leg and gives a sharp tug, pulling me under, and this time when I kick, I can't break free.

More hands, and still the voices, bubbling and laughing and whispering. Hands grip my wrists, my legs, my hair. Fingers crawl over my chin, force their way in past my lips, scrape against my teeth as I try not to scream, knowing it will only let the water rush in.

I flail against the gripping hands. They tighten painfully, craggy nails scraping across my skin. I thrash one hand away and reach for the surface, but it's too far away; I grasp at only cold water. I can't hold my breath much longer. I can't get loose. My lungs burn, and in a moment I'll have no choice but to surrender.

The last thing I'll see is nothing at all. Only darkness.

And then—light. A soft, golden light, filtering weakly through the water. Briefly, it illuminates the shapes around me. They're almost human, with withered torsos and gaping, broken-toothed mouths, huge clouded eyes and hollowed cheeks, ash-gray hair billowing in the water around them. Beneath their breastbones, their bodies turn to tatters.

The light hits them and they scatter. Their movement is jerky, nauseating, but it tears them away from the light and in a moment they have vanished. I struggle for the surface, but my vision goes to spots. I reach for the light.

A hand plunges through the water and closes around my wrist, hauling me upward. Seconds later I'm being pulled over the edge of a boat, which rocks alarmingly. I spill into the belly of it, coughing and gasping as water puddles beneath me.

"Ho, there. Air's for breathing, now, not water," a low rumble of a voice says. I peer up. The light shines behind the man sitting in the center of the boat, but I can see the broad outline of his shoulders and the silhouette of his hat, wide-brimmed and crumpled as if jammed down on his head. "Let's get you out of the dark, then, miss."

He gets a grip on the oars of the little boat and turns it with a few practiced movements. Around us, the darkness is a solid shell, but it can't press in past the limits of the light. I'm still struggling to breathe normally; the first word I attempt comes out as a sputtering cough.

"None of that, now," he says. "You just hold tight. We'll have you out in a moment."

"Who are you?" I manage.

"Oh, now, there's an interesting question," he says. "Interesting on account of it not having much meaning anymore. Who I am is a man on the road, and that's all that's mattered for some time now. You can call me John, as some fair few have, though I can't rightly recall whether any did so before I stepped through the Liar's Gate."

"You're a traveler?"

"I was," he says. "But those days are behind me. There's no leaving this place for old John, but don't worry yourself about that. I've learned to abide well enough. And here we are."

We edge out of the darkness, back onto the glimmering path of light. John finishes his stroke and sets the oars a moment while he reaches behind him, fetching the source of the light. When he turns back, he's cradling a hand in both of his. It's been cut off just below the wrist, a bit of bone protruding from the desiccated flesh. The fingers cup a candle, melted almost all the way down, fat globs of wax spilling over the palm. He puffs his cheeks to blow it out and wraps the whole thing tenderly in a cloth he pulls from inside his jacket. Then he puts the bundle inside a wooden box at his feet and taps the lid as if to assure himself it's secure.

"What—" I say, but realize before I ask the question there's really no answer that will make it make sense.

"There are two ways to survive the road. One of them is following the rules, the other is learning how to break them in just the right way," he says. "Not much left of that trick, and the cost of its acquisition was dear, but as it's saved one life, at least, I'll call it a worthy price."

In the lighthouse's beam, I can see him more clearly. He's white, with a russet beard streaked with gray and a broad, weathered face. His clothes are as rumpled as his hat and old-fashioned, though I don't know enough to say whether the fashion is eighty years out of date or a hundred and eighty. One of his eyelids droops, and the cheek on that side is scored with deep scars.

"I'm Sara," I say.

"Oh, that I know," he replies. "And your next question's going to be about your friends, who will have fetched up to shore by now, as soon we shall in turn. We've been waiting for you awhile now. There was some doubt as to whether you'd make it."

"We?"

He doesn't answer. The shore is in view, gleaming gray at the end of the light. The others' boat is there, leaning drunkenly against the shore, pulling free and wandering back with every breaking swell. There's no sign of them. I lick my lips, taste salt.

"They're just fine," he tells me. "You've come through the worst of it, now. For this stretch, at least."

Then there is only the slap of the water against the hull, and then the scrape of sand as he drives us all the way up onto the shore. He steps out and grabs hold of the prow, hauling it up another foot before holding out his hand to steady me. I shiver, a cold breeze cutting right through my wet clothing, and he settles his rough woolen coat around my shoulders. It helps a little. I chatter out a thank-you, but he only smiles and ducks back to the boat to fetch his box.

With the box, and the hand inside it, tucked under his arm, he heads up the beach and the slope beyond, leaving me to follow.

I've got no particular reason to trust him, other than the fact that he just saved my life, but I also have no other options and no direction to go but straight up the last sliver of light to the next section of road.

Sand gives way to scrub, which gives way to the road, and the path of light ends. John pauses, pats his sides, and then turns back to me. "Ah. In the pocket there, if you please," he says, pointing to the coat hanging limply around my shoulders.

I get at the pocket awkwardly and find a flashlight inside. There's tape over the bottom, and initials—*M. N.*—in Sharpie. I decide not to wonder about who it belonged to. I hand it up to him and he uses it to light our path. We walk another few hundred yards through shallow hills, trudging up and down, which at least warms me.

Up ahead, a puddle of light spills over the road. A campfire. And the figures around it—

"There are your people," John says. "Go on, then. They'll be eager to see you, but these old bones don't move so fast anymore. Take the light, then, I don't need it."

I accept the flashlight from him wordlessly—because I can't manage words. They're alive, all of them. *I'm* alive, a fact that finally sinks in as I lope along stiffly, my bare feet slapping the stones. I run as fast as I can and it isn't fast enough. I resent every second it takes me to cross the distance to them.

Mel spots me first and lets out a whoop, running to meet me. I slow down, but she still slams into me and wraps her arms around my sodden shoulders.

"Sara! Oh my God, she wasn't lying. You're okay? You're you?"

"I'm me," I say, and then, before I can think better of it, I kiss her.

The kiss tastes of ocean water, and a damp strand of hair gets stuck between our lips, but I don't care. I don't care who's watching, either, only that Mel is there and she's kissing me back and there's one thing, at least, that this road can't take from me.

When we break away, she bites her lip, flushed. Mel, shy—that's new. "Turns out waiting is a terrible idea," I say, and she laughs. And then I look past her, and see Becca, cheeks streaked with tears that haven't yet had the chance to dry. Mel follows my gaze and steps back. Gives Becca room to come forward.

Becca draws in close. She puts her hands to either side of my face and leans her brow against mine. "Don't you dare do that again," she whispers. "You're my little sister. I'm supposed to be looking after you."

"I'm older than you now, remember?" I say. "Also taller." I hug her, and this time her answering embrace is quick and sure.

"Barely." She steps back and grins, relief pouring into her expression. Then she clears her throat—what she always does when she's trying not to cry. My gaze skirts past her, and for the first time I notice that they weren't alone by the fire.

A girl stands backlit, wearing a white dress, a blue ribbon around her waist. Her hair is red brown, and falls in loose curls to the middle of her back.

"That's—" I begin.

"Lucy," Becca says. "We found her."

"More like she found us," Anthony says. He's a few steps back, close enough to the fire that the orange of its light is still stronger than my flashlight. "She and that other guy. We were going off track, I guess, and then suddenly they were there with this light. He just reached out and yanked our boat back on track and went with us the last couple strokes, out of the dark. Lucy asked where you were. She knew your name. She knew all our names. And when we told her what had happened, she hopped over into our boat and told the guy to go after you."

A dozen half-formed questions come to the tip of my tongue, but none of them are complete enough to voice. I stare at Lucy, who's close enough she can probably hear everything we're saying, but far enough away she isn't intruding too obviously. She stares back. Then she lifts a hand and waves a little, a fluttering of her fingertips.

"She said she wanted to wait until you were here to talk too much," Mel says. "And you're soaked. And I can hear your teeth chattering from here. Come on, let's go up near the fire."

She throws an arm around my shoulder. I lean against her a

little and catch Becca's hand, just my fingertips hooked to catch hers, on the other side. Kyle and Anthony trail behind.

We reach the firelight and Lucy dances back a bit, elegant little steps to give us room to maneuver. I get close enough to the fire to feel the warmth before addressing her.

"Hi. I'm—"

"Sara," she says. She smiles, cheeks dimpling. "And I'm Lucy, if you hadn't guessed."

John tromps up behind us and then past, turning sideways with muttered apologies to fit by the group. He goes to the far side of the fire, where a stool sits next to a pile of boxes and bags, and sets the box with the hand on top of it.

"Did you encounter any problems?" Lucy asks him.

"Oh no," he says, blowing out his cheeks. "Just the usual sort of hungries, and the candle's burning low, but you knew that."

He rummages in a bag beside him and pulls out a length of wood and a small knife, and sets to carving it with a level of concentration that suggests he'll have no part in the following conversation.

"John's been on the road for quite a long time," Lucy says. "Even longer than I have. I wouldn't have survived its trials without him, but he's—he's not what he used to be." John shows no visible offense at this, only whistling and working his knife into the wood.

"He's the man your brother saw you with," I say.

Lucy blinks at me. "My brother?"

"Your brother followed you into the woods, and he saw you

get on the road with a man in a broad-brimmed hat," I say. "That's what the newspapers said."

"Ah," she says. "I think someone may have told me that story before. Sometimes I have trouble keeping track. I've worked hard not to lose my senses quite as much as dear John, but I'm hardly immune. I am eighty years old, after all. Even under normal circumstances, my memory might falter." She smiles. "I didn't know my brother was following me. John was already playing ferryman back then. He's a very *good* person. Or was. He could have gotten off the road, but he decided to stay behind, and risk himself going back and forth to help people along. He told me I should turn back, but I was quite set on traveling."

"Why?" I ask. "If he warned you, why would you—?"

"It calls to some people," Lucy says, a little wistfully. "It's lonely. It calls to the ones it thinks can make it to the end."

My skin prickles. Maybe it's just the cold. "Can you help us get to the end?" I ask.

She sighs. "The thing is, this *is* the end," she says.

Seven gates. Everything we've come across has been consistent in that, at least. "We've only been through . . ." I count them off in my mind.

"Five," she says. "The Liar's Gate, the Sinner's Gate, the Blind Man's Gate, the Gate of Many Doors, the Sailor's Gate. Sometimes they have different names. Sometimes they come in a different order, and the details of each change to suit the traveler. But to get here, you passed through five. I know. There ought to be two more. Come with me."

She turns and walks into the dark. John stays put, whittling his stick and whistling through the bristles of his beard.

Lucy leads us down another hill and up the side of the next, then stops, pointing.

At the base of the hill is a wreck of shattered stone. An eruption of the earth, and the road beyond it utter ruin. Brambles grow over the hills beyond, and then a thick snarl of trees, a forest that stretches to the dark uncertainty of the horizon. Here and there I think I can make out a paler patch among the shadows, far beyond the limits of our flashlights, where another scrap of road remains.

Mel moans as we come to a staggered stop. "That's it?" she says. "It just ends? Then how do we get off?"

"You have to leave the road," Lucy says.

"But if we leave the road, we die," Anthony says, taking another step toward the end of the road and squinting as if a solution will reveal itself.

"It isn't that clear-cut," Lucy says. She looks at me. "Sara left the road."

"When I was running after Kyle," I say. "How did you know that?"

"I've been keeping an eye on you all," she says. "When I can."

"That beast would have killed you if Trina hadn't stopped it," Becca says.

"But she did stop it," Lucy says. "And while the words are one of the more explosive things to find their way onto the road, they're hardly the only tools at our disposal. The gates may be gone, but enough of the road remains to follow it—if you have the right connection to it, and to your destination. You all have keys, I presume. Have you all used them?"

I think through quickly—Becca must have used hers at some point, because she nods. Kyle opened that first gate, Anthony opened the gate after the water, Mel handled the third—which leaves me, and the gate at the beach.

"Good," Lucy says. "That ties you to the road. If you're careful, and stay focused, it should be enough. Well. Could be. But we don't have any option but to risk it."

"We?" I say.

Lucy blinks at me. "Isn't it obvious?" she says. "I'm coming with you."

EXHIBIT M

Email sent from Rebecca Donoghue to Andrew Ashford

April 29, 2017—Ten days before interviews

To: Andrew Ashford
From: Rebecca Donoghue
Subject: help

My sister gave me your name. My name is Rebecca Donoghue. We live in Briar Glen, in Massachusetts. Something happened. I don't have time to explain.

Look up Lucy Gallows. I have pictures. I'll attach them here, I think I can do that.

We need help. Something's wrong. Sara said you could help us. She said Miranda told her, but Miranda's dead so I don't know how that could be true.

I can't explain.

I'm attaching the pictures.

Please come. Please help.

Please.

INTERVIEW

REBECCA DONOGHUE

(Audio only)

May 4, 2017—Five days before interviews

The background of the recording is noisy—clinking plates and silverware, the murmur of voices. It seems to be a public place, probably a restaurant.

ASHFORD: Miss Donoghue. Rebecca.

BECCA: Becca, please. No one calls me Rebecca.

ASHFORD: Becca, then. Do you mind if I record this?

BECCA: Why? To give to the police?

ASHFORD: I try to avoid contact with the police whenever possible. I can assure you that I will do everything I can to see that this recording, and the rest of the materials I may collect, will not come under scrutiny by anyone other than myself and my associates.

BECCA: Associates, huh?

ASHFORD: Mostly just Abigail. You'll meet her later. My point is that any information you share will be quite safe with us.

BECCA: What more do you need to know?

ASHFORD: A great deal, actually. But for now, let's talk about why you emailed me. Often when people call me, what they're looking for is confirmation. Someone who can tell them that what they saw was real. That they aren't crazy.

BECCA: I don't need anyone to tell me it was real.

ASHFORD: No, you said you needed help. What sort of help?

Becca hesitates. Someone drops a plate and swears in the background. Then something shifts in her tone; she has come to a decision, decided on a course of action.

BECCA: There's something wrong with my sister.

ASHFORD: Wrong how?

BECCA: She did something to her.

ASHFORD: Who did something to your sister, Becca?

BECCA: Lucy.

ASHFORD: Lucy Callow? The girl who disappeared in the fifties?

BECCA: We shouldn't have trusted her. But it was the only way to get home. And now Sara is . . .

She takes a shuddering breath, her voice trembling at the edge of tears.

BECCA: You have to help her. Please. You have to save her.

ASHFORD: Miss Donoghue, I promise you that we are going to do everything we can.

SUPPLEMENT B

Email from Andrew Ashford to Abigail Ryder

May 5, 2017—Four days before interviews

To: Abigail Ryder
From: Andrew Ashford
Subject: Briar Glen Setup

Abby,

We are going to need a secure location. At least two rooms to use for interviews, with sturdy locks. Soundproof, or at least in an area we are unlikely to alarm any neighbors.

Please approach this as a standard interview. We want the subjects to be comfortable and to trust us. We will collect standard written statements from all of the survivors who have agreed to talk to us. Given the police involvement in this case, we need to tread cautiously, though it appears that the usual effect is in place and the matter is being mysteriously overlooked and forgotten by the authorities. Convenient enough for us, I suppose. It isn't as if they would be able to help in these circumstances.

I want everything recorded. Multiple angles in the interviews, if possible, and I want you to review all of the material that Miss Donoghue has supplied and make copies for our records. Pay attention to every detail.

One of them is lying.

—Andrew

25

HERE IS WHAT Lucy tells us.

She came this far with John, all those years ago. She had an easier time of it than most, and John already had a great deal of experience by then. They got this far, and could go no farther because John couldn't leave the road, but he assured her that once he shepherded another lone traveler here, they could hazard the journey to the end. He had sent others that way, but did not know if any of them had made it.

She waited for a very long time. It was years before anyone else came, and when they did there were two of them, and she could do nothing but wave them onward. Years after that, John discovered another lone traveler, and together the two of them attempted an escape. It was a failure. The things beyond the road killed Lucy's companion, and she barely made it back to the road herself.

She begged John to leave with her, but he could not give up his task, his purpose. Nor was he certain that he could leave the road anymore. And so she waited. And waited. And became, perhaps, a little bit less of our world, and a little bit more of the road's. She learned to watch among its curves and turns, in what she called the gaps between moments—sneaking looks at who was coming. Who might need John's help. She learned to whisper to a few travelers, though she could rarely manage to whisper anything that would provide real guidance.

She watched travelers die—most of them. She watched them reach the end of the road—a few of them. But in sixty-four years, she hadn't yet found someone who would take her with them.

"That's why we came to get you," she says. "That is, we would have helped in any case and we would have helped sooner, but going back—it makes you more part of the road. I've only done it once. I could tell that if I did it again, I'd be like John, and never get away at all. But the point remains: there are five of you. We can leave together. Two and two and two. I can finally escape this place. And I can show you all the way home."

She smiles, eyes sparkling. She still looks ready to prance down the aisle at a wedding. She looks pristine, especially next to the rest of us, with our bumps and bruises and torn clothes and bedraggled hair. Perhaps her smile is a little too wide. Perhaps her skin is a little too perfectly pale.

"What is it like? Past the end of the road?" Mel asks. I'm at the edge of the group. Becca stands with me, both of us silent, as if we're listening to some sound, some hum in the air, that only we can hear.

Find me. More memory than sound.

"Less and less anchored in reality," Lucy says. "It's difficult to explain, and it's different for everyone. There is a certain cohesion to the road. You may trust, to some extent, that what you see is the same as what the person standing next to you sees. It becomes less true, out there. More like a dream. It's disorienting."

"All the more reason to be glad we have a guide," I say. Lucy's cheeks dimple.

"Do you mind if we talk among ourselves for a minute?" Anthony asks. Lucy shakes her head cheerfully.

"Of course not. Take your time. I have waited this long," she says, and heads down the road a ways to give us room.

Anthony drops his voice. "Do we trust her?" he asks.

"Why wouldn't we?" I say. He frowns at me, as if he isn't sure how to answer that. I frown back at him.

"She's helped us get this far," Becca says. "Sometimes her whispers were all that kept me going."

"Becca's right," I say. "She and John saved me on the water. The least we can do is help her get free of this place."

"You don't think it's a bit weird?" Mel asks.

My brow furrows. "Which part?"

"She used exactly the same phrase as Grace. 'Two and two and two.' And I think Grace heard her, too. That's what she was yelling about at the end, wasn't it?"

"It's not Lucy's fault that Grace was psychotic," I argue.

"Why are you pushing so hard on this?" Mel asks, sounding bewildered, and I'm suddenly not sure I know. Except that I trust Lucy. I like her. It feels like coming home to an old friend, finding her here, and I want more than anything to help her.

Becca saves me from needing an answer. "Because it's the only way we all escape."

"Five of us," Kyle says. I've almost forgotten he's there, he's so withdrawn. "And I'm guessing that even if it would last long enough, they're not going to just give us that candle. But we shouldn't trust her."

I want to tell him that he's wrong. I look at Becca, and I'm surprised to see anger flickering in her expression—anger at the others, the same as what is brewing in me. Why is she angry? Why am I so certain?

I still don't remember.

We talk awhile longer. Argue, maybe. In the end, the only thing that matters is what we've already said: this is our only option. And then . . .

The more I try to remember, the more it frays. I remember we decide to leave at daybreak. The sky is already turning gray. I search it horizon to horizon. There are no crows, and this means something.

You want the rest of the story? Here it is. We walk off the road, each of us with one hand in our partner's, the other clutching a key. We walk to the gates of Ys. We walk through the dark. We walk out again, into woods whose name we know.

Not all of us. But you knew that already.

What is it you don't know? What is it you're looking for, in all of this? We walked out of the dark. Isn't that what matters? Some of us made it out.

You want to know who.

Is that it? You want to know who made it out, and who didn't.

And I don't know why I'd think that. And I don't know why I don't know the answer.

There's something wrong with me, isn't there?

What happened in the dark?

INTERVIEW

SARA DONOGHUE

May 9, 2017

ASHFORD: What happened in the dark?

Sara doesn't answer. She hunches her shoulders, sitting almost
sideways in the chair to point her body away from him.

ASHFORD: That's what you wrote, at the end of your statement. "What happened in the dark?" But you were there,
Sara. You're the only one who was there for all of it. You're
the only one who knows for certain.

SARA: But I don't. I can't remember.

ASHFORD: I understand, Sara.

SARA: You do? Because I don't. Why can't I remember? I
can't remember what happened, and I can't remember
Nick, and I—there was something I forgot, and then I remembered, and now it's gone again, but I told you, didn't
I? I told you?

Her voice is pleading.

ASHFORD: You mean Miranda.

She lets out a sigh, shuts her eyes.

SARA: Yes. Miranda. I—there's something important. Something she told me.

Her fingers tap on the table.

ASHFORD: When did you write those words on your arm, Sara?

She looks down at her arm, pushes the sleeve up a few inches, frowns at the writing on her flesh.

SARA: I don't remember.

ASHFORD: Do you remember why you did it?

SARA: I was trying. To remember.

ASHFORD: But you don't remember *what* you were trying to remember.

Sara lets out a hysterical giggle and rakes her fingernails over her scalp.

ASHFORD: There's no need for that, Sara. I want you to look at me a moment.

She lifts her eyes to his reluctantly.

ASHFORD: You've been tapping out a pattern. You repeated it verbally earlier, when you said you wanted to tell me about Miranda. And you've written it on your arms.

Sara is stock-still, breathing thinly between her teeth.

ASHFORD: I've been going through your testimony, Sara. I noticed what you said to Mel in the lighthouse. "Count the crows." I think I may know what it means. What that pattern you keep tapping means.

SARA: Don't.

ASHFORD: I want you to think about school, Sara. I want you to think about sitting on the back steps, the day the message arrived. I want you to think about what you saw.

SARA: I saw Vanessa.

ASHFORD: Before that.

SARA: Trees. And—

ASHFORD: Yes?

SARA: I don't know. A crow.

ASHFORD: Yes. Try to fix that image in your mind, Sara. Now I want you to think about your dream. The dream you had of Miranda. What did you see in the sky?

SARA: Birds.

ASHFORD: Crows. How many of them?

SARA: Five.

Her fingertip taps out the number against the tabletop. Ashford nods encouragingly.

ASHFORD: Good. And then—

SARA: After the gate. After the dark. There was a crow screaming. And then—and then in the town. The crow that attacked that man.

ASHFORD: One and five and one. One and four and three. What were the four and the three, Sara?

SARA: There were so many, after the flood of dark. But—but then they flew away, and there were four left. And the crows flew up from the trees in the lake and there were too many to count, but then there were three on the gate, waiting. I'm sure. There were three on the gate.

Her knuckles rap three times, sharp and steady against the table, and she locks eyes with Ashford.

SARA: One and five and one. One and four and three. And two crows in the eaves of the house. And five crows when I ran to save Kyle. And two—and two crows—

ASHFORD: Where did you see two crows, Sara? Think. Remember. Please.

SARA: The gate before the beach. After Jeremy and Trina. I went down to the gate by the beach, and I sat down. The sun was setting. The light was red over the water. I remember thinking it looked nothing at all like blood. Jeremy's blood was darker. It was thicker. And two crows landed on the gate. And then—and then—

Her fingertips twitch. Ashford slides a pen and paper toward her.

ASHFORD: One and five and one. One and four and three. Two and five and two. You can do it, Sara. You can remember.

She begins to write.

26

AND THEN I'M not alone. Someone is sitting with me, a presence more sensed than seen. I turn my head—just enough to make out her shape, shot through with the dying light like sun through murky water. I can count the bones of her hands.

"Hello, Sara," Miranda says.

"You can't be here," I say. I can't turn my head all the way to look at her; fear claws through the numb shell I've built around me. "You were lost. In the dark."

"It wasn't the dark," she says. "It was the sunrise. It's harder to exist in the light. I'm less real."

She stretches out her hand. It shifts, becomes more solid, then the bones and muscles and veins glimmer below her skin again. She pulls it back.

"What are you?" I ask in a hushed whisper.

"Dead," she says, with a harsh laugh. "Which I suppose doesn't clarify things much here."

"You're a—ghost?"

"Yes. I died a long way from here." I turn to face her now. She smiles a little, sad. "I'm sorry I stayed away so long. It's harder, here. It's not just the daylight. It's the road. I don't belong, and it knows it. It's easier to hide from it at night. I think I'm safe for a little while, though. And we needed to talk."

"Why?" I ask. "Why are you here? Why are you—are you helping us? Or—"

"I died—I was killed—and then I woke up," she says. "And I didn't know where I was or what I was supposed to be doing, but I found the road. Or it found me. It catches things. Lost things. Like me."

"Like the creatures in the house?" I ask.

"A bit like that. Though I'm not as lost as they are. I've got a good hold on who I am. So far, at least. It might last. Might not. The point is, while I was wandering the road in those first few days after I died, I found your sister."

"Becca. She didn't say anything."

"I didn't show myself. I didn't know how to hide from the road, not yet, and for someone—some*thing*—like me, if you draw its notice—well. Once the road notices you, you start to become part of it. You lose the ability to leave. So I only watched.

"Becca talked to herself sometimes. She talked to you, too. And I knew that you would come, eventually, because you're her sister and that's what sisters do. I brought you the notebook." I frown, thinking of Isaac. *She left you a map.* I thought he'd been talking about Becca. He must have gotten them confused, his mind too addled by the road to distinguish the living girl and the dead one. Miranda continues. "I helped, what little I could without the road noticing me. Without her noticing me."

"Without Becca noticing you?" I ask, confused.

She shakes her head. "Think, Sara. You're getting so close to her now. This might be the last chance you have to remember."

"Remember? I . . ." I look away. There's something at the back of my mind. A dream I had, maybe. The memory of a voice whispering in my ear. *Find me.* Not Becca. "Lucy," I say. "I didn't—I didn't come here for Becca, did I?"

"Of course you did," she says. "You would carve through a hundred worlds to find your sister. She used that love, Sara, but it was real."

"I was having dreams about Lucy," I say. "I could hear her calling me. Telling me to find her. I can still hear her. But I can't—" I shudder. *Find me*, a soft voice whispers, and I feel the sensation of fingertips dragging over the backs of my hands. "Why can't I remember?"

"Places like this do strange things to memory. Make it malleable. There are things that take advantage. The echoes took Nick from you." The name means nothing to me; it slides away. "They're hungry, bitter things, but their motives are simple, at least. What she's doing is more complex."

"And what is that?"

"She's altering your memories, but she's also making you . . . open," Miranda says. "Vulnerable. She needs you, you see. To escape this place. She's greedy for life. She'll take yours if she can."

"Take mine? How . . . What . . ."

"Listen. I will tell you as plainly as I can," Miranda says. "Since you first started having the dreams, she's been shaping your mind and your memory. Because if you know what she is and what she wants, you'll try to stop her. She'll hide every memory you might use against her. She'll hide this one, too, because I've told you what she's doing. And if you can't remember, you can't fight her."

"Help me, then," I say, desperate. I can feel fingernails of fear against my throat; I know Miranda is right.

"We don't have much time. The eyes of the road are on me," Miranda says. "And once you cross the water, I won't be able to follow."

"Then how do I stop her?" I ask, the only question that seems to matter.

"I don't know," Miranda says sadly. "I don't even know if you can. But if you can remember, maybe you have a chance. I can't give you your memories back, but I can help you make a map back to this moment. And if you can remember this, remember what she is and what she's doing, maybe you can find the rest of the memories she's hiding. Find the truth."

"A map?"

"A trick," she says. "A trail of memories so inconsequential she won't think to erase them. If you can tie those memories to this conversation, it might be enough to uncover it."

"Like what?" I ask.

"Something small, but concrete. A pattern you can remember," Miranda says. "It could be anything. A color. A phrase you've heard along the way. It can be anything, as long as you remember it. And as long as she won't think to destroy it."

My eyes flick to the gate, to the two crows crouched there. They've been here the whole time—there was a crow in the tree when I talked to Vanessa, that day in school. And more on the road since, alone and in groups.

Miranda follows my gaze. She doesn't need me to say anything at all; it's like she knows what I'm thinking. She nods. "Count the crows, Sara. All of the crows you've seen along the way. Remember them. Follow them back to this moment, and remember me."

She stands. The light carves through her. Voices tumble behind us, coming toward the crest of the hill. The others will be here soon.

"And Sara? I have a sister, too. Find her, if you can. She works for a man named Andrew Ashford. They can help you. Tell Abby—tell her I'm sorry. Tell her to stop looking for me."

And then Miranda is gone.

One of the crows on the gate croaks, shaking his wings. "Two," I whisper, my finger tapping twice, slowly, against my thigh.

INTERVIEW

SARA DONOGHUE

May 9, 2017

Sara stares down at the page she's written. Slowly, deliberately, she sets the pen to the side. And then she begins to tear the page in two.

ASHFORD: Sara, don't—

He reaches for her. She slaps his hand away.

SARA: Don't! Don't touch it. You can't—

They grapple with the pad of paper. He wins, pulling it free of her as she shrieks.

SARA: It isn't true! None of that is true. I lied. I lied to you. Nothing happened. I sat alone. I sat alone until they came to find me. None of that is true.

With every word, the frantic strain in her voice settles. Her hands go flat against the table. She looks levelly at Ashford. He skims the page, glancing quickly between the words and the girl.

SARA: It's nonsense.

ASHFORD: Is that so.

SARA: I don't know why I wrote it. None of that happened.

Ashford remains silent.

SARA: You don't believe me.

ASHFORD: I believe that you are telling me the truth, as you understand it. Some memories are hard to hold on to. But I think this one is important. I want you to think about the crows, Sara. I want you to count them. They're bread crumbs, leading you to the memories you've lost. Miranda gave you a tool. Hold that in your mind as long as you can. I'll be back in a moment.

SARA: Where are you going?

ASHFORD: I think it's time that you spoke to your sister.

PART V

THE TRUTH

EXHIBIT N

Excerpts from interviews conducted in 1963

"I've never stopped waiting for her to come home. Like nothing ever happened. It would be so like her. She was such an imp. That's why we thought for such a long time that it must be a prank she was playing, because she was upset that her sister was getting all the attention."   —*Irene Callow, mother of Lucy Callow*

"She was a little shit. She'd always been a little shit. She ran off into the woods because she couldn't stand not being the center of attention for once."

—*William Callow, brother of Lucy Callow*
(unpublished)

"The girl's dead. No ghost story changes that she went into the woods and died. If you ask me, her brother did it. That cockamamie story about a disappearing road. He was hiding something. And pissed at her for running off. Always thought so. But without a body, what could we do?"

—*Jack Brechin, Mass. State Police (unpublished)*

Note from Mark Watts,
reporter at the Briar Glen Beacon, *to his editor:*[10]

I've been working on this too long. I'm starting to dream about her. I'm turning in what I've got along with the rest of my notes. If you need more, you can get someone else to finish it.

Do you want to know where Lucy went?

---

[10] Local records indicate Mark Watts left Briar Glen shortly after publication of the interview. Unable to locate forwarding address.

INTERVIEW

SARA DONOGHUE

May 9, 2017

The door opens slowly. Rebecca Donoghue enters, followed by Andrew Ashford. A bruise mottles Rebecca's cheek, and her left eye is slightly swollen. Bandages cover her arms at random intervals. Sara sits placidly, staring down at her hands, which are folded on the tabletop. Abigail Ryder is the last to enter, and at Ashford's nod she takes up a position in the corner, her hand on the syringe in her pocket.

BECCA: Hello, Sara.

Sara mutters something but doesn't look up.

BECCA: Dr. Ashford said that you might be ready to talk. About what happened.

SARA: What about what happened?

BECCA: He says that you need to remember on your own.

Sara lets out a sound between a whine and a moan, like an animal in pain.

SARA: I don't want to.

BECCA: Sara, you need help.

SARA: I don't need help. I'm fine. Except that I'm locked up in here.

BECCA: You aren't fine. You haven't been fine since we left

the road, and you know it. You're the one who—you told me to call them. You begged me.

SARA: She's lying.

She looks at Ashford. Her eyes are dark and glinting with intensity.

SARA: Don't you see? What we pulled off that road wasn't her. And she's trying to confuse you. She's been messing with my memory. Making me remember things that aren't there.

BECCA: That's not true.

ASHFORD: This isn't productive. Sara, all we want is the truth. All we want is to know what happened when you left the road.

SARA: She turned on us.

ASHFORD: Lucy?

SARA: No, *her.*

She points to Becca and lets out a strangled laugh.

SARA: But you don't believe me. You think I'm the one who has something wrong with me, but it's only what she's done to me. She's not even Becca, don't you see that?

Becca presses a hand to her mouth, turning her eyes away as if she can't bear to look at her sister in this state.

ASHFORD: If that's the case, then it's all the more reason for you to tell us what happened, Sara.

Becca comes around the table, pulling a chair with her. She sits beside her sister and covers one of Sara's hands with her own.

BECCA: It's going to be okay, Sara. But we have to talk about what happened.

Sara lets out a sigh and leans her head against Becca's shoulder.

SARA: I'm so tired.

BECCA: I know.

Sara touches one of Becca's bandages gingerly.

SARA: Did I do that to you?

BECCA: It's not your fault.

SARA: I did, didn't I? I hurt you.

BECCA: You saved me, Sara. You fought so hard to get to me. But you have to keep fighting a little longer. Think about the crows, Sara. Think about the crows, and write it down.

SARA: You'll stay?

BECCA: I'm not going anywhere.

In the corner, Abby leans against the wall, watching closely. Sara's fingers tap out the now-familiar rhythm. Ashford slides a pen and paper toward her. She picks up the pen, but doesn't yet begin to write.

BECCA: We were getting ready to leave the road.

SARA: That's right. Lucy said she knew the way.

BECCA: Mel and Kyle paired up. And then we argued about who was going to go with who. You said Anthony and I should go together, but I wanted to go with you. Except I didn't want to say that, because that might make Anthony feel bad, and—

SARA: And then Lucy chose.

BECCA: Lucy chose you.

Sara fixes Becca with a steady look.

SARA: Are you sure about that, Rebecca? You don't remember what happened in the dark, do you? It isn't that I need to remember on my own. It's that you can't. You've tried, and you can't.

BECCA: Sara . . .

SARA: Maybe I'm not the problem at all.

BECCA: Do you really believe that?

SARA: I don't know. Do you?

Becca looks away. Sara sighs.

SARA: I'm sorry. I'll try to remember. We were at the end of the road . . .

She writes.

27

"I WILL GO with Sara," Lucy says. It cuts short our argument—our not-quite-an-argument, none of us wanting to state anything too firmly because then we'd be forced to acknowledge that it *is* an argument. We're standing by the ruined end of the road, and daylight is seeping over the horizon. It catches on Lucy's skin and slides over it the way it should, and a tension I have been holding in my chest without realizing it eases. I'm not sure why, except that it has something to do with sunrise—and with bones.

"Are you sure?" I ask. "Becca's more experienced."

"All the more reason to spread out our knowledge," Lucy says. She glances at Kyle and Mel, who paired up without any discussion or objections. "It's unlikely we'll be able to stick together once we leave the road. I'll do my best to keep you all in sight, but we need to plan to be alone in our pairs."

"So how do we find our way? How do we stay alive?" Mel asks.

"You need to keep your destination fixed in your mind," Lucy says. "The gates of Ys. Do whatever you need to in order to keep that name in your mind. There are still traces of the road. Try to follow them. They'll look different to all of us. But the rules are the same. Stay to where the path *should* be, and you'll be safe. Or safer."

"This sounds impossible," Mel says.

"But it's not. Other people have gotten off," Becca replies. I find myself nodding.

"There's one more gate before the gates of Ys," Lucy says. "It's wrecked, but obvious. If you get there, stay there. It's a safe point and we can find each other again. Past that is the dark. The last stretch before we reach the gates of Ys."

"And then?" I ask.

Lucy hesitates. "I've never gotten that far," she says. "I lost my partner. I couldn't get through the dark. But I think if you get through the last gate, if you get to Ys itself, you can just . . . leave."

"Sounds straightforward," Mel says drily.

"It sounds like something we can't possibly prepare for," Becca says. "Which means that we should just go for it, before we talk ourselves out of it."

"I agree," Anthony says. "We can do this. And dark or no dark, whatever you do, don't let go of your partner's hand. We survive by sticking together."

"Don't let go," I echo.

Lucy nods, smiles encouragingly, and reaches out her hand to me. I hesitate the barest fraction of a moment before taking it.

I hardly hear the click of Becca's camera.

The light is strengthening. It makes Lucy almost glow, her veins a blue tracery under her milk-white skin. Her hand is warm and very much alive, but still the hair on the back of my neck prickles, and I cast an uncertain look at Becca. But she is busy putting away the camera and whispering with Anthony. Which of them is confessing worry and which offering encouragement, I'm not sure.

"Let's begin," Lucy says primly, settling a cloth satchel over her shoulder. She gives me a dimpled smile, waves farewell to John, and takes a prancing step. I follow behind less gracefully. We pick our way over the last few contiguous stones of the road. I try to make out the shape of it snaking through the trees, but I can only be certain of fragments here and there.

"We'll make it," Lucy assures me with confidence I envy. "I've been this way before."

"You didn't both make it," I remind her.

"You're stronger than he was," Lucy says. "And you have better friends." She doesn't explain what she means; she steps off the stones, and I follow.

The world pulls itself apart. There is no other way to describe it. Colors separate. Matter reorganizes itself and then becomes chaos and then becomes a new order. We stand in a forest, in a desert, in the middle of a city square with people bustling past us, gray eyes fixed on the ground. I stagger, but Lucy steps through one world and then another with dogged determination.

The air whispers and thrums around us.

Where are you going?

            Where is she taking you?

    I know you.

                I know her.

        The gates are open.

The sea rushes in

Coral and bone

Where are you?

Who are you?

The whispers grow into a forest, and we stand among its trunks. An ancient forest, trees too big for three men to wrap their arms around. The canopy so thick that only speckled light filters down to us, shivering with the shapes of leaves. We stand on a patch of road, seven stones knocked up against each other. I pant. Lucy grins, cheeks pink and eyes bright.

"See?" she says. "It's not so bad."

I can still feel reality pulling apart inside of me.

"No time to waste," she says.

"Wait—" I begin, but she's already stepped off our little island and—

—and into the sea. It closes over us, deep and dark and filled with echoes. Whale song and weeping. I hear my name and start to turn, taking in a breath before I think. Water rushes in, but I don't choke. A man stands—floats—stands beside me, staring ahead, wrapped in cloth like a funeral shroud, his mouth gaping and mournful.

We're all coral and bones since she let the water in. They get the story wrong. They say that, besotted and foolish, Dahut opened the gates for her lover, and the tide came and snuck in after. But her lover was no man of blood and bone and breath. It was older, greater, than any man. It sang to her of destruction, and she let it in. To cover every part of her. To devour every part of us. Do you understand?

And a laugh. We've moved on. Another step, another ten, I can't tell. We shouldn't be able to walk, surrounded by dark water, but walk we do. And now a woman walks with me.

We're all coral and bones since she let the water in. They get the story wrong. They say it was an accident, that she forgot to close the gate against the tide, but it isn't so. Dahut opened the gates to a power more ancient and terrible than we could comprehend and spread her arms in welcome. But the wise men of Ys called to the sea, and drowned all of Ys to stop her. Do you understand?

I don't, I want to tell her, but she is already gone, and a child walks beside me, our feet stumbling over silt and stone.

We're all coral and bones since she let the water in. They get the story wrong. She opened the gates, but she drowned before she could let her lover in, and the gates were shut once more. Yet she persists. The road persists. She draws them in, the travelers, sings to them that they may come to Ys and she might escape, and find her lover again. The sea cannot drown him forever. The road cannot hold her forever. Do you understand?

I gasp, and we are on dry land again. Another cluster of stones, a remnant of the road.

"What did you see?" Lucy asks, head cocked. "What did you hear?"

"I'm not sure," I say. "There were—we were under the water—and there were people down there with us. I think they were talking about Ys."

"A scholar came down the road once," Lucy says. "He said that the city of Ys was a French myth. He said it bore some similarity to the things about Ys he'd heard on the road, but there were differences, too, and he never did decide whether it was just a story the road manifested for him, or if it was the truth behind the road's illusions."

The story is shifting and sliding in my mind. Dahut, this woman, was trying to let something—something ancient and terrible—into the city. She failed, but the city was destroyed, creating the road. At least that's what I think Lucy is telling me, what Becca told me before.

The road calls to some people, I remember. Becca heard Lucy calling. What did Lucy hear, to lure her to the road? Ys? Dahut? "What do you think?" I ask.

"I think it's real," Lucy says. "I think there was a city called Ys, and a woman called Dahut who drowned it. I don't know about the rest of it—this ancient power, the reason Dahut flooded the city. But I don't think it matters, do you? It doesn't matter *why* we're here, only that we are, and we want to escape."

It's one of many moments where her age strikes me—the depth of it. She's not just older than fifteen. She's been here decades. A lifetime. How much must that change you? But she smiles her dimpled smile, and looks over her shoulder, and the moment passes.

"Look," she says.

I glance back. Behind us is not water but a hill that drops away, and at the bottom, fields of golden wheat spill in all directions. In a gap between the wavering stalks, Mel and Kyle run, hand in hand, Mel's bag thumping against her back with each step.

"They're running from something," I say. I can't make out Mel's face but I can imagine the fear etched on it. I start back toward them. Lucy holds me in place. "We need to help them," I protest.

"They'll be all right," she says. "And if they aren't, there's nothing we can do from here. We need to get to the gate. We're almost there."

She steps off the stones. And we are—

In the woods. I know these woods and I don't. We're in the Briar Glen Woods, but they're younger, with slender trunks and too much light, and a voice calling.

Lucy. Lucy, where are you?

Lucy, I didn't mean to.

Goddammit, Lucy.

Lucy's hand trembles in mine. Her eyes are wide. She suddenly looks like layers of her have been peeled away. Decades. She is a child, shivering beside me.

"We have to go," she says. "We have to get away from here. He's coming."

"Who's coming?" I ask, but her hand has slipped from mine, and she's running. Vanishing between the trees.

I see her—or is that her, there? Lucy and an echo of Lucy, Lucy and a memory of Lucy. A child and—and whatever she's become. Both of them running.

I run after.

Lucy!

That voice. It booms between the trees, impossibly deep and

impossibly loud. Footsteps crash, thunderous, and I think of the beast, but when I look back there is only a young man in a formal shirt, sleeves rolled up to the elbow, his hair mussed. He looks like her.

Lucy, come back, you idiot child!

She's beside me, but it isn't her—it's the wrong her, the echo-memory, the child as thin as tissue paper.

"We have to go," she tells me. "He's going to catch us." She reaches out to take my hand, but I flinch back. Echo-child. Not real. Not right. *He's coming.* Each step takes him six feet, ten, the ground crawling to bring us together, and before I can move, he catches her.

He seizes her by the shoulders and he bears her up, and slams her back against the trunk of a tree, onto the jutting spike of a broken branch and he pushes her back to pin her there, the wood sliding bloodlessly through her middle, and she screams and she thrashes but he presses farther still.

She stops screaming. She hangs limp. He steps back, as if checking to make sure that the picture he's hung is level, and then he turns to me.

She's such a brat. Do you understand?

"Sara." My name hisses between clenched teeth. Lucy—the real Lucy—is up ahead, crouched at the base of a tree, her whole body shaking and her eyes wide with terror. "Sara, this way. Quick." She beckons, her hand outstretched.

I dash around the man. He lunges for me, but his grip strikes my shoulder and slides right off. Lucy holds her hand out to me, and I can see every muscle of her body tensed, desperate to flee.

I catch her hand, and together we sprint between the trees. They tilt, folding in toward us, like a trap snapping shut in slow motion, and still his footsteps crash behind us. The pale ribbon of a patch of road gleams between the trees, a promise of safety—or something like it—but it's so far away. We aren't going to make it. He's going to catch us. Unless—

Ys. We have to get to Ys, I think, as I have been thinking as often as I can remember, but I shift the thought in my mind. *Focus on me*, I think. *Not Lucy. Me.*

I direct the thought at—I'm not entirely sure. The road, I suppose. And I feel something hungry turn toward me. It's all mouth and tooth and wet. The forest falls away abruptly, and the crashing footsteps vanish, knife-cut quick.

We stumble to a walk. We aren't in the forest any longer, but a park. A familiar one.

"I'm sorry," Lucy says. "That old fear lives in the body. I thought I'd left it behind, but I suppose it still has power."

I'm not listening; my eyes are fixed on the path ahead. It leads up to a bridge, and beyond that the stones of the road, but between us and our destination a girl and a boy stand on the bridge.

Me. And Anthony.

"What, it's all my fault?" the other me asks, glaring at him.

"We all loved Becca," he says.

This is the way it happened. That night on the bridge. This is the conversation we had.

"It doesn't matter," the other me whispers. "It doesn't matter now."

"No. It doesn't," Anthony says. "Because whatever happened then, I'm here for you now. I don't know if this is a prank or a trap or if there's really something hiding out in the woods, but I'm not letting you go alone."

"And what about the others?"

"If you ask them, they'll come," he says.

The other me shakes her head. "They won't. Especially not if they know—"

"You don't have to trick them into being your friends."

"Can you promise me that? We haven't spoken in months, Anthony."

He looks away. "Trina would come."

"If I asked? Maybe. But if you ask—if you tell them you're worried about me, and you know I'm going to go alone, that I need support . . ."

"You want me to lie to them. Sara, you don't have to do this."

"Yes, I do. It's the only way I can be sure they'll come. And if Becca's really still alive, we should all be there to try to find her. I'm right. About all of it. You know it."

He's silent for a long while. "Sara. Did you send the text?"

The other me doesn't answer. She snaps a photo of the dark water, frowns at the screen.

Anthony sighs. "I don't get why you assume that none of us care enough to go with you. All you have to do is ask."

"Really?" the other me asks. She reaches for her phone. "Let's see."

Her voice fades. Lucy is tugging me along, and with every step toward the bridge, it grows more indistinct, until it's only mist, and so is everything else—mist roiling around us, and nothing at our feet but tendrils of it, cold and damp, until the ribs of the gate rise from it, dark and brutally bent back until the top almost touches the ground. Lucy halts. She looks sidelong at me.

"That's what you're running from?" she asks.

"It's my fault," I say. I look back into the formless mist, my hands cold and limp at my sides, as if waiting for the illusion—the memory?—to reappear. "All of it is my fault."

INTERVIEW

SARA DONOGHUE

May 9, 2017

BECCA: Is that really what happened?

Her voice is soft. Gentle, but wounded.

SARA: I don't know. I remember seeing it on the road. And I didn't remember that before. But I thought I remembered the way it happened, and that wasn't it. I didn't tell Anthony to get the others. I told him I didn't need him to come. I told him I didn't need any of them to come.

Ashford clears his throat.

ASHFORD: Sara, we got access to Jeremy Polk's phone records. There are some text messages on there between him and Anthony.

SARA: And?

ASHFORD: It isn't clear-cut, but . . . Here, I have a printout. I can show you.

He takes a moment to find the relevant page in his briefcase and hands it to Sara. Her brow furrows as she reads it.

EXHIBIT O

Text messages between Jeremy Polk and Anthony Beck

Jeremy   **Anthony**

4/18/17

How'd it go? Why did she want you to
meet her at the bridge?

                                    It's complicated.

Complicated meaning I was right
and she's nuts?

                        Complicated meaning complicated

                        I'm going to go to the woods.

With her?

                        Yeah. And whoever else will come.

                        I would really appreciate it if you came, too.

Sure.

Really? I thought I'd have to

talk you into it.

No worries. If she wigs out and stabs
you with scissors I want it on film.

That's not funny.

I'm serious. Girl's unhinged.

She lost her sister. Cut her some slack.

This is me cutting her some slack.
So did she send the text message?

No.

You mean no, she didn't, or no,
you don't want to think she did?

I mean stop asking.

You know you're an asshole, right?

Yup.

You ever think about not being an asshole?

I'm saving my spiritual growth for college.

Anyway, ignore me. I know she's your
friend and she's been through a lot of shit.

I've got your back whatever happens.

I knew you would.

You're a great guy, Jeremy.

But seriously, work on the asshole thing.

We've got plenty of life ahead of us.
I'll get around to it.

INTERVIEW

SARA DONOGHUE

May 9, 2017

SARA: That doesn't prove anything.

ASHFORD: He says that you asked him to meet you at the park.

SARA: Did I?

BECCA: Sara. I think what you saw on the road is true.

SARA: And Lucy's brother impaled her on a branch, then?

BECCA: Maybe it's not that literal, but there was a reason you saw that.

SARA: I felt guilty. Maybe that's what the road came up with to make me feel *more* guilty. I'm not lying. I don't remember that happening—telling him to convince the others to go.

She grabs at Becca's hand, her gaze imploring.

BECCA: I believe you. I believe you, Sara. But you're forgetting things.

SARA: Why? Why can't I remember what really happened? What's *wrong* with me?

She turns to Ashford, her voice raw and demanding. Abby straightens in the corner, ready to intervene, but Sara stays seated.

ASHFORD: Your guilt over your friends' deaths makes it difficult for you to think about that night. Because of that night, you blame yourself. Your mind shies away from it naturally, and so it's an easier memory to hide away in the recesses of your brain. And then it is easier to hide other things alongside it. It serves as a kind of deterrent, to keep you from questioning your false and missing memories. I believe that memory is key to what Lucy is doing to you—what she is making you forget.

SARA: You mean what happened in the dark.

ASHFORD: That's part of what I mean, yes.

SARA: And what's the other part?

ASHFORD: One thing at a time.

SARA: You keep saying that.

ASHFORD: I'm not doing it to be cruel. You need to do the work yourself, Sara. We can't do it for you. And you do want to, don't you? You want the truth, and you want to be whole again.

Sara's fingernails scratch the table's surface. Her head lolls to the side, her eyes half-closed.

SARA: Sometimes I do. Sometimes I—sometimes I—

Becca seizes her hand.

BECCA: Stay here, Sara. Count the crows. Follow the path Miranda made for you. Remember.

SARA: I don't want to hurt you again.

BECCA: You won't.

SARA: No. You should go. I don't want to hurt you again. Please. It's not worth it. I—

ABBY: I'll keep you from hurting anyone.

ASHFORD: Abby.

But Sara looks fixedly at Abby.

SARA: Promise?

ABBY: You want to protect your sister, right? It's the most important thing to you. And it's part of why you've been holding back. Because you're afraid of what happens if you open certain doors. I get that. And I promise. If I think you're going to hurt her, I'll stop you.

SARA: Are you sure you can?

ABBY: Yeah. I'm sure.

Sara nods.

SARA: Good. Okay. Then we can try again.

ASHFORD: Are you certain? I don't want to push too far too fast.

Sara frowns faintly.

SARA: No, I think we have to do this. I think we have to do it soon. I think . . . I think we're running out of time. I am. Running out. I . . .

Her brow creases, smooths. Her next words are a whisper.

SARA: Do you understand?

28

THE OTHERS CATCH up to us not long after. I don't know if I've already forgotten by then—the bridge, what I saw. Even now that I remember what I'd forgotten, I don't remember when it was I forgot. Is that strange?

Mel and Kyle find us first, and I panic, because Becca and Anthony should have been before them—but they're less than a minute behind, racing out of the mist and fetching up near us with identical stricken expressions.

"That was a trip," Mel says, underselling it by a mile. She shows her teeth, but it isn't a smile. I want to ask what they saw, and I can see the same question on their faces, but no one speaks it out loud. One confession will demand the rest, and I don't think any of us can quite bear that.

"This is it, then," Anthony says. "The last gate."

"Not the last," Lucy says. "There's one more." The gate to Ys itself. And from there, a way home.

We clamber over the broken gate, helping each other across. On the other side the road sticks out into the mist like a broken-off dock. No one moves.

"We've come this far," I say. "We can do this." I reach out and take Becca's hand, then Mel's. Mel grips Kyle's hand tight, and Anthony takes the other, Becca and Anthony closing the ring— Lucy dropping back, away, giving us the moment. We held hands like this before we stepped onto the road. A ring of us, and so many gone now.

"You came for me," Becca says. "All of you. I don't know how to make that up to you. How to make it worth everything you've been through. Everyone we've lost."

"We did this for you. Not because of you," Anthony says. "Don't feel guilty. Feel . . ."

"Loved," I say softly. "We came, all of us, out of love. For you. For each other. Even Jeremy, even though I doubt he'd appreciate me saying it."

"Way too much of a bro for that touchy-feely stuff," Mel agrees with a tilting smile, and we chuckle. "Sara's right. We're here out of love. Because of what all of us were willing to give up for it. Especially Trina. She loved you more than anything in the world, Kyle, and she would do what she did a thousand times over again if she knew it would get you home. And so we're *going* to get you home."

"I hope I'm worth it," Kyle says.

"I hope I'm worth it, too," Becca says. They share a look that settles from pain into a kind of peace.

"We all get home," Anthony says. "That's how this ends. Every one of us."

"Every one of us," we all echo.

The circle breaks. Anthony keeps hold of Becca's hand, and

Mel lingers near me a moment. We don't have the right habits yet—the small things to comfort each other, to connect not as friends, or not friends alone, but whatever we're becoming. We have to settle for an out-of-place smile, a gaze that lingers a second longer than it might have yesterday, a brief touch of her hand against mine.

Then Lucy steps up, her smile sweet, and slips her hand into mine once more.

"It isn't far now," she tells us. "Soon this will all be over."

"Should we go first?" I ask.

"We'll go first," Kyle says. "I mean, if that's okay. I just want this over with." His eyes shift away from mine.

We watch silently as Mel and Kyle walk into the mist, turning into shadows before they vanish.

"Ready?" Lucy asks me.

"Ready," I lie, and we walk after them.

The road is surprisingly intact here—few stones that manage to touch one another, but the edges clear enough, speckling the ground at semiregular intervals. The mist leaves us mostly blind, but that's a kind of blessing. I don't want to see what's around us.

Because of the mist, we don't see the dark until we're almost in it. We hardly acknowledge it, except to rearrange our grip slightly, more securely.

"Almost done," Lucy tells me—or maybe she's talking to herself. We step past the border of the darkness, and into that strange, echoing space.

I count steps. One, two, three, four. That urge is there—
letgoletgoletgo—but I grit my teeth against it, and Lucy's grip
never wavers.

And then she stumbles. Her breath is labored, and her grip
tightens against mine with an alarming sort of desperation.

"Lucy? Are you okay?" I whisper.

"Hold on," she says. "Here, hold—hold my arm."

She slides her hand through mine, guiding my palm up to her
upper arm so I can grip and leave her hands free. I hear her rummaging in her bag, and then—light. I blink rapidly in the sudden
luminescence. She holds the severed hand with its candle in the
palm. There isn't much left of it, but she sets it at our feet. We're
still among the scattered stones, soft grass growing up around
them.

"What's wrong?" I ask, and then I see that she's bleeding.
Her hair hid it at first, but the blood trickles down her neck and
pools in the dip of her collarbone, soaking into her dress. Her eyes
are glassy, and she sways. "What happened? Oh my God. What
should I—what should I do?" I ask.

She peels her lips back from her teeth. "What happened is
Lucy's brother is a bastard," she says. "And there's nothing you
can do. Not unless you can travel back sixty-five years or so and
stop him from slamming a rock into her skull." *Lucy. Her* skull. I
blink in confusion, but I don't have time to think about it.

The blood comes thicker, faster. She staggers. Her knees
buckle. I lunge to catch her on instinct, but all I can do is lower
her to the ground as she wheezes.

"What do I do?" I ask again.

"It's all right," she tells me, her voice faint. "I knew it would happen. It's why I had to turn back last time. Lucy was dying when she stepped onto the road. This close to the end, it catches up with her, that's all."

"What do you mean, Lucy was dying?" I ask. "You're Lucy. What—"

"It's why I couldn't use her to get away," she says. "But you and your sister—you're both so receptive. I never had to try very hard to get you to hear me. Lucy was like that. Pity about the dying." Something moves behind her eyes, and I realize I was wrong. Lucy isn't decades older than she looks.

Those eyes have the weight of centuries.

"You're Dahut," I whisper.

She grins. "And you are my way out of this prison," she says. She reaches out, and before I can pull away, she seizes my hand. Something rushes out of her, cold as the sea, and into me.

And

    I

        cease.

VIDEO EVIDENCE

Retrieved from the camera of Becca Donoghue

Recorded April 19, 2017, 12:49 a.m.

BECCA: Something's wrong.

ANTHONY: Just keep recording.

At first the phone records only darkness. Then, light ahead, the surface of it strangely opaque, though a figure can be seen dimly, kneeling.

BECCA: Why do you want me to record this? We should just go up there.

ANTHONY: I want a record of this. I don't trust Lucy. And that camera's way better than the one on my phone.

BECCA: Then you take it.

She hands him the camera, then pulls him forward. The distance between the camera and the light seems to shrink, fold, faster than it should, and then they stand within the circle of light.

Sara crouches near the flickering candle. Lucy lies in a pool of blood nearby.

BECCA: Oh my God.

She rushes forward, dropping to her knees beside Lucy. She searches for the source of the blood and tries to stanch it with her hands.

BECCA: What happened? Sara? *Sara.*

Sara jerks, gaze snapping into focus.

SARA: I don't know. She just collapsed.

BECCA: Where did all this blood come from?

SARA: I don't know.

She stands, lifting the severed hand with her. The candle wax puddles in the cupped palm and spills along its creases. A liquid drop rolls free of the rest and falls to the ground.

SARA: We have to go. The candle won't last.

BECCA: Do we leave her?

SARA: We don't have a choice.

Becca straightens up. She looks down at her hands, frowns, and wipes her hands on her shirt.

BECCA: Do you hear that?

ANTHONY: Hear what?

BECCA: Nothing. It's . . . it's quiet.

She looks disturbed.

ANTHONY: Let's just get out of here.

He hands the camera back to Becca.

<Recording ends.>

29

THERE ARE THINGS I am not supposed to tell you.

There are things I don't remember.

There are things I don't know.

Sorting out one from the other is harder than you think. I'm not sure I've done it right. I'm not sure what the things are you need to know, and I'm not sure which things I've told you are true.

Because not everything you've been told can be true, can it?

This is true:

I don't know how long I am gone, in those moments after Dahut takes hold of me. When I exist again, when I wake, I am in the dark—but it is not the darkness of the road. It is a maze. It is a house. It is a cage. I am running, chasing someone. *Lucy*, I think, but the name is as slippery as a dream. *Dahut*, I call, and laughter echoes back toward me.

The house unmakes and remakes itself, but there is an order to it. A will, a malice, an architect with a careful hand. Doors vanish behind walls. Corridors are carved where they should not be, false paths to fool my memory.

I don't know how long I'm in this place, feeling the deepest parts of myself brutally rearranged, but I wake to darkness, and it is the darkness of the road. And in the darkness is a sound—

The sound of waves.

"Don't move," Becca whispers. Her questing fingers find my arm. Her breath catches in time to Anthony's, and I know that they've found one another as well.

"What happened?" I ask.

"The light went out," Anthony says. "Just now. Didn't you— but I think we're there."

Light shines all around us. Not the light of the candle, but a green-cast light, sliced narrowly into shafts that stretch from some vast height to the ground at our feet. I tilt my head up, still half-lost and uncomprehending, my mind lurching from one thing to the next without being able to conceive of the connections between them.

Becca makes a sound—*ta*—behind her teeth, startled and wondering, as the light grows stronger.

We stand on a cobbled street. Around us, buildings rise to domes and spires and minarets, a glorious confusion of architectural styles, their sides overgrown with fringes and folds and rivulets of varicolored coral. The light above filters down as if through a great expanse of water, and I can see the wrinkling surface of waves, but we are no more drowned than when I walked with Lucy through that unformed space. What we passed through there was like a dream; this has the substance of skin, of stone. A solid thing, more real than not.

The severed hand lies at my feet. The candle is burned down to nothing, a puddle of wax and a smudge of soot that used to be the wick. Spent.

"What is this?" Anthony asks. He and Becca are barely touching, the last two fingers of his hand softly bent around hers. Her fingers dig into my arm, gripping tight.

"Ys," I say, with a certainty that girds my ribs like iron. "This is Ys."

"There they are," says a voice, and I turn. For a moment the girl is a stranger, the smile on her face inexplicable. And then I know her—Mel. Relief and affection rush in, but they never quite reach me, as if restrained behind a pane of glass. Kyle is with her, running toward us down the cobbled street. Mel reaches me and catches my hands. I should feel something more, I'm certain, but I am focused instead on the cool, dry texture of her palms. "You made it. Where's Lucy?" she asks.

"Something happened to her," Anthony says. "She's dead."

Mel swallows, but just nods. Lucy was a stranger, and we're all out of grief. "But we made it," she says. "This is Ys, isn't it?"

Somewhere beyond us, through the maze of buildings, comes a deep, reverberating sound.

I move toward it, pulling free of Mel's hands. Her fingers slide from my arm without resistance, and a moment later I hear the others' footsteps behind me.

Anything wooden has rotted through, but stone still stands. The buildings are empty. We don't check inside to be certain, but they have a loneliness to them, a hollow way of watching us, that makes it clear. And it's clearer still when we turn a corner and find them.

The crowd stands before the gates of Ys. The women wear long skirts in colors to match the coral, and jeweled pins adorn the hair piled in lush arrangements on their heads. The men wear tunics belted over leggings. Some people carry lanterns. Most stand empty-handed. They no more belong to one era or country than the buildings; they're the sum of a hundred imaginations, not quite real, not quite in agreement.

The gates are massive. Taller than ten men, and not wrought iron but solid stone, carved with a pattern of waves. Every face in the crowd is turned toward them. Every face—including a blonde girl, her features sharp, her form muscular and lean.

"Trina?" I say, but the moment I step toward her, the crowd seems to shift without moving at all, and she's gone. I halt, pain lodged in my breastbone.

A boom sounds through the air, and the gates shudder with the force of a blow. The crowd tenses, a thousand intakes of breath making a seething, wave-dragged sound. The tension bleeds out slowly.

"That . . . that's the gate?" Anthony asks. We're still a ways back from the crowd. They don't seem to have noticed us—or if they have, they don't care that we've come. "That's the gate we're supposed to open?"

"I do *not* think we should open that gate," Becca says.

"But that's the way home, isn't it?" I ask. I drift a step forward. "Through the last gate." I want to open it. I need to open it. Someone is waiting behind it, I'm sure—waiting for me to set them free.

"No," Becca says, catching my wrist in a tight grip. "That isn't the way home. Can't you feel it? Whatever's past there, it's . . ."

"Hungry," Mel finishes, shuddering.

"Ys drowned for him," Becca says. Her eyes are unfocused, and her body sways slightly. "Ys the drowned, Ys the drowning, Ys long since lost. We walk among its bones. We speak to its memories. Ys is the end of the road. And the end of the road is Ys."

"Becca?" Anthony says, but she seems not to hear him, to see any of us. She sways forward.

"I can hear it. Now that it's quiet, I can hear all of them. The drowned," she says. "They stand guard, to keep it shut. The gate. To keep him out. Dahut's lover—Dahut's master. She draws us here, and we feed the road. We feed it by traveling it. We feed it by dying. We keep it alive so that she stays alive, and someday she'll escape it. Someday she'll wake him up, and open the gate, and we will have to drown the world to stop him."

The others shift uneasily. I reach for Becca's hand, hush her. "Stop. Don't listen," I tell her, surprised by my own urgency. "Everything we know says we need to go through the last gate. That's how we get home." She turns half-blind eyes on me. The boom comes again. Something knocking on the door. Something knocking to be let in.

"The old story about the road," I say. "It says that if you reach the end, you can ask for something. A wish. What if that's what's past the gate? What if whatever's through there could . . ."

"Could what?" Kyle asks. "Bring them back? Trina? Jeremy? Vanessa?" He shakes his head. "No way. Becca's right. That's not our way home."

"Then what is?" I demand.

Becca turns. She raises her hand, and points. And there it is— the darkness, waiting. "There," she says. "That's the way home."

"Or it's just another trap," I say.

But the others are listening to her, I can tell. Mel moves close to me. "I think she's right, Sara. She's been on the road longer than any of us. She's the one that could hear Lucy. I think we should listen to her."

"We can't," I say, looking back at Anthony and Becca. "We can't go through the dark. Not with only five of us."

"We don't have a choice," Anthony says.

"We can't all make it. We won't have another miracle," I say. "The candle is gone. No one is coming to save us. If we go through the gate—"

"That gate isn't to keep us in," Anthony says. "Don't you hear that sound? It's to keep something *out*."

The sea cannot drown him forever. My lips are dry and taste of salt.

"We'll make it," Becca says. "We'll find a way."

Anthony shakes his head. "Sara's right. Basic math. Odds and evens. We can't break the rules, not this late in the game. If only four make it, that's better than none of us."

"I don't accept that," Becca says. "We'll figure it out. I was in this place for a year and you *found* me, do you know how impossible that is? We—"

The panic in her voice breaks something inside of me. The last bit of my reckless hope vanishes—or maybe some last scrap of defiance wakes up, for a moment.

We can't open the gate. Whatever lies beyond it, I can feel its power—like heat or frost, already almost painful. I don't need to know what it is to know that it is nothing I care to be responsible for unleashing. If what the road whispered to me is true, this whole city was drowned to stop it from getting in. And every traveler that has passed by—every one of them chose the uncertain dark.

And we have to choose it, too.

"All right," I say. "Mel, take Kyle. Get out of here."

"But—" Mel looks between the three of us. But she knows what we need to do—Kyle has to survive, more than any of us. She doesn't want to leave us behind, but she doesn't want to die, either. Who would?

She steps in close to me one last time. Her kiss is light and chaste, and I want it to last forever. "See you on the other side," she says. Like she's making a promise that's my job to keep.

"Go. And don't stop until you're home," I say. "Don't wait in the woods, just get Kyle to safety. We'll find each other later."

She nods reluctantly. "Be careful," she tells me. She looks toward the waiting dark. "This was a lot more fun when we were kids, and it was all a game."

"Just thirteen steps," I remind her.

"Or in my case, seven, and then Tommy Jessop ran up and sprayed us with Silly String," Mel says, trying to smile and failing utterly.

"You'll make it," I promise her. She nods—and then she's gone.

We watch them walk toward the dark, hand in hand. Mel looks back. Kyle doesn't.

They vanish into the dark.

"Becca," I say. I look at Anthony. "Can you give us a minute?" I ask him.

He hesitates, then nods. He walks a little ways away. Out of earshot if we drop our voices. I pull Becca toward me, linking both my hands with hers. Our brows touch. She trembles and the movement passes through me like an echo.

"One of us has to stay," I say.

"You want to stay behind," Becca says, anger clipping the words.

An answer lodges in my throat.

Because I should. Shouldn't I? I want my friends to live. My sister. My best friend. How could I choose one of them to leave behind? It has to be me. It should be me. Yet something has changed, and it sends a sick shiver through me. I fight against it, not entirely aware that I am fighting, trying to put the order of myself back the way it should be. "You have to go," I say, halfway to what I mean. "You know you do. Otherwise this—all of this? It's for nothing."

"I don't accept that."

"I know you don't want to hear it. But you know that it's true."

"Then you've got to come with me."

I want to protest. *They will not die because of me.* It should be Anthony and Becca, but I can't say it.

"I already made my choice," Becca continues. "In the boat, when you fell . . . I was reaching for you. It's you. I choose you."

And still I say nothing. Instead, I grip her hands tight and shut my eyes. Something passes between us in that moment, a force I cannot describe, and a tension loosens in my chest.

Anthony clears his throat. We look up in the same movement. He's tucking his phone in his pocket.

"I think it's obvious what has to happen," he says. "I'm staying."

Guilt knifes through me, but he continues before I can say anything to contradict him.

"We don't have to . . . Of course you're going to pick each other. You should. I agree. It's the right choice. And I'm saving you from making it. I'm volunteering." His face falls into a smile. "Besides. Maybe if I stick around awhile, some other fool will—will—" He can't finish. Can't scrape up enough belief or hope to voice it.

"This isn't fair," Becca says. She crosses to him in three quick strides and throws herself into his arms. He wraps her up, and I turn away, walking a few paces to give them one last moment together.

It's a little while before footsteps approach behind me, and Anthony taps on my shoulder. I turn. Becca is hunched in on herself, staring off into the distance.

"You shouldn't have to stay," I say.

"Hey. I can't let Jeremy go out a hero and upstage me," Anthony says. "Wherever we go after this, he'd never shut up." He scrubs his hand over the back of his scalp. "Look, Sara. I know things aren't great between us right now."

"You think that matters?" I ask.

"It matters," he says. "We might not want it to, but it does. We haven't been talking. We haven't been friends like we used to be. I wasn't there for you, and you were, let's face it, kind of a jerk."

"Definitely a jerk," I tell him. He smiles.

"I don't want you carrying that, when you leave here. Pretend we had the time to work it out. To be friends again, best friends, the way we used to be. Promise?"

My vision blurs with tears. I don't stop them from falling. He hugs me, and I can't remember the last time he did that.

"Be strong. Get Becca home. And don't you ever look back," he whispers. He breaks away, his own cheeks wet with tears, fear he doesn't want to show deeply etched in his features. As he pulls away, he slips his phone into my bag.

And then there is nothing but goodbye.

We come through the dark. Count the steps in twinned whispers, hands clutched together tightly against the urge for release. We come through the dark, and we leave Anthony behind, and some rewritten part of my soul is triumphant.

I think I understand now what happens next. Better than I did then, at least. Then, I didn't even think about what I was doing. It was instinct, automatic action, unexamined. We step out of the dark. My hand is still wet with Lucy's blood—the same blood that stains Becca's palms and her shirt, one lonely streak marring the hollow of her throat where she swiped her hand unthinkingly. We emerge stumbling, and our hands unlink. The road is already vanishing behind us, and as Becca blinks, sunlight-blind, I vanish, too. I slip away.

I hear voices in the woods—police, searching for Trina. I hope they'll find Becca. I don't remember how I get home, but the next thing I can consciously recall, I am in the bathroom Becca and I have shared all our lives, washing dirt from my feet and blood from my hands. Then I'm crawling under my blankets and lying awake in the early morning light.

The police come to get us not long after. I hear my mother downstairs, her voice rising in shrill disbelief. When she comes up to get me, I pretend to still be half asleep, to not understand what she's telling me.

Becca is alive. She's back. But there's a problem. And they want to know if I've seen Trina Jeffries or her brother.

They don't ask about the others yet. As if the road is making them forget, look the other way. They never ask about them together; it never occurs to anyone to notice that all of them vanished on the same night. Last night. We didn't miss a single sunrise here, however much time passed on the road.

In the end, they decide that Trina Jeffries ran away after attacking her stepfather. Kyle goes home. He tells them about what Chris did to him. It doesn't matter for Trina. They're looking for a girl undone.

And Becca—eventually, Becca comes home. They can't find any blame to attach to that blood. If any of them wonder about the other teens who didn't come home, they don't wonder long.

I am sitting in my room when she returns. Dad is home. Pretending he never left, though that won't last long. Becca promises she can find her way upstairs, and she makes her way up alone. I listen to every step. She knocks on my door, pushes it open.

We had seen each other at the police station, but it wasn't like we could talk about what happened. She gives me a hollow look.

"Where did you go?" she asks.

I have been waiting for her to ask me this question since I left her behind, and I don't have an answer for her. "I don't know," I say. "I don't remember." I want to tell her that there is something wrong with me, but I don't. I want to tell her that I have changed, been changed, but I don't. "Mel made it home okay. Kyle, too."

"Good," she says, her relief palpable. She crosses to me, sits beside me. "I don't remember what happened after Anthony and I stepped into the dark."

"You don't?" I say, surprised. Or maybe not surprised. "I'm missing things, too."

"What happened to Lucy and Anthony?"

"I—" I know the answer, and then I don't. We all walked into the dark. Becca and I walked out. It's all I know.

My fingertip taps out a strange rhythm on the bedspread. Becca takes my hand.

"What matters is we're safe," she says firmly.

"We're safe," I agree. I am wrong, of course. And so is she.

We aren't safe at all.

INTERVIEW

SARA DONOGHUE

May 9, 2017

Sara's head hangs low. Her hands rest in her lap, palms up.
They look like the wings of a broken bird, bent wrong, limp.

ASHFORD: That's it, then. That's what you remember?

SARA: You seem disappointed.

ASHFORD: I had hoped . . .

SARA: I've figured some things out, though.

ASHFORD: Oh?

SARA: Can ghosts possess people, Dr. Ashford?

She cocks her head to the side. Becca is tense beside her.

ASHFORD: In my experience? Yes.

SARA: The road called to people. But it wasn't the road itself. It was Dahut. She needed someone who could be her
vessel, to carry her off the road. She thought she'd found
that vessel, with Lucy. But Lucy was dying. Her brother
had attacked her in the woods, before she reached the
road, and so she couldn't leave it. But an innocent girl like
Lucy—people wanted to rescue her. People came when
Dahut called with Lucy's voice. It wasn't really Lucy calling to Becca. It was Dahut, using Lucy's voice. Her face.
And I—I think I heard her, too.

ASHFORD: I believe you are correct.

SARA: Becca and I got out. But it wasn't just us, was it? Everything that's wrong with my memory. The things I remember that didn't happen. The things I don't remember that did. Could she have done that to me?

ASHFORD: It's possible.

SARA: I see.

There's a knock on the door. Abby opens it, nods, and lets Mel in.

SARA: You're all here, then. But not Kyle.

ASHFORD: We weren't able to bring Kyle in, due to his legal situation. We thought it better not to complicate that for him.

SARA: You mean you couldn't get past his lawyer.

ASHFORD: That, too.

MEL: Sara. We're all here to help you.

SARA: Because I've been acting crazy.

She draws a spiral on the tabletop with her fingertip.

ASHFORD: If Lucy—or Dahut—is using you, we don't have much time. The better she establishes her hold, the less likely it will be that we can remove her. You'll lose yourself, piece by piece, and she'll be all that's left. She's using your guilt to hide, Sara. Using your friends' deaths.

SARA: Using them.

ASHFORD: Your guilt. Your pain. She's hiding herself behind the memories that you would be glad to be rid of. I don't believe she's controlling you, not directly. Influencing, maybe. But it is Sara Donoghue that we've been speaking to.

Sara laughs bitterly.

SARA: Oh, if you're sure.

ASHFORD: We can help you, Sara. And it makes it much, much easier to root her out now that you've located the hidden memories yourself. It makes it harder for her to hide from us, and easier to remove her without . . .

SARA: Without what?

ASHFORD: The process can be damaging. This will minimize it.

SARA: It's dangerous?

ASHFORD: Yes. There are absolutely risks involved. I won't lie to you about that. But it's also our only option. Given the length of possession, it's likely we don't have long at all before she's entrenched thoroughly enough that she can't be removed.

SARA: I've felt like I was going crazy for weeks. I . . . This is why I attacked Becca?

ASHFORD: Becca was trying to get you help. The spirit would be strongly invested in stopping that.

BECCA: But I did get you help. They *are* going to help you, Sara. You're going to be okay.

She squeezes Sara's hand and gives her an encouraging smile. Mel hangs back, frowning, arms crossed. Abby arches a curious eyebrow in her direction. Mel leans in toward her and whispers something, and both young women slip out the door. Ashford looks after them momentarily, a puzzled expression on his face, before turning back to Sara.

ASHFORD: This isn't going to be easy, Sara, but your sister and Melanie are here to help ground you in your real memories. Your real self. With their help, I'm confident that we can remove the malign spirit.

SARA: And then my memory, everything—it'll go back to normal?

ASHFORD: I can't promise that. But you will be yourself. Able to move forward.

BECCA: You asked me to call them, Sara. You knew you needed help. Let them help you.

SARA: Then do it.

ASHFORD: I'm glad to hear you say that, Sara. This will be much easier with your cooperation. Now if you'll excuse me, we have preparations to make. Becca?

BECCA: I'll stay here.

ASHFORD: Are you sure that's—

BECCA: I'm staying here. I'm not afraid of my sister.

She puts a possessive hand on Sara's shoulder. Sara hunches over the table. Ashford hesitates, then nods.

ASHFORD: Very well. I'll be back shortly.

SUPPLEMENT C

*Text messages between Abigail Ryder
and Andrew Ashford*

Ashford   **Abby**

Where did you go?

                              Checking something out.

Specificity, Abigail.

                           Mel said something was
                             bothering her, Andrew.
                    Specifically Anthony's phone.

What about it?

                         Sara said that Anthony gave
                       it to her. But we don't have it.

                 As far as I know, no one else does,
                  either. I checked the police report, it
            says he took it with him when he "ran away."

Seriously, I know that this stuff makes people's
brains into goo but how do you just decide that
five teenagers "ran away" on the same night and
it's not connected or suspicious?

It's a survival mechanism, and a
canny one our species has developed.

Better to ignore such things
than to become part of them.

Sure. But point is, we're going to the Donoghue
house to see if we can find the phone.

Mel says she knows where Sara used to hide
things when she didn't want Becca to find them.

Why wouldn't she want Becca
to find the phone?

Don't get started on the
de-ghostening without me.

I would remind you that time is
of the essence.

VIDEO EVIDENCE

Recorded by Abigail Ryder

Recorded May 9, 2017, 9:16 p.m.

The camera pans across a fairly unremarkable bedroom. A few art prints adorn the walls—a woman with a birdcage for a chest, a manipulated photograph of a girl falling from the sky over a field of wheat, a painting of a girl plucking a star from the night sky. A desk sits against one wall; a twin bed, gray sheets, rumpled, against another. Melanie Whittaker steps into frame and crosses to the closet.

MEL: If she hid it, it should be in here.

ABBY: Do you mind starting from the top, introducing what we're doing? For the official records.

MEL: Official?

ABBY: I mean. Ish. Ashford's a stickler.

Mel turns to the camera.

MEL: Okay. Um, this is Sara Donoghue's room. Sara and Becca have always been really close, but even close sisters occasionally want to keep things private, so Sara would sometimes stash things where Becca couldn't find them. And I know where, because I'm a bad influence and it was usually my fault she had something worth hiding. So.

She turns back to the closet and slides it open, then crouches down. She runs her fingers along the near side of the floor.

MEL: Yup. This bit of carpet comes up, and then this bit of wood comes away, and there's a little gap, and . . .

Mel pulls free a phone, brushing dust from it.

MEL: Shit. Here it is.

ABBY: Can you confirm that is Anthony Beck's phone?

MEL: I think so. Out of juice, though.

ABBY: Let's get it charged and see what was worth hiding.

INTERVIEW

SARA DONOGHUE

May 9, 2017

The door opens. Ashford enters, looking grave. Becca and Sara sit side by side, Becca with her arms around her sister, whispering to her, an expression indicative of a wearied but determined attempt at comforting on her face.

ASHFORD: Sara, we've made our preparations. I'm going to need you to come with us.

Sara takes a deep, shuddering breath.

SARA: You said that this was risky.

ASHFORD: It is.

SARA: What could happen?

ASHFORD: I'm not going to mince words. You might not survive the process, Sara. And if you do, it could cause further damage to your memories and even your personality. And that is only in isolating the spirit; extracting it is more difficult still. But I have years of experience with this sort of thing, and Abigail is remarkably talented with exorcism. Miranda sent you our way for a reason. She knew that we could help you.

SARA: All right.

ASHFORD: You're certain. I don't want to do this without your consent.

SARA: It's better than . . .

ASHFORD: I understand.

BECCA: It'll be okay. You're going to get through this, Sara. I'll be right with you.

Together, they rise.

ASHFORD: Actually, Becca, I would prefer to have a few moments to get your sister situated before you join us. It will help . . . I suppose "calibrate" is a reasonable word. You and Mel will be brought in once Sara is properly in place and we have a good sense of the baseline energies in play.

BECCA: I . . . Okay. I have no idea what any of that means, but okay.

ASHFORD: Wait here, and Abby will come to collect you in just a moment.

He beckons to Sara, who walks meekly to him. His hand on her shoulder, he guides her out. The door shuts behind them, and Becca settles back into her chair.

Several minutes pass. Eventually, frowning, Becca rises. She walks to the door and tries the knob. It's locked.

Slowly, she turns back and looks straight at the camera, sitting in the corner of the room. Her mouth curls in a slight, sly smile. She speaks softly.

BECCA: I missed something, didn't I?

VIDEO EVIDENCE

Retrieved from the cell phone of Anthony Beck

Recorded April 19, 2017, 12:49 a.m.

The spires and domes of Ys rise, coral obscuring the precision of their architecture with tumorous bulges of reds and blues and pinks. Sara and Becca stand, fingers laced, locked in silent, urgent conversation.

ANTHONY: I don't know why I'm recording this, but . . . I don't know. Something's not right.

His voice is so soft the microphone almost fails to pick it up.

ANTHONY: When we found Sara in the dark . . . Something was wrong. Something is wrong.

Suddenly, Sara wrenches her hands free from Becca's. She collapses to her knees, hands over her face, a sound between a scream and a moan trapped behind her lips.

ANTHONY: What's wrong?

Anthony runs toward them, dropping the phone into his pocket. The picture is half-obscured, but the sound is clear.

BECCA: I don't know. We were just talking, and then—

SARA: No no no she's in here she's drowning me I can't get her out.

Sara looks up between splayed fingers, her eyes red-shot and frantic.

SARA: You have to leave me here. Get out. Run, now.

ANTHONY: What? No. What are you talking about?

BECCA: It's her.

Anthony looks at her, bewildered. Becca retreats a step, clutching herself with both arms.

BECCA: Lucy. It's Lucy. I can hear her, in Sara's voice. I don't know how, but it's her.

SARA: Not Lucy.

Her voice is different. Still strained, but calmer. Her hands drop into her lap. She draws a deep breath.

SARA: But close enough. I chose wrong.

ANTHONY: Is Sara—is it like Vanessa?

SARA: Not like Vanessa, Anthony, no. Vanessa was unmade and a poor facsimile constructed of her. I've merely slipped inside Sara's skin, but she's fighting me more than I thought she could. And you're not going to stop, are you?

Her eyes unfocus slightly as Dahut addresses the last words to Sara. Then they snap back into focus, and Sara bursts to her feet, frantic.

SARA: Just get out of here! She wants to escape. She wants to start over. She'll find a way to let that thing out into the world. If you leave me here, she can't—

Her voice cuts off abruptly. Her whole body shakes, then stills, and she draws heavy breaths through clenched teeth.

SARA: You won't stop fighting as long as you can feel me in here, will you? Fine, then. Easier to fix your memories and find a more hospitable home.

She steps toward Becca.

ANTHONY: What are you doing?

He moves to interpose himself.

SARA: It's all right. Isn't it, Becca? Come here.

Becca, mute, her lips slightly parted, steps forward before Anthony can stop her. She takes Sara's hand. The gesture is delicate, like dancers coming together as the music begins.

There is a flicker in the air beside the girls. A figure appears. A girl. Lucy Callow, her dress white and crisp. Her hair flutters in a wind that touches nothing else. And then she isn't Lucy at all, but a woman with sharp, high cheekbones and a regal pose, her hair adorned with gems. Then Lucy again, delicate and sweet.

Just as swiftly as she appeared, the girl is gone. Anthony grabs both sisters and pulls them apart; they offer no resistance. The angle of the phone in his pocket makes the picture nearly incomprehensible as he says the girls' names in turn, frightened and confused.

BECCA: Anthony. There's no point in panicking. This is what you wanted. They both live. For a while longer, at least. You stay here. It doesn't really change anything.

She steps close to him, only a portion of her torso visible.

ANTHONY: Just let her go.

BECCA: No.

The video barely catches the glint of the knife in her hand—the knife Becca used to carve the walls of the endless halls, not long but sharp and gleaming. Anthony doesn't even have time to react or defend himself. Her arm jabs forward three times, driving the knife somewhere below his ribs, the poor angle of the camera obscuring the exact location. He staggers back. The camera angle changes abruptly, as if he's fallen to his knees, and the phone falls, clattering to the ground. The camera faces straight up, recording Anthony from below. He gasps, his breath wheezing.

SARA: No. No . . .

She stumbles toward Anthony and sinks down in front of him. Her hands move to cover his, to stop the blood.

BECCA: It's all right. It might not even kill him. But it should keep him from interfering any more than he already has. And you won't remember it. Your memories are still scabbing over. You don't have to remember any of this. It will be peaceful.

Sara's arms go around Anthony's neck. She holds him tight, her shaking evident even with the contorted angle that barely reveals a sliver of her side.

Anthony's voice is a whisper.[11]

ANTHONY: My phone. Take my phone. Don't let her see. Remember—remember that. I gave you my phone.

The phone scrapes as Anthony awkwardly lifts it and tucks it into Sara's bag, their positions hiding the motion from Becca/Dahut.

ANTHONY: Remember.

SARA: I will. I'll remember. I promise.

Another moment's fumbling as Anthony finds the button to stop the recording, and then the video ends.

---

[11] Audio is unclear in original recording, but Ashford has employed a specialist to decipher the contents.

EXHIBIT P

Witness statement regarding attack in Briar Glen City Park

April 30, 2017

FRANK MICHAELSON: The two girls were walking together. An Asian girl and a white girl. I thought I maybe recognized the Asian girl, but I'm not sure. Maybe I saw her on the news or something? They were just walking along, and talking, and then the white girl started screaming and threw herself at the other girl. Really going at her.

OFFICER BAUER: Did you hear what she was saying?

MICHAELSON: I think she was saying "get out." "Get out of here."

OFFICER BAUER: Are you sure she was saying "here"?

MICHAELSON: What else would she be saying?

OFFICER BAUER: One of the other witnesses thought she heard "her."

MICHAELSON: "Get out of her"? How does that make sense?

OFFICER BAUER: Thank you, Mr. Michaelson.

EXHIBIT Q

Text messages between Sara Donoghue and Becca Donoghue (deleted)

Recovered from phone records

Sara   **Becca**

4/27/17

Do you still hear her?

                                                Hear who?

You know who. Lucy.

                        I don't know what you're talking about.

I still have dreams but now I can't tell
if they're memories or something else.

                        Sara, you need to stop thinking about this.

                                                It's over.

But what if it's not? Something happened.

In the dark.

                        We survived. That's what matters.

                                 Forget the rest.

I need to remember. There's something

I'm supposed to remember. About Dahut.

                           It's better if you don't.

That name I told you about,

Ashford? I looked it up.

                    Sara, you said yourself you don't know

                            where you heard that name.

                           It's probably nothing.

It's not. He's a professor.

Or he was a professor.

There's not a lot online, but I think he

investigates paranormal things.

I think he could help.

There's nothing to help with anymore.

He's probably just a crackpot.

I need help.

You don't.

I want to call him, but I can't. I keep trying.

Maybe you haven't called him because you know you don't need to.

Please, Becca. I need your help.

I'm not going to enable this obsession.

EXHIBIT R

Text messages between Sara Donoghue and Melanie Whittaker

Sara   **Mel**

4/28/17

Mel, I need your help.

> Anything.

There's someone. This man. Becca knows.

She needs to call him.

Please.

You have to make her call him.

There's something wrong with me
and he can help.

> You just got done yelling at me that there
> was nothing wrong with you.

I can't think

I can't remember

It comes and goes

Please

Please

Mel the road

4/30/17

Jesus, sorry. I think I got a little too drunk.

                                                  Since when do you drink?

When do you think I started drinking?

But I'm fine.

Seriously, I don't know why I was freaking out.

There's nothing "wrong with me"
except horrible trauma.

So we've got that in common.

I'm calling Becca.

I'm going to make sure she calls that guy.

You don't have to.

I kind of think I do.

Because if this is anything like the last time you
"drunk texted" you're not going to remember this
conversation tomorrow, and it's getting really
fucking obvious that there _is_ something wrong
with you. You need help and I'm going to make
sure you get it.

Don't worry, Sara. We're looking out for you.

EXHIBIT S

Emails recovered from the drafts folder
of Rebecca Donoghue

To: Sara Donoghue
From: Rebecca Donoghue
Subject: (none)

Help I

To: Sara Donoghue
From: Rebecca Donoghue
Subject: (none)

i need help i

To: Sara Donoghue
From: Rebecca Donoghue
Subject: gone

She's gone, but she's not gone. Only for a few minutes, maybe. I can already feel her trying to take control again. It's

To: Sara Donoghue
From: Rebecca Donoghue
Subject: wake

Lucy did something to me only she's not Lucy at all and now I keep waking up and it's another day and I'm in another place and I don't understand what happened.

To: Sara Donoghue
From: Rebecca Donoghue
Subject: listen

A moment ago I was with you and I tried to tell you something was wrong, but I think she messed with you too. She spent so long whispering to me it was like she could just step inside me and she already owned me but I think she couldn't control you and I think that's why she left. Why she picked me instead. I think she had to do something to you to make you forget instead. But you need to remember.

What happened to Anthony? What did I do?

To: Sara Donoghue
From: Rebecca Donoghue
Subject: Mel

Mel called and I didn't understand what she was talking about. But I sent that man an email. Ashford? I told him I needed help, but I don't know if I made any sense. I sent him a bunch of photos. That was easier than writing. They were already on the computer. I hope he

To: Sara Donoghue
From: Rebecca Donoghue
Subject: (none)

I haven't sent any of these why can't I send them I can't even make myself push the mouse over

To: Sara Donoghue
From: Rebecca Donoghue
Subject: (none)

I'm waking up less and less

To: Sara Donoghue
From: Rebecca Donoghue
Subject: (none)

I love you.

To: Sara Donoghue
From: Rebecca Donoghue
Subject: goodbye

[no message text]

EXHIBIT T

Transcript of phone call to Rebecca Donoghue

May 1, 2017

BECCA: Hello?

ASHFORD: Hello, is this Rebecca Donoghue?

BECCA: Yes, who's calling?

ASHFORD: My name is Ashford. Andrew Ashford. You emailed me about a recent incident you were involved in.

BECCA: I . . . I'm sorry. That was a prank. I'm sorry to waste your time.

ASHFORD: I know that it may be difficult to trust anyone right now, Rebecca, but I want you to know that I believe you.

BECCA: Really.

ASHFORD: You said that you needed help. Your message wasn't terribly clear . . .

BECCA: I don't need help. Really. You don't need to bother.

ASHFORD: Miss Donoghue, do you know a young woman named Miranda Ryder?

BECCA: No, I don't.

ASHFORD: Your message included a photo of her.

BECCA: Did it?

ASHFORD: Miss Donoghue, I have already told you that I

believe you. And I believe that I can help you. My assistant and I are already on our way to Briar Glen.

[*Silence*]

Miss Donoghue?

BECCA: It isn't me. It's my sister, Sara. Something's wrong with her. Something is very, very wrong with her.

ASHFORD: Tell me more.

FINAL INTERVIEW

SARA DONOGHUE

May 9, 2017

ASHFORD: I realize that this must be quite jarring.

SARA: You're wrong.

ASHFORD: You've seen the evidence for yourself. You've seen the video.

SARA: No. There's nothing wrong with Becca. It's me. I'm the one that—

ASHFORD: We all thought so, Sara. Becca is cogent. Her story is consistent. Utterly consistent. She only has the one memory gap, and that—I think that was her way of trying to keep you from being able to ask her about what happened. Even a false story might jar something loose. Sara, the influence of Dahut's spirit on you was fleeting. She could only manage rough manipulations. Shoving memories into a hole, building slapdash memories over them. She had a year to whisper to Becca. And then she simply stepped through the door she'd built for herself.

SARA: No. It has to be me. I can feel it. I'm . . . wrong.

ASHFORD: What you feel, Sara, is guilt. Survivor's guilt. And the more classic kind. You were the one who sent that text message to your school, weren't you?

SARA: I thought it was the only way they'd come with me, if they thought it was real. And I got them all killed.

ASHFORD: But you saved your sister. And she still needs your help. We can still free her. But you will need to be strong. You will need to be unflinching.

SARA: I . . .

ASHFORD: Anthony's last act was to make sure you had that video, Sara. His last act—saving you both, in more ways than you understood. And you hid the phone, because some part of you knew the truth.

SARA: She's been Dahut. Ever since we came out of the dark.

ASHFORD: It looks that way.

SARA: Then I didn't save Becca at all.

ASHFORD: Not yet. But you still can.

SARA: What do I do?

ASHFORD: I'll show you. Don't worry. We'll be with you every step of the way.

SARA: "Whatever walked there, walked alone."

ASHFORD: What's that?

SARA: Nothing. It's from a book.

She stands.

SARA: I'm ready.

VIDEO EVIDENCE

Donoghue Exorcism

Recorded by Andrew Ashford

May 10, 2017, 12:34 a.m.

Video is fragmentary, lapsing frequently into black or visual
and audio distortions that make comprehension impossible.

A man speaks in a calm, clear voice. The language appears to
be Aramaic.[12] An image flickers into view: Becca Donoghue,
pacing at the edges of a circle of chalk surrounded by strange
symbols, perhaps lettering of some kind. Andrew Ashford
stands to the north of the circle; it is he who is chanting.
Melanie Whittaker stands to the east, Abigail Ryder to the
west, and Sara Donoghue, back straight and eyes fixed on
her sister, to the south.

The image turns to black; a sound like howling wind drowns
out all else, followed by an electronic squeal and then a ca-
cophony of other sounds, impossible to distinguish.[13]

The next clear sound is a woman screaming.

Seconds later, an image flickers briefly into view. Melanie
Whittaker stands against a wall as if flung there. Ashford

---

12 We have been unable to translate but are reaching out to experts.
13 Ashford has marked this audio for further analysis. Unfortunately, we were unable to
obtain copies ourselves.

has stumbled back. Abigail Ryder remains in position, hands moving swiftly in strange, mathematically precise configurations.

Sara Donoghue remains. Her sister stands at the edge of the chalk, inches away, teeth bared and pupils filling her irises.

The video cuts out. Here and there, fragments of shouting can be made out, syllables isolated until they have been stripped of meaning.

ASHFORD: It's not working. We need to stop this.

ABBY: No. We're not stopping yet. I just need—

Audio cuts out. Video and audio cut back in several seconds later. Only Sara remains beside the circle. The others have fallen back. Becca Donoghue stalks back and forth along the inner edge of the chalk. She licks her lips, her head moving like a snake's.

BECCA: They died because of you. All of them. You can't even remember poor Nick. Vanessa? You weren't even her friend. You didn't even notice she was gone when you *did* remember her, and then you were perfectly happy to kill her, weren't you, just to save Trina. Perfect Trina, who died anyway. Died saving *you,* and was it worth it? You know it wasn't.

Sara Donoghue does not flinch. She reaches out her hand, across the barrier of chalk.

ABBY: Don't—

SARA: I found you once, Becca. I'll always find you.

Becca flinches back from the hand.

BECCA: She's already gone. There's no point to any of this.

You failed. You tricked them all. Brave Jeremy. Anthony, so loyal he lied to you for a year about his feelings for Becca so he wouldn't hurt your fragile little ego, because he knew you couldn't stand to be anything but the center of attention. Mel, sick with love and too afraid to tell you, but oh, you enjoyed finding out about that, didn't you? Back to being the shining star.

Sara laughs, bright and sad.

SARA: You don't understand her at all. You don't understand us at all. I wanted to shine as bright as her, because she was the most beautiful thing in the universe. My sister. The brightest thing.

Sara steps forward. She stands at the very edge of the circle now.

ABBY: Do *not* step over that circle, Sara!

SARA: It's all right.

Sara Donoghue takes another step forward, breaking the barrier of chalk, her hand still outstretched.

Abby lunges forward. Ashford catches her by the shoulder, restrains her.

ASHFORD: Wait.

Sara's hand hovers in the air.

SARA: Becca. It's time to walk out of the dark.

Slowly, her sister reaches out.

Video cuts out. It does not return.

ADDITIONAL MATERIALS

This concludes the contents of Ashford File #74. We have, however, located additional materials that you may find of interest, included without additional charge.

As to your primary question, we are confident that Abigail Ryder was unharmed during the events in Briar Glen, and we have confirmed that Miranda Ryder is deceased. We will continue to attempt to track down Abigail Ryder's current location.

Do not attempt to contact us. No previous means of doing so will be operable after you receive this message.

SUPPLEMENT D

"Me Again: A Self-Portrait" (Photograph)

September 17, 2017

Posted on photography forum by lostgirl151

Becca Donoghue sits cross-legged on a white bedspread, body forward, face in profile as she looks to the left. Her hair falls around her face; her expression is distant. The photograph is in black and white. Somewhat artful, expressive, but largely unremarkable; the compelling, strikingly beautiful subject is all that sets it apart, until one notices the standing mirror at the edge of the frame.

In the reflection, Becca's form is captured, almost a perfect reproduction of the scene—except for the faintest shadow of a second figure sitting beside her. One can almost make out the features of a girl, her hand raised, reaching toward Becca but not quite touching her. In the reflection, Becca's gaze, turned away, reads as rejection. Defiance, perhaps. There is something desperate in the shadow-figure's reach; Becca remains beyond its grasp.

Comments on the post compliment the subtle, surreal touch and ask about the techniques used to manipulate the image. Lostgirl151 never replies. This is her only post on the forum. The username does not return any results in general searches.

SUPPLEMENT E

Instagram post by Melanie Whittaker

August 7, 2017

Melanie Whittaker's Instagram is infrequently updated. Photographs are mostly of coffee, books, and dogs, along with a handful of selfies.

In a set of three selfies, clearly taken in quick succession, Melanie Whittaker and Sara Donoghue sit at a table at an outdoor café. Sara has cut her hair shorter, just below her chin. Though it is clearly a warm day, she wears long sleeves. Her expression is melancholy in the first frame, distracted as Mel grins for the camera. In the second, she seems to have realized that Mel is taking the picture; she looks across the table in apparent surprise. In the third photo, a slight smile bends her lips. She is not looking at the camera. She is looking at Mel.

The post is tagged #threepointtwoweekaversary #itsathing #lazygothaesthetic

SUPPLEMENT F

Video posted online by anonymous user

Akrou & Bone *video game fan forum*

"Weird in the World" sub-forum

Subject: Anyone know this kid?

An embedded video clip shows Kyle Jeffries sitting on a picnic table in a park. It is late evening, and the park is abandoned. Kyle doesn't seem to be aware that he's being filmed. He speaks softly; the words are inaudible, but the rhythm is slow, deliberate.

The wind shifts. A brief stretch of words reaches the camera and the microphone: "—cup the hand—writhes it beneath—"

The air in front of him buckles, wavers, distorts. Something seems to be weaving itself into being. It has almost the shape of a person—or it might only be a trick of the light.

Kyle stretches out his hand. Smoke rises in faint coils from his palm. It threads through the air to the figure, as if pulled by a draft, and the figure solidifies just a little bit more—

And then the rhythm of Kyle's words falters, and the figure, the trick of the light, vanishes. Kyle's hand drops. He sags, seemingly weary.

The video ends.

SUPPLEMENT G

Security video

Gas station, Point Brook, Pennsylvania

A standard view of a gas station at night. A car pulls up to the pump. Andrew Ashford gets out of the driver's seat; Abigail Ryder exits the passenger side, says something to Ashford, and gives a mock salute. She heads toward the gas station store and disappears inside.

Ashford begins pumping gas. A young woman steps into frame, across the car from Ashford. He seems to sense her presence and looks up. It is difficult to identify the young woman, whose back is to the camera, but she bears a clear resemblance to Miranda Ryder.

Ashford speaks to her. She seems to respond. He glances back toward the store, where Abigail has gone. Then he nods.

A young woman sets something on the trunk of the car. And then she steps back. The shadows are thick at the edge of the frame, and the video quality is poor; it is impossible to be certain that she vanishes before she reaches the edge of the frame. It is natural to assume she simply steps out of view.

Ashford picks up the small object that the young woman left behind, and tucks it into his pocket.

Abigail Ryder exits the store. She tosses him a bottle of water.

He seems about to tell her something.

He doesn't.

He finishes pumping gas. They drive away.

Turn the page to read a newly

discovered transcript.

We have uncovered new information related to your last inquiry, regarding the item that Miranda Ryder gave to Dr. Ashford. We have determined that the item originated on an island called Bitter Rock.

Further investigation has uncovered a fragment of what appears to be one of Dr. Ashford's files. However, there are no other references to this file; the number is duplicated with an unremarkable case of a fraudulent haunting in Arizona. We have retrieved only a partial transcript and a photograph.

Our supplemental surveillance of Dr. Ashford revealed more information. The relevant items are enclosed.

VIDEO EVIDENCE

Recorded by Dr. Andrew Ashford

Bitter Rock, Alaska

Recorded June 9, 2013

Dr. Ashford stands on a rocky slope, punctuated here and there by bristly shrubs. The camera, mounted on a tripod, takes in a wide field of view, but it is obscured by the mist that rolls through. Just discernible at the edge of the frame is the movement of waves against a pebbled shore.

Ashford seems to be waiting for something. He stands with his hands in his pockets, eyes trained on the formless mists. A female voice speaks from behind the camera.

UNKNOWN: What are we waiting for, Dr. Ashford?

ASHFORD: That depends on who you ask.

UNKNOWN: I'm asking you.

ASHFORD: And I would tell you it's a monster. One to be avoided at all costs.

UNKNOWN: What if I asked Landon? Or Ryder? What would they say it is?

ASHFORD: They would tell you it's a god.

A bird lands on the rocks near him, watching him with a curious tilt to its head. It is a white bird, with the narrow, elegant wings of a tern—and a splash of scarlet at its neck. The red-throated tern, endemic to the small island of Bitter Rock.

The bird examines Ashford for a moment longer. It startles, taking flight in response to some unseen threat. Ashford tenses. And a shape appears.

One might be tempted to call it an angel. It has the body of a man but it also has wings—six of them, stretched out like dark and ragged shadows from its shoulders. It moves through the mist in stuttering leaps, like a film missing frames, and as it moves it makes a sound like the screech of a bird layered over a low, hollow moaning.

ASHFORD: Then it *is* here. This means . . . The gates we thought destroyed, they're still out there. Not just the Gray. Ys, Abalus, all of them.

UNKNOWN: You've seen enough. We have to get—

The shape turns. It has no discernible eyes and yet its gaze seems to burn into the camera. Its wings flare out. It seems part of the mist made solid—no, as if the mist is all an extension of its own form, as if it has covered the whole horizon.

The creature screams, and the air fills with the sound of a thousand wings beating in frantic flight.

The video cuts out.

SUPPLEMENT

*Phone call between Andrew Ashford
and unknown woman*

September 13, 2017

WOMAN: Andrew. You never call unless there's something wrong, so—what's wrong?

ASHFORD: I need your advice.

WOMAN: This is about the exorcism business? Massachusetts?

ASHFORD: No, no. That's resolved. At least, for the time being. Some traces of the spirit rooted themselves too thoroughly to be entirely banished, but Becca is strong. Dahut has no power over her any longer. Though I fear she will always haunt Ms. Donoghue's dreams. This is about Abby.

WOMAN: The Ryder girl. You still have her in hand?

ASHFORD: Not how I would put it. She remains in my custody. Miranda—Miranda's ghost—gave me something. She asked me to pass it along to Abby. It's . . . it's from Bitter Rock.

There is a beat of silence.

WOMAN: Miranda didn't know—

ASHFORD: No. I made sure of it. Neither of them had—has—any idea.

WOMAN: If Abby goes to Bitter Rock, that will change.

ASHFORD: If Abby goes to Bitter Rock, there's a good chance she won't survive.

WOMAN: That would not be . . .

She trails off. When Ashford speaks, his voice is sharp with warning.

ASHFORD: What are you suggesting?

WOMAN: I'm not suggesting anything. You've made it clear that conversation is off the table.

ASHFORD: Abby is under my protection. Until I decide otherwise. She doesn't know anything, and I'll keep it that way.

WOMAN: Then get rid of that thing, whatever it is. Destroy it.

ASHFORD: I—

UNKNOWN: Andrew. Keep her away from Bitter Rock, whatever you do. Or you risk having the decision taken out of your hands.

Call terminated.

Acknowledgments

First and foremost, thank you to my husband, Mike, for his tireless support through every stage of this book and all the others, and to the rest of my family for putting up with me while under deadline—especially Mr. O, who sometimes tried to help with the typing.

Many people offered editorial expertise, critique, commiseration, brainstorming, support, and dedicated hard work in shepherding *Rules for Vanishing* from an odd little concept to a polished final manuscript. So thank you to:

The truly sensational No Name Writing Group—Shanna Germain, Erin M. Evans, Rhiannon Held, Monte Cook, Corry L. Lee, and Susan Morris; my tireless agent, Lisa Rodgers, and her UK partner-in-crime, Louise Buckley; my fabulous editor at PYR, Maggie Rosenthal; my also fabulous UK editors at Walker, Annalie Grainger and Megan Middleton; and my meticulous copyeditors and proofreaders on both sides of the ocean: Marinda Valenti and Abigail Powers at PYR and Kirsty Ridge at Walker.

I am privileged to have Dana Li as my cover designer once again, and she continues to knock it out of the park. Simón Prades's hardcover illustration is beautiful, spooky, and perfect. I am deeply grateful to both of them for lending their artistic skill and talent to creating a stunning cover. And Jim Hoover's great work on the interior layout helped bring this peculiar book to life.

I have the great fortune of having not one but two wonderfully creepy covers to enjoy. So thanks to those who worked on the UK edition: Leo Nickolls, for the haunting illustration, Maria Soler Canton for the design, and Anna Robinette for the typesetting.

A special thank you to my expert readers/consultants, Meriah Hudson and Beth Bienvenu, for their insight. Any errors and missteps remaining are entirely my own. Thank you also for those who helped with thorny questions of all sorts at various stages, especially Mat Murakami, Day Al-Mohamed, and the Thrills & Chills crew.

Finally, thank you to Ms. Bean, who arrived just in time to have the final pass of the manuscript read aloud to her, and who will probably grow up a little weird as a result. If it's any comfort, with parents like these, that was inevitable.

Dying for more?

Keep reading for a sneak peek
of Kate Alice Marshall's upcoming
OUR LAST ECHOES
for more in this eerie universe.

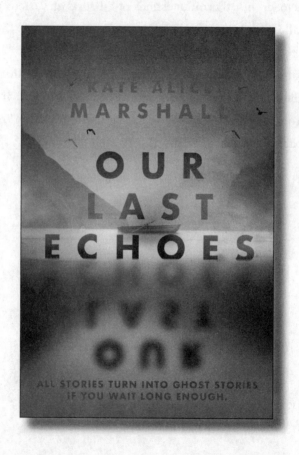

INTERVIEW

Sophia Novak

SEPTEMBER 2, 2018

The camera is positioned to one side of a study. Bookshelves line the walls; a heavy wooden desk in the center of the room is covered in orderly but prolific stacks of folders, books, and papers. A photograph on the desk shows Dr. Andrew Ashford standing with Miranda and Abigail Ryder, his wards, in front of a sycamore tree.

In the chair in front of the desk sits a young white woman: Sophia Novak. She is blonde, in her late teens. Her features are solemn, her skin sun-weathered. Dr. Ashford appears from behind the camera and sits opposite her, in the chair behind the desk.

ASHFORD: There we go. Ms. Novak, was it? Is it Sophie or Sophia?

SOPHIA: Either one is fine.

ASHFORD: I see. Thank you for coming all this way.

SOPHIA: I thought I should. Abby said—she talked about you a lot.

ASHFORD: The file Ms. Ryder compiled is incomplete. Her notes are fragmentary and I'm having trouble piecing together exactly what occurred. I hoped you could fill in the blanks.

Sophia seems to have expected this. She reaches down to a backpack beside her chair and pulls out a spiral-bound notebook.

SOPHIA: I wrote it all down. Abby asked me to, but I didn't get the chance to give it to her.

She slides it across the table to him. Ashford rests his hand over it but doesn't open it yet.

ASHFORD: What happened on Bitter Rock, Ms. Novak? What did you two find there?

Sophia smiles a little, almost sadly.

SOPHIA: Nothing but echoes.

SOPHIA NOVAK

WRITTEN TESTIMONY

1

MY EARLIEST MEMORY is of drowning.

I only remember bits and pieces. The darkness of the water; the thick, briny taste of it; the way it burned down my throat when I gasped. I remember the cold, and I remember hands, impossibly strong, pushing me under. And I remember my mother lifting me free. Her voice and her arms wrapping around me before the warmth of her slipped away.

But I've never been to the ocean. Never choked on saltwater. So I have been told all my life. My mother died in Montana, hundreds of miles from any ocean. The water, the darkness, the cold—they're nightmares, nothing more.

Or so I thought, until Abby Ryder asked me what I knew about Bitter Rock.

The first tendrils of mist seethed past on the wind as the boat bucked. Droplets trembled on the few strands of hair that had escaped my tight braid.

"It's just ahead," Mr. Nguyen shouted unnecessarily: there was no way to miss the island, as grim and foreboding as the name Bitter Rock suggested. But I would have known we were approaching the shore even with my eyes closed. The sea had been a constant since we left the shore; the water had sloshed, sucked, and slapped at the sides of the boat. But now a new sound reached us: a sibilant crashing of water meeting rock.

The engine thrummed through me, singing in my bones. I knew this place. I knew those sounds, even though I shouldn't. The thought sent a shiver through my core, but I couldn't tell if it was fear—or relief. I knew this place. There had to be a reason— an explanation. An *answer*. In my pocket, my hand closed tightly around the small wooden bird that was all I had left of my mother. *We're here,* I thought.

Mr. Nguyen piloted us past sharp black rocks to a tongue of weathered wood—a dock, but not much of one. The engine puttered, then cut out, and Mr. Nguyen leapt to the dock with a nimbleness that didn't match the ash-gray patches in his hair. He didn't bother to tie the boat off. He wouldn't be staying. He hadn't even wanted to bring me in, not with the storm threatening to sweep down and cut off the island from the mainland, but I'd talked him into it.

"You're sure this is where you want to be?" he asked.

Was I sure? Was I sure that I should be here, three thousand miles from home, chasing the memory of dark water? Tracing the footsteps of a dead woman?

Yes.

"I'll be fine," I told Mr. Nguyen. "Will you be okay getting back? That storm looks bad."

"I'd rather face the storm than stay here." He helped me off the boat, catching my elbow when my foot skidded on the wet boards.

"Thanks," I told him, pulling away. "I've got it from here."

He gave me a long, unblinking look. Like he was trying to decide whether to talk me out of it. But he'd tried on the mainland and he'd tried on the way over. I guess he decided he'd done all he could. "Be careful," he said at last. "Nothing good happens here."

I could have told him, *I know.* I could have told him, *That's why I've come.*

Instead I only nodded and turned away.

I didn't have directions to the house where I would be staying, but it wasn't like there were many options. The beach led to a road, and the road led in two directions: west, to the Landon Avian Research Center; or east, where the few houses on the island were located. It was after hours, so no one would be at the Center. I turned east.

The island was equal parts rock and clinging grass. The wind made the grass hiss, like the island already disapproved of my presence. I kept my head down. The strap of my bag dug into my shoulder and across my chest.

If I hurried back, I could still catch Mr. Nguyen. I could tell him that I'd made a mistake. I could go home—except there was no home to go back to. Now that I'd graduated high school, I was officially aged out of the foster system. The only thing I had left was a ghost, and this was the only place I knew to look for her.

I remembered almost nothing about my mother. A blue jacket. Her hand cupping the back of my head as I pressed my face against her thigh. Her voice barely hiding a laugh. *Come on, little bird. Bye-bye, little bird. Good night, little bird.*

Joy Novak died in an accident, fifteen years ago. I was three years old, and I didn't remember any of it. I only knew what they told me in foster care, and it wasn't like my foster parents knew any details. I wasn't able to find any either, when I went looking. One dead woman didn't make a ripple in a world where worse things happened every day, and I'd started to accept a future in which I never knew what her last moments had been like, or what kind of accident had claimed her.

And then I'd gotten a phone call. The girl on the other end had asked what I knew about my mother's disappearance. The word had been so unexpected that at first I hadn't heard it at all. I assumed she was asking about her *death*. So when Abby asked me about what my mother been doing in Bitter Rock, Alaska, I'd told her she'd made a mistake. *My mother died in Montana,* I'd told her. *I don't think she'd ever been to Alaska.*

So you believe she's dead, then?

That's when I realized what she'd said. *Disappearance.*

I still didn't believe her. Not until she sent me the photo: my mother and three-year-old me on a beach.

Turns out there were answers. I was just looking in the wrong place.

Gravel crunched under my feet. A pale bird winged toward me. The splash of red at its throat was vivid as fresh blood. A red-throated tern—the bird Bitter Rock was famous for, in certain scientific circles. It was a perfect match to the wooden bird in my pocket, its wings barred with black and white. The colors flashed at me as it flew overhead, and I tracked its progress.

The western point of the island rose in a hill, and at its top crouched a blocky gray building—the Landon Avian Research Center, or LARC for short. It was the only reason anyone came to Bitter Rock. It was the reason my mother had been here, at least according to Abby, and so I'd lied and wheedled my way into a summer job interning for one of the lead researchers.

The tern flew over the hill and disappeared northward. Heading, I assumed, toward Belaya Skala—Bitter Rock's headland, connected to the main island by an unnavigable isthmus of sheer rock and home only to birds. Though that hadn't always been the case. At least three times before, people had tried to gain footholds of one kind or another on that side of the island.

Every time, it ended in disaster. Disaster that left not corpses, but questions—which had never been answered. This island had swallowed up dozens of people. Now I was here, alone and unsure of what I was facing.

Suddenly it crashed over me, the immensity of what I was doing stopping me in my tracks. My mother was just one name among many, and these islands had eaten them all, and left behind nothing—not even bones. Who was I against that?

I turned on the road, a plea on my tongue— *Wait, I've changed my mind*. But Mr. Nguyen was a blot on the sea, too far for my voice to reach. I dug my fingers into the strap of my bag, sick with the sudden conviction that this had all been a mistake. There was a strange vibration in the air that seemed to settle in my chest and radiate out through my limbs. It made me queasy, like I stood on the lurching deck of a boat with the rumble of the motor beneath me.

I blinked. Mr. Nguyen's boat was gone. I searched the horizon for him—he couldn't have gotten far enough to vanish, not yet. Fear skittered over my skin. I gritted my teeth. It was fine. I wasn't leaving anyway. I was letting my nerves get the better of me, that was all.

My eye caught against a shape jutting up from the waves.

It was a man standing in the water. He was up to his thighs in cold surf, facing away from me. He wore an old-fashioned army jacket that flapped in the wind. He stood canted to one side, like he had a bad leg, with his arms dangling into the water. His head hung forward.

That water had to be freezing. What was he doing? I stood rooted for a moment, torn between concern and caution. I drew forward haltingly. That buzzing in my bones was almost an ache. I licked my lips, wanting to call out, but afraid to. "Hello?" I managed at last, still far away, lifting my voice above the crash of the surf.

His shoulders jerked back. His head snapped up. He started to turn.

I knew immediately I'd made a mistake. I scrambled backward, a yell lodged in my chest, desperately wanting to steal back that word, to stop him from turning, because I was sure, in a way that I could not explain or defend, that I did not want him to turn.

Rough hands seized my arm and yanked me around, and now I did yell. A huge man loomed over me, his hand gripping the meat of my upper arm. His face was half hidden behind a huge gray beard, an orange knit cap jammed down over his blunt forehead.

"You," he growled, brow knit. "What are you doing out here?" His voice was thick with a Russian accent. He smelled of damp, salty sea spray and stale cigarette smoke. Drops of moisture jeweled the bristles of his beard. A half-healed blister balanced at the edge of his bottom lip. One of his eyes was almost entirely white, the skin around it ropy with a starburst of scarring.

"I—I—" I stammered. Fear surged through me, and my breath caught in my throat.

But fear wasn't useful. Not now. I shoved it away—not just repressing it, but flinging it away from me, into the void—the other-place that was always waiting. It bled away in a rush, and I gave a small shudder of relief.

"Get your hand off my arm," I said, cold and flat.

He peered at me through his good eye. "Do you know me?" he asked.

"No," I said, bewildered.

He let go abruptly and took a half step back. I just stared at him. I wasn't afraid, and there would be a price for that later, but for now I needed the calm. The empty. I did know him, though—didn't I? It was like I remembered him from a dream. Or maybe a nightmare. "What were you looking at?" he asked, brusque and demanding.

"I saw—" I twisted back toward the water. The man was gone. In his place was a tree that must have been uprooted on some other shore and dragged here by the tides, blackened by the water and pitching as the waves rolled it. Out in the distance, Mr. Nguyen's boat continued its steady retreat. Not vanished at all. The tree— I'd seen the tree, and somehow I'd thought it was a man.

The explanation leapt into my mind, comfortable and reassuring and false. I swallowed. No. I knew what I'd seen.

Read Kate Alice Marshall's
critically acclaimed
I AM STILL ALIVE

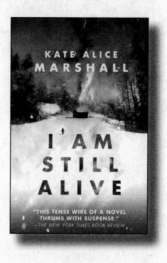

"This tense wire of a novel thrums with suspense . . . [This book] just might be the highlight of your summer." —*The New York Times*

"[A] twisty survival story that I tore through compulsively. You won't regret the hours that disappear when you read this one."
—Nancy Werlin, National Book Award honoree and *New York Times* bestselling author

"I couldn't set this book down—the words actually made me shiver. It's *Hatchet* meets *The Revenant*, infused with fierce, undaunted girl power." —S.A. Bodeen, award-winning author of *The Raft*

"If *Hatchet* was your favorite book in grade school, but you wish it was filled with much more girl power, then *I Am Still Alive* is the book you've been waiting for." —Bustle

"A gripping adventure." —*The Wall Street Journal*

★ "A taut, gripping page-turner with a strong female hero to root for." —*Kirkus Reviews*, starred review

★ "A thrilling blend of wilderness survival and revenge, this is an engrossing read from a writer to watch." —*Booklist*, starred review